Queen's Surrender

(To a Higher Calling)

The Jamieson Legacy

By

Pat Simmons

Queen's Surrender

(To a Higher Authority)

By

Pat Simmons

Developmental Editor: Chandra Sparks Splond
Final Proofreader: Darlene Simmons
Beta Reader: Stacey Jefferson
Interior Design: Kimolisa/Fiverr.com
Cover Design: Ultrakhan22/Fiverr.com

Praises for Pat Simmons Novels:

5.0 out of 5 stars Must read

After reading this book I wanted more, I hope you have a story for Queen and Phillip something beautiful is brewing there 😊 I love this family so much they encourage each other and always speak the truth. Having Christ is plus for me, I enjoyed this book can't wait to read what's coming next. Ms. Simmons you have touched my heart with your books. God Bless you and your creativity🖤

—Amazon reader on *The Guilty Generation*

5 out of 5 stars Beautiful love story.

This book was a beautiful love story!!! I could not put it down. I would recommend this book to everyone! It's a must read. It had me shouting, crying, and so joyful. I love the scripture references.

—Amazon Reader on *The Confession*

5.0 out of 5 stars Beautiful Story of Love and Family

Pat Simmons has written a story showcasing the power of love and family. I smiled and cried as Daniel and Saige's story progressed. Pat handles a very emotional issue beautifully and reminds us that God's will is always perfect, even when we want Him to do things differently. I will think about this story for a while as I meditate on how He does all things well. Are you looking for a Christmas story that will warm your heart? You don't need to look any further than *Christmas Greetings* by Pat Simmons. Great job Pat, if I could I would give a rating of 6 stars.
—Reader Leslie Hudson

Special thanks to

Readers and book clubs who support my work: thank you reading, encouraging me, telling others, posting reviews, and overall blessing me

To my author sisters. There are *soooo* many to name, but a shoutout to the CBLR and the Fun Friday crew. The sisterhood bond is special.

My writing village:
Beta reader: Stacey Jefferson
Author's assistant: Jackie Roberts
Developmental Editor: Chandra Sparks Splond

District Elder Ron Stephens for his consultation and Agent Latoya Smith with the Arthouse Literary Agency for securing the audio rights for Queen's Surrender to Recorded Books. How exciting to bring the Jamiesons to life. Be on the look out.

Cheerleaders: husband Kerry Simmons and cousin Darlene Simmons
Love you all

In loving memory….

Kym Lovanne Eastern Stepney
1976-2021

Oh, the stories we could tell.
I will miss your smile, love, laughter, and being your aunt.
I will forever praise God for sharing you with us.
To God be the glory for His lovingkindness.

Chapter One

Queen Jamieson never missed a party. Galas. Banquets. Soirées. Receptions. Pool parties. No matter whatever the occasion, she graced the host with her presence. It was shameful to learn from Giselle "Gigi" Jamieson Jacobs, her older half-sister, Queen's name was left off the guest list of an epic celebration.

The payback: crash the party. Three hundred and fifty miles was nothing. Distance didn't deter her as she was en route from Tulsa to St. Louis.

What did she care it was a birthday celebration for her three-year-old twin cousins, Camille and Gabriel Jamieson? A party was a party in her book she thought as she glanced out the window seat of her airplane.

"Sorry. I thought you knew. Gabrielle has been planning it for months," Gigi had said during their regular weekly phone chat. As the children's godmother, Gigi and her husband Jacob, who lived in Connecticut, were expected to be in attendance.

Seconds after the wheels touched down at Lambert International Airport, Queen unbuckled, stood, and stretched before she reached to unlatch the overhead compartment. A gentleman intercepted and smiled.

"I gotcha, beautiful." He was tall, handsome, and dressed in a business suit—nice. She was drawn to the professional type. "Which one is yours?"

"The red paisley with the queen luggage tag." She pointed.

"Yes, you are." His lopsided grin did nothing to flatter her.

Queen's name was a conversation starter. Sometimes, she engaged. Other times, like now, she thanked and dismissed the stranger. Queen knew a flirt when she saw one. She was the master of the technique herself.

Not today.

Making her way down the ramp, Queen followed the signs to exit the terminal. She rounded the corner, and the Jamieson sisters, eighteen-year-old Kami and sixteen-year-old Victoria didn't contain their excitement to greet her.

Half-siblings, they were young when placed in the foster care system, unaware the other existed until a chance meeting in high school. The experience in the system was horrific for Victoria who suffered abuse and neglect, while idyllic for Kami, who flourished after Parke and Cheney Jamieson adopted her. Once they learned of Victoria, Parke and Cheney adopted her, too.

The Jamiesons. Queen couldn't be prouder of her bloodline. Certified genealogists, her cousins had tracked their kinfolks back to 1770 in Cote d'Ivoire, Africa. Queen believed her family held the record for the most half-siblings and half-cousins but embodied whole hearts. After losing her sole sibling, Suzette, to complications of lupus, her halves made her complete again.

She returned the girls' smiles as she continued toward them. Whenever Queen visited the Gateway City, she spent time with these two. Kami and Victoria's closeness reminded her of the relationship she had shared with Suzette. Kami flew into Queen's arms while Victoria watched.

Rocking Kami from side to side, Queen motioned for Victoria to join them. She did. In a few months, the sisters would graduate from high school. Victoria's impressive I.Q allowed her to skip to grade levels.

Queen fingered the silkiness of Kami's hair and admired Victoria's straight mane. Their resemblance was remarkable since they had different dads. "Wow. Aren't my two nieces beautiful?" On paper, they were fifth cousins, but in the Jamieson family, children were taught to address adults as Auntie or Uncle.

"Not like you. These cute guys are staring at you, Auntie," Kami gushed and giggled. "Don't look now. One's coming—"

"Excuse me. I didn't have time to introduce myself on the plane. I'm Karlton Jennings. I would love to buy you a drink or take you to dinner while you're in town." He pulled out his business card. "I noticed you aren't wearing a ring."

There was no way she would give this man a call. Queen allowed nothing to get in the way of family time. However, she played along. Lowering her lashes, she flirted back and accepted it to be polite and dismissed him. "Thanks."

She brushed a kiss on Victoria's cheek. "Pretty as your big sister. You're coming to the twins' party with us, right?"

Victoria scrunched her nose and was quick to say, "Nah." She held up car keys. "Grandma BB taught me how to drive, and I got my license yesterday, so I'm dropping you both off."

Queen stilled her movements and did her best to mask her concern. She stuttered, "O-okay."

Kami and Victoria didn't stifle their laughs.

"Just teasing, Auntie. I've had it for a couple of weeks. I'm going back home. Y'all can catch a ride with Grandma BB and Chip and Dale who are already there."

Patting her chest, Queen gave Victoria a side-eye. "I was about to snatch those keys." Minutes later, Queen relaxed in the front passenger seat. Destination: Cameron's house. "You are really a cautious driver. Grandma BB taught you well."

"She drives like Grandma BB too," Kami teased. "Slow."

Victoria stuck out her tongue. "Thank you, Auntie. She told me not to speed, but if I accidentally drove too fast, which I haven't yet," she was quick to add, "to tell the officer I belong to Grandma BB, and he will look the other way."

Every law enforcement officer within miles of Ferguson knew of Grandma BB. Queen had never seen the woman in action, but believed the rumors were true about the shenanigans of the eighty-something gun-toting woman. She wasn't scared of anybody.

Soon, they arrived at her cousins' home in Ladue, near the Washington University campus where Cameron was a professor. Partygoers' cars lined the private street, including the long driveway to their estate. The celebration was in full swing.

"Are you sure you don't want to stay for a little while?" Queen tried to coax Victoria who had suffered trauma at the hands of foster fathers and avoided all men, including the nice guys like the Jamiesons. After Parke and Cheney adopted her, Victoria chose to live with Grandma BB, because trusting her new stepbrothers was a slow process.

"Yeah, I'm sure." Her facial expression betrayed her. The longing was there.

"Okay, sweetie." Queen didn't hide her disappointment. "Be careful. Text Kami when you make it home."

Victoria rolled her eyes. "You sound just like my sister."

"Trust me. Sisters are the best gift parents can give a little girl, so hold her close."

God had given Queen twenty-five years and three months with Suzette. Not a day longer.

While waiting for Kami to get out of the car, Queen admired the mansion that stood majestically among the others. The neighborhood screamed money, which was the perfect fit for a department head at a prestigious private university. She was blown away with the five bedrooms, six baths and forty-eight plus hundred square feet of living space.

All the Jamieson men, including her half-brothers, had large homes for gatherings. None this majestic, but roomy. Her relatives were doing well. Queen was no exception. As a senior mechanical engineer in Tulsa, she lived in luxury.

Kami looped her arm through Queen's and synchronized their steps along the path. "I'm glad you're here."

"Me too. Is Victoria going to be okay?" Queen's heart bled for the girl.

"She's got God, Grandma BB, and me. We'll make sure of it, Auntie."

As they approached the stone-and-brick archway to the front door, Queen heard laughter and music. Turning the knob, she grinned and stepped inside. *Yeah, this party is so worth crashing.*

Heads turned. Cousins, big and small, mobbed her, screaming their delight.

"Gigi just told me to expect you. You look fabulous. Love the hair." Rubbing her swollen belly, Talise, Queen's sister-in-law, and a licensed stylist, nodded her approval at Queen's mass of natural curls.

"Why didn't you tell us you were coming?" Ace, Talise's husband, engulfed her in a hug.

"Can't tell you all my secrets, big brother."

An impromptu Soul Train line formed as Queen danced her way through the opening like a celebrity, receiving hugs and kisses until she caught sight of the guests of honor—the twins. She received a five-second acknowledgment before they gave chase to their small cousins.

Queen twirled around when someone tapped her shoulder. She turned into the arms of Gigi. "Hey." Their bond was stronger than their embrace. Gigi sutured the wound of losing Suzette—almost. After nine years, time had not healed the loss. Both had dark brown skin and long hair, but a person would have to look hard to see a resemblance between these half-sisters.

Gigi was part of Samuel Jamieson's first family. To her, he had turned his back on his wife and children with his cheating. To Queen—the third family—Samuel was a kind, caring father who regretted his past indiscretions. Kidd and Ace filled in the gap. They were evidence of Samuel's sins with Sandra, and to their disgrace, Samuel never married their mother.

Because of Samuel's two marriages and one known affair, Queen would always have family. She cherished the regular phone talks they had getting to know one another and making peace on behalf of their father.

"Break it up, you two, and share." Eva, the other expecting sister-in-law, married to her brother Kidd, said as the hug with Gigi lingered.

Kidd lifted Queen from the floor. Before her feet could touch down, Ace hefted her higher as if to outdo his older brother.

"Let me go. You two have bench pressed my weight enough." Queen giggled as they did as she requested.

Making her way to the kitchen, Queen found the Duprees—Gabriele's mother and the twins' maternal grandparents—Dr. Bernard and Mrs. Veronica Dupree, replenishing food platters.

Two of their handsome sons were in attendance. Queen wasn't interested in either of their single status. She made sure they knew it. Where was the third, an evangelist turned pastor?

Philip. He was fascinating, but unaffected by her charm. She enjoyed their harmless banter about Philip, who lived God's will versus Queen, who preferred her own free-will lifestyle. He didn't judge her choices—most of the time—and she respected his choices—most of the time. Perfect harmony sometimes.

Before she could ask about his whereabouts, the front door opened. A hush silenced the guests as heads turned. The six foot, three inches of conditioned muscle dressed in casual attire, the epitome of top five most handsome men in the world, entered with a smile that could make a woman say, "Yes, Lord," except for Queen.

She was accustomed to men being tongue-tied over her allure and vying for her attention. Queen had dated handsome men before, worked with and mingled with them at events, but Philip—*whew*—he had something extra.

He oozed confidence while embodying humility. His charisma would make any woman surrender to him, not realizing he was the front man for the Lord. He seemed untouchable.

Philip's smile, the hugs, the handshakes—they were all there, but something was off. Queen studied his body language. His grin, showcasing incredible white teeth, was in place. His greetings generous, not forced, but there was a hint of weariness that flashed on his face then retreated.

Queen folded her arms and leaned against the counter, biding her turn for a greeting. She shivered when his eyes captured hers. Despite her ankle boots' three-inch heels, he towered over her. He smiled, but his eyes didn't twinkle. "Queen, it's good to see you. Nice hair."

She'd gone natural months ago, giving her hair a rest from the heat process, then decided she liked the look. "Same here. The silver strands on your chin make you look distinguished." She lifted her brow. Flirting was second nature to Queen but flirting with him wasn't advisable. Somehow, he had the upper hand. Philip could lure a woman into a false sense of attraction with his undivided attention, but it was all for the gain of his ministry.

"Yeah." His eyes didn't sparkle. "And each one was hard earned." Gabriel and Camille screamed their uncle's name, and

Philip scooped them up, smothered them with kisses, and excused himself with a farewell nod. Queen felt his absence at once—or maybe it was his energy. His spirit.

Munching on treats and listening to Gigi, Queen watched him make his way to the buffet table and stack a plate too small for food he was about to consume. "I'll be back." She followed Philip's path, kissing Parke and Malcolm's children, until she stood next to him.

Philip blessed his food and had his mouth open for the first sample. Queen took the plate out of his hand.

"Walk with me," she demanded.

Why had Philip allowed Queen to interrupt his hot meal? He was mentally exhausted and famished.

He loved family and the souls he encountered as a pastor. But now? He could strangle some congregants at the church where God had directed him after the Lord told him to cease his worldwide evangelism ministry. He was not in a sociable mood, including Queen's company.

At least she didn't ask for a nibble of his chicken. Those would have been fighting words. She seemed patient as he cleaned the bone and swiped another drumette off his plate before she looped her arm through his and nudged him out the side door.

"Good, huh?" Mischief danced in her eyes as he faced her.

"More would have been better." He could feel a smile rising from his chest, despite his irritation with her. A one-dimpled smile that rivaled her mesmerizing long lashes, Queen was as regal as her name. Her wild mane magnified her personality. Dark skin glistened with good health under the sun's rays.

Besides the beauty that she was, he was drawn to her radiance, vibrancy, and the calmness she possessed. He liked that about her. A woman true to her convictions.

Philip knew well what the Scriptures said about the lust of the eyes, so he made sure not to admire too long the hand-carved figure that God had molded.

Speaking of eyes, she had her brothers' eyes—same unusual shade of brown—smart, intense, and in her case, seductive. The woman knew how to command attention without trying.

"What's going on with you?"

She squeezed his arms, and his biceps flexed in response. Flawless in her appearance, she lifted her delicate chin and walked ahead—that was another production.

Each step and movement of her body was in sync and deliberate. She didn't walk, she glided or strutted to her destination.

Most women weren't intimidating, but this lady had a way to dumbfound him. He searched for a Scripture, any verse to reign his mind back in. *Finally, brethren, whatsoever things are true, are honest, are just, are pure, are lovely, are of good report; if there be any virtue, and if there be any praise, think on these things.*

Philippians 4:8. Got it. Philip nodded at the Word recalled to his mind. *You need a wife.* Now where did that thought come from?

"Philip," Queen said with a distinct dialect, "I want to know what's going on with you. Don't lie me. You're a pastor, remember?" She was in a demanding stance that dared anyone to cross her.

Did the woman just scold him? He stiffened. Her assumption could be debatable—not the sinning part, but being the angel of one of God's houses, shepherd of God's sheep, or overseer was more than a notion. Was he that transparent? "What gave me away?"

"Your eyes." She seemed shocked, as if he should have known. After a few seconds, Queen gave him an innocent smile and arched a brow. "Spill it. So, what, I've got a rebellious streak when it comes to church, but I'm concerned about you."

God, will this woman understand the workings of Your ministry for me to spill my guts? He stalled, wondering, then believed her. "One more bite." Philip devoured more drumettes and wiped his fingers.

"I'm thinking…" He exhaled. "I'm not cut out to be a pastor." He admitted his weakness with a shrug.

She stepped back. Her movements were graceful as her hand found its way to her waist. "Philip Dupree, you were born to win souls for Christ." Her tone defied him to argue with her assessment.

"Says the woman who has yet to be won." He grunted.

She laughed. "Yeah, well. I'm coming—maybe. I kinda like myself the way I am. Why change now?"

"Because we all were born in sin and shaped in iniquity." Philip wasn't a walking Bible, but with Queen, he knew to win her soul, she needed to hear the Scriptures to believe. "Stubborn woman."

Queen jutted her chin. "Stubbornness has been my wall of strength. Otherwise, I would crumble under sorrow."

There were so many Bible lessons he could give on that one, but not now. When Philip smacked his lips, he tasted the sweet and spicy sauce from those wings. "I feel the honeymoon is over."

"What? You're married?"

Fear struck Queen's face. The intensity was enough to make Philip's belly ache from laughter, so he tempered his amusement.

"How come I wasn't invited? Nobody told—" She became annoyed with each word. Her eyes flashed like fire, her nostrils flared, and she balled her hands. He had never seen her so fierce. Momma bear. Dangerous.

Philip held his stomach and released an uncontrollable hoot.

"What's so funny?"

"You. It was just an expression."

"Oh." Queen relaxed as she blushed, then shoved him toward the front gate. "The next time you speak in a code, give me the heads up. I need to vet the chick—I mean first lady of the church. You can't marry just anybody." She *hmphed* as if she were about to go to bat for him.

A Jamieson to the core. They loved hard and were a force to be reckoned with for one of their own. If only Philip could convince Queen to join the Lord's side.

"That I agree." He stuffed his hands into his pants pockets. "What I meant was I'm the trial pastor for one year. I'm seven months in, and God's people are worse than toddlers on a diaper strike, and the board is blaming me for the division." He shook his head. *Good grief.*

More than once, Philip questioned God calling him to pastor. He consulted with his confidant, Bishop Henderson, who once was an evangelist then elevated to pastor and recently bishop.

"Growing pains," Bishop Henderson had assured him.

And then it was his older brother. Drexel gave him a pep talk, too. "Everything will work out. This is new."

Philip wasn't consoled. Had he been wasting his time? Meetings with the deacon board like the one earlier in the day frustrated him. Those men held his future as the leader of their flock in limbo. "This experience makes me wonder if I heard God's voice… Can I be honest?"

Queen linked her fingers through his as if it was a natural gesture between them. It wasn't, so he should break away, but her touch comforted him. "That's the only way I know you." Her eyes revealed she believed that.

"I feel like bailing." There. He'd said it aloud. Now how would God and others judge him?

He wasn't expecting her to laugh, but Queen did. "The pastor's running scared. Why?"

"It's not funny." But he chuckled anyway and shrugged. "I'm second-guessing things."

She frowned. "What do you mean?"

"I'm seriously thinking about returning to the evangelism field."

She twisted her pouty lips. "You once told me God doesn't make mistakes, but if you're not feeling it, leave."

The mind of a carefree woman. "It's not that simple, and yes, God doesn't make mistakes, so I guess this is all on me."

"Philip, you're not making sense. One thing I know about you is you're deliberate. I'd never describe you as confused."

He rubbed the waves of his hair. His life made little sense after the three-month honeymoon period with the church folks expired. They had welcomed him with open arms. People seemed like they had a hunger for God's Word, and souls were saved every time the church doors opened. Why did anyone have complaints? Plus, the congregants had his number on speed dial 24/7.

"I'm thinking about giving it up. I mean evangelism is no picnic either in God's harvest, but when the revival ends, members are back in the hands of their pastor."

Queen frowned. "In other words, no attachments. *Hmmm.* Philip Dupree, you're not a quitter, and you're going to show them who's boss." She jabbed a finger in the air as the wind played with a curl in her thick mane.

"Yes, ma'am." He gave her a salute and steered her back to the house, not realizing they had walked as far away as they had.

"Queen, you're one of a kind. Thanks for the pep talk." He grinned.

"In another life, I'd be a therapist. Be glad I'm not billing you." She squeezed his arm again, and he responded by covering her hand with his. As they turned up the long driveway, he. spied their family watching them through the windows with no shame.

When they walked through the door, everyone scrambled to fake positions on the furniture. Some poses seemed rather uncomfortable.

"What are you all up to?" Queen asked.

"We're lookin' out the window at you and Uncle Philip," Camille tattled on her family.

"There's nothing to see. Now—" Philip slipped off his jacket—"where's the food?"

"This conversation isn't over," Queen whispered close to his ear.

He eyed her. "Trust me, it is. I'm good."

"If anybody's going down at your church, it won't be you. Not on my watch." Queen strutted away. With her wild curls, skinny leather jeans, short, tailored jacket, and ankle boots, Queen should have thrust her fist in the air in a show of black power.

Before Philip left the party, Drexel took him aside. "I see Queen has her claws in you."

His older brother was a judge in Illinois. Whenever Drexel could, he made the ninety minutes weekend drives to St. Louis to see their sister.

"Queen is an in-law," Philip reminded the man who'd had a crush on Queen since the first day they'd met.

"That woman should be an out-law to all men on earth, especially you. She'll take you down, bro." Stuffing his hands in his pockets, Drexel returned to the party.

Philip was immune to a woman's clutches. He had nothing to worry about.

Chapter Two

Nobody messes over Philip. He was Queen's hero.

So, what you goin' do about it? A voice in her head taunted. What could she? Whatever his church folks were putting him through was almost enough to make her pray against their foolishness. Queen didn't have that spiritual power to make something happen, so there had to be another way.

In the kitchen, Philip and his father were the kings of the castle, as his mother and sister catered to Philip with all his favorite dishes. He seemed to be back to his usual charming self.

Maybe my job is done, she mused to herself as she cast one last glance at Philip before joining the women in the hearth room. She took a seat next to Gigi on an oversized ottoman to watch the entertainment.

Grandma BB did a step show routine from her college days, decades ago as a member of Delta Sigma Theta Sorority, Incorporated.

Queen was impressed. For a woman in her eighties, nineties, or whatever her certified birth certificate stated, her movements were smooth.

Kami shouted, "Go Grandma. Go Grandma. Go…" Others added to the chorus and soon, the woman mimicked the Harlem shake, the Moonwalk, then she broke out with Hammer Time moves. That was all Queen needed. She stood and joined her, followed by the small children.

When Grandma BB attempted a split and couldn't get up off the floor with ease, her escorts, Chip and Dale—retired Las Vegas performers turned personal assistants—came to the rescue. They were careful not to scuff her trademark Stacy Adams shoes that clashed with whatever ensemble she wore. Once on her feet, Grandma BB smiled and took a bow to hearty applause and laughter.

Chip suggested they take her home. "Right. Got to have energy for our morning exercise."

Slipping on her jacket, Kami said goodbye to her parents.

Kami stayed at Grandma BB's, too, to keep Victoria company and get to know her half-sister. Although Grandma BB wasn't a Jamieson by blood, the family welcomed her as everybody's grandmother. Parke and Cheney were okay with the decision.

Queen grabbed her things to go with them. She gave Gigi a heartfelt embrace.

"Aww, you're leaving already?" Gigi didn't hide her disappointment. "It's tradition you stay here to hang out with me."

"I know." It was torture for Queen to leave her big sister, too. "How about next time? I want to spend time with Victoria."

"Gotcha. She needs us—all the Jamiesons."

"In smaller doses." Queen demonstrated with a small crack between her thumb and forefinger. "We are a lot to take in."

"You think?" Gigi laughed.

The goodbyes were as much a production as the welcomes. Queen made her rounds, hugging her brothers, rubbing her sisters-in-law's swollen bellies, and accepting a to-go plate for Victoria.

When Queen made her way to Philip, the sparkle had returned to his eyes. There was nothing that kinfolks and food couldn't fix. She hugged him, then rubbed the hairs on his chin. She did it to annoy him, but today it felt odd. If they were a couple, it would have been an intimate gesture. They were family—sort of—in-laws.

"Remember, I believe in you and dare anyone to mistreat *my* Philip." She winked and turned to leave, but he grabbed her hand.

"Am I *your* Philip?" The smirk he wore made her chuckle.

His flirting skills were impressive. His voice dropped a tone, and he stared into her eyes taunting her to blink. The man didn't know she was more trouble than she was worth. Queen had left a trail of heartaches since she was old enough to wear heels.

"Of course, you are, as long as I'm a Jamieson. That's a promise." She stepped out of his hold and turned around to say goodbye to the others.

"Will you be at church tomorrow?" It was Philip's customary closer between them.

Any other day, she had a smart retort, but words escaped her, so she shrugged and left with Kami, Grandma BB, and her escorts.

During the short ride to Grandma BB's spacious home in historic Old Town Ferguson, Queen relaxed against the headrest and closed her eyes. After a demanding work week and the travel, fatigue was playing hide-and-seek with her.

By the time Chip parked in the driveway, Queen opened her eyes and yawned as Dale waited to help her and Kami out.

In the house, Victoria greeted them in the great room, snacking on a bag of chips. "Did you have a good time?"

"Yes," Queen answered, "but it would have been better if you had hung out with us. Mrs. Dupree sent you a plate."

"They always do." Victoria lowered her lashes. "Maybe one day I'll tag along, but..." her voice faded. "I know the Jamiesons love me, but I'd rather avoid men and boys over the age of five. Bad memories."

Grandma BB, who had claimed her favorite oversized chair, got a second wind and suggested a pajama party once everyone showered and changed. "Then we can have a girl talk."

A hot bath—sweet news to Queen, but not the girl talk. Her mission had been accomplished. Sort of. Queen did crash a party, although family needed no invitation to visit.

Refreshed and dressed in their silk pajamas, courtesy of Queen's previous Christmas gifts, Kami and Victoria strolled into Grandma BB's master suite. Pairs of Stacy Adams shoes in various colors lined the back wall. They were not her late husband's.

Queen stared at the girls. "I can't believe in two months, the Jamieson sisters will graduate from high school. Victoria, this must be exciting. You've earned your G.E.D at sixteen and received numerous scholarship offers." Queen patted her chest with pride. "I'm glad Parke demanded both his daughters walk across stage at the graduation ceremony."

Victoria's face glowed. "Yeah, but he didn't have to do that." She rubbed her hand on the smoothness of her pajama pants.

"We're talking about my cousin. As your father, Parke's going to make sure you get everything you deserve and then some. We can't change the past, but we can make sure your future is bright."

Kami grabbed Victoria's hand. "She's almost as smart as me."

"Smarter." Victoria stuck out her tongue.

"So, what are your college plans?" Queen asked as Grandma BB's soft snore made them giggle, including Grandma BB. Was the woman listening or dreaming?

"I'm already taking online college courses," Victoria said. "I'm thinking about law school to become a judge."

"Excellent." Queen grinned. "That's my niece."

"Auntie," Kami interrupted, "I don't know if that's a good thing for Victoria." She exchanged a glance with her sister, who shrugged. "She would sentence every man to life without parole."

"Oh no." Queen thought about her brothers, cousins, and every innocent Black man. "Humph. Not a good career choice. Women are accomplices in crime too. Convicted sex offender Jeffrey Epstein had help."

"Yep, and foster mothers," Victoria said, snarling. "They were tone deaf. So much for calling for help."

Kami squeezed Victoria's hand. "We're here now. Nobody messes with a Jamieson. We have your back, and God has you, too."

Quietness filled the room before Kami perked up. "I've applied to three top schools, but like Pace stayed in St. Louis to attend Wash U, I won't leave my sister either." Kami's no-nonsense expression meant it wasn't negotiable. "Wherever she goes, I'll go."

Parke and Cheney adopted Kami and Pace, and then had two sons together.

"That's what I'm talking about." Queen gave her an imaginary fist bump from across the room. She envied their unbreakable bond like the one Queen had with Suzette until her last breath. "Both of you are welcome to apply at the University of Central Oklahoma in Edmond, which is close to me." She put her hands together in a praying manner.

The previous summer, Kami had visited Queen. They had so much fun. When Kami left, Queen considered moving to St. Louis to be closer to her siblings and cousins, but she couldn't. She had deep roots in Tulsa.

"You two are always complimenting my clothes and know how to make your outfits pop. If you're interested in that industry, the University of Central Oklahoma has an expanding curriculum in fashion design."

Pumping money into the program had been Queen's brainchild to keep Suzette's memory of her passion alive. She had attended the Academy of Art University in San Francisco because top students could present at Fashion Week in New York City. When Suzette was diagnosed with lupus, she transferred to UCO to be close to home, but her health declined, and Suzette never graduated.

Every year, Queen encouraged the department to offer more scholarships, and she asked fashion bloggers and influencers to help recruit potential students. Queen's goal was to put Tulsa's program on the map!

"No disrespect, Auntie," Victoria seemed to fumble for words, "but everything about you screams, 'Look at me.' I don't want that attention. I know God cleansed me from the filth of those dirty scums, but I'd rather they not look at me."

"Let me let you two in on a secret." Queen paused. "The hair, clothes, and attitude, that's all Suzette. I'm the brainy one. She was the glamour girl who would have lit the runway if she had lived."

Hmmph. Grandma BB stirred and sat up. "Oh, no. You're both, dear. Take it from the oldest diva here. I know my share of pain. I haven't lived…" She mumbled her age, "and not learn how to move on. Henry would have wanted that." Grandma BB's eyes lit up. "I'd have remarried in a heartbeat to experience the deep unselfish love I shared with him."

"I don't believe in love. It's not in my future." Victoria seemed sad at her own declaration.

"Mom and Daddy say God holds the future," Kami said. "Uncle Philip told me Jesus died for us to get our lives back on track."

Sounded like something he would say. Queen mused. That was her Philip, a man with an encouraging word and kindness to a fault, which was why he needed her backup.

"I'm going to church, but the life I wanted was taken away from me." Victoria shrugged.

"The devil is a lie!" Grandma BB rolled her neck. "I've seen you mime at Restoration Temple. You're working through your pain. Once God restores you mentally, physically, and spiritually, those losers are going to meet their day of reckoning. Elder Winnie Jordan Scaife knows how to call on heaven for y'all." Grandma BB looked smug.

"Oh, so you're a member now?" Queen blinked her surprise and snickered.

Grandma BB folded her arms like a defiant toddler. "Ain't nobody got time to be a member. I go to watch Victoria." She *hmmphed* for emphasis.

Queen snickered. A fellow holdout in the Jamieson clan.

"I can't wait to get to that fierce level, so I'll never be a victim again." Victoria gritted her teeth as if she were about to pounce on her prey. "The church's young women's ministry has helped me a lot."

Queen nodded. "I get it, Victoria. Trust can be a long time coming. Miming in church? I've got to see this."

"Then come to service with us in the morning." The expectancy on Victoria's face made Queen say yes.

Take that, Philip Dupree. *Church, here I come, even if it isn't his.*

One day, Queen. One day, God is coming for you, and you won't be able to say no, Philip whispered the final Amen to his morning prayers. He chanced a text to invite her to his church again.

I'm getting ready now.

"Yes, Lord. Finally." Philip's heart pounded with excitement—until he read on.

Victoria does a mime routine, so I'm curious to see her, then I'm flying out. I would say maybe next time, but you would hold me to it.

He snickered. **Yes, I would**. At least she was going somewhere. Philip had heard Elder Scaife at Restoration Temple was a fireball and preached the gospel to scorch stony hearts. Maybe the Word would prick Queen's heart to say, "I surrender, Lord."

How about dinner, and I'll drive you to the airport?

When he didn't hear back right away, he took that as a no. While tying his tie, Queen called him. "Sorry. Applying makeup takes concentration."

He snickered and abandoned his task. "Woman, you're perfect without it."

"*Awww*, Philip, don't make me blush. I brushed enough blush on my cheeks."

Ummm-hmmm. Interesting. He didn't know he had that power. When she said that Kami and Victoria were cooking a meal afterward for her, she changed her flight to enjoy it with them. That was two strikeouts.

"How about a ride to the airport?"

"I look forward to it."

Philip imagined her smile, and he grinned. "Me, too, Queen."

She told him what time to pick her up. As he was about to end the call, her husky voice yelled, "Wait! Preach, Philip, preach."

His cheerleader. "God will." When they ended the call, he wondered what it was going to take for Queen to be saved. Philip knew the answer: repent.

And that's what stood between God and man. No one wanted to admit their imperfections and a desire for repentance.

That's your job, God whispered. *Preach the Word; be prepared in season and out of season; reprove, rebuke, and encourage with every form of patient instruction.*

Timothy 4:2. It was like a golden text for all ministers. He gave the Lord a salute, finished dressing, then locked up his two-bedroom spacious apartment the church had provided him. Queen's "I believe in you" echoed in Philip's head as he stepped into his SUV, which he had purchased before relocating from the East Coast.

Philip smiled all the way to his destination. "It's going to be a good day. Yep." He had heard from the Lord, and he'd see Queen off. The whipped cream on the cheesecake would be to see souls hungry for salvation, not for socializing or to show off their wardrobe.

He arrived and parked with a warning to the devil. "My church is a saving station, Satan, so you're on enemy territory."

Entering the building, Philip waved at members as he headed to his office before Sunday school. Nathan Davis, the deacon assigned to be his armor bearer, had become more since Philip came on board last year. They seemed to share the same sentiments when it came to not compromising the Christian walk. Both single, the two of them would attend local baseball games, go bowling, or meet up somewhere to watch games.

"Morning," Nathan and others greeted him. "Ready to feed God's sheep?"

"Only if they're hungry," was the standard exchange between Philip and Nathan on Sunday mornings.

"I'm starved." He patted his heart and followed Philip into his office. "How did it go at the birthday party with your family?"

"Refreshing, filling," he said, patting his belly, "and entertaining. Let me just say my sisters-in-law know how to throw a party. They are indoctrinating my three-year-old niece and nephew on the proper way to celebrate."

Nathan laughed. "Wish I had a big family, that way a person always has a friend."

"True." Philip hung his coat and rested his briefcase in the chair. "It's three of us Duprees—you've met Drexel when he's driven down from Springfield to watch the Cubs beat up on the Cardinals, but those Jamiesons," Philip shook his head and chuckled, "they're an army of God's soldiers."

"I hope they decide to fellowship with you at Total Surrender." Nathan looked hopeful as if the church lacked members.

"Right now, they're comfortable at their own places of worship. Maybe in the future, after I'm installed as pastor." During the trial period, some Jamiesons had dropped in to visit on Sundays

Minutes later, they walked out of his office and into the sanctuary where various classes were scattered for the Sunday school lesson on forgiveness.

Once that session concluded, the praise team worshipped with melodies from heaven until Philip stepped into the pulpit for the sermon. He never lacked confidence when it came to preaching. Why did Queen's whisper of "I believe in you" give him a boost as he opened his Bible? He put aside his prepared notes on Philippians 4 after God diverted him to another passage.

"While some might strive for riches, processions, and popularity, our focus is to live godly, which is invaluable. You can't live holy in the flesh—I get that. But once you receive the

Holy Ghost, you have supernatural power to live for Jesus. In 1 Timothy 6:6–9: there is a cash-in value of godliness. *But godliness with contentment is great gain. For we brought nothing into this world, and it is certain we can carry nothing out. And having food and raiment let us be therewith content. But they that will be rich fall into temptation and a snare, and into many foolish and hurtful lusts, which drown men in destruction and perdition."*

Philip preached hard until God's voice became silent. He appealed to his audience the benefit of repenting and the rewards of salvation. Several came to the altar for prayer, four wanted the water-and-fire baptism.

While the congregation lifted praises to God, more people wanted to take part in the salvation process. Soon, two ministers prepared themselves to perform the baptism, and helpers assisted the candidates to change out of their church clothes.

Half an hour later, a hush descended throughout the sanctuary as Philip folded his arms and turned his attention to the pool behind the pulpit.

The baptism candidates, dressed in all white, were standing in the pool. Two ministers lifted one arm as the other hand gripped the back of the garment.

"My dear brothers and sisters, upon the confession of your faith and the confidence in the Holy Word of God, we indeed baptize you all in the mighty name of Jesus Christ—for salvation exists in no other name under heaven given to men by which we must be saved—for the remission of your sins. You shall receive the gifts of the Holy Ghost, and the Lord will fill you with heavenly tongues, according to Acts 2:38."

The church shouted, "Amen!" The candidates were submerged in water and reemerged. Some spoke in heavenly tongues; others praised Jesus.

Philip's heart rejoiced with thanksgiving. This is what his mission was all about—salvation. When would Queen concede to repentance? He would continue to give that request to the Lord.

"Good service," Nathan said afterward and patted Philip on the back. "I'm heading out to dinner with some of the saints. Do you have any dinner invites from some of the single sisters?" He didn't hide his amusement as he stroked his goatee, which was grayer than Philip's, yet he was a couple years younger.

"Not funny, I didn't come here to dinner hop with the sisters like some folks bar hop. I think I'm safe if I accept your invite. Let's go." Philip grabbed his things.

At the restaurant, Philip enjoyed the fellowship with other deacons and two married couples, getting to know more about them outside of church. However, there was no subtle way to watch the time so he wouldn't cause Queen to miss her flight.

Nathan treated him when the bill arrived.

"Hey, I was about to take care of that." Philip thanked him and checked the time again.

"You have somewhere to be?" Nathan gave him a curious stare. His friend knew Philip's personal schedule, which most times was open, if it didn't include family functions.

"An in-law who flew in for the twins' birthday yesterday needs a ride to the airport, and I offered—rather I asked if I could take her." Philip didn't want to add the latter part, but he trusted Nathan with the truth as they walked out of the restaurant together.

"Your family goes all the way out for parties. One day, you've got to let me tag along as your plus one for the cake and ice cream. Who knows, we could end up related one day."

Philip threw his head back with a hearty laugh. "You'll get an invite. Most are married, and the one I'm taking to the airport—whew. God would have to put her in a spiritual straitjacket to yield to His will because she's not coming freely, trust me."

"One of those holdouts, huh?" Once they were at Nathan's vehicle, they patted each other's back in a brotherly hug.

"She is until the end," Philip mumbled as he continued to his SUV, hoping it would be sooner rather than later.

In no time, Philip parked in front of Grandma BB's house and hiked the stairs to her front door. He nodded to Chip and Dale who were on their way out. They exchanged fist bumps.

Her escorts appeared older than Philip's forty years, but they remained in good health to keep up with the feisty widow. Grandma BB's morning exercise regimen comprised them jogging beside her scooter at top speed. Kami had snapped a photo and shared it on social media.

"Queen is holding court in the house. I thought Grandma BB was high maintenance. Man—" Chip—or maybe it was Dale—shook his head. They didn't look alike, but sometimes, Philip couldn't keep them straight.

"I heard that," Grandma BB yelled from down the hall. "My late husband left me plenty of money to maintain the lifestyle he wanted for me, including your salaries and year-end bonuses."

"She's got a point." Both men laughed. "We're out of here."

Since Victoria now lived there, certain sections of the house were off limits to male guests. Philip took his seat in the front parlor. Soon, he heard the unhurried tap of Queen's heels as she rolled her luggage. She appeared in the doorway and waited for him to lift his head and give her the attention she sought.

Philip obliged and stood. He walked toward her smiling face and reached for her small designer carryon while inhaling her perfume's subtle scent.

God, save this woman for mankind's sake. "You look pretty." He would have to get use to her hair wild with natural curls instead of the long flowing black hair he was accustomed to seeing. Yet, she owned that look.

"And you're handsome, pastor."

He and Queen were almost out the door when Kami turned the corner and gave him a hug. He kissed her hair and squeezed tight. Last year, the devil had enticed her away from holiness with a first boyfriend, but the Jamiesons weren't having it.

Satan had crossed the line. Fasts were called and prayer lines crammed. By the time Philip made it to Tulsa for a tent meeting, Kami was more than ready to repent and return in full force to the Lord's house.

He was glad to have his old sweet, affectionate niece back instead of the defiant disobedient one. God knew Kami would need restoration to minister to her sister.

They chatted a few minutes, then Philip checked his watch and spied Victoria in the corner. She wasn't out of sight, but out of any man's reach. Philip offered a smile and waved, which was warily returned. He would continue to pray for her deliverance. Facing Queen, he asked, "Ready?"

She nodded and strutted out the door. Once she was strapped in, Philip pulled away from the curb.

"I missed you at church today." He glanced her way. "I was hoping to look up and see you there."

"I was in someone else's pew." Queen patted her chest and choked. "Victoria needed me more. She performed her mime ministry to 'I Will Wear a Crown.' Whew, I felt her raw emotions. She had me in a trance." Queen sounded breathless.

Pleased she had been affected, Philip patted her hand. "God will stir your spirit if you let Him."

Queen squinted at him. He wasn't sure if it was because he hadn't removed his hand. "I almost was persuaded."

"Almost in heaven is not in heaven."

"My Philip is back." Queen shook his hand from hers and clapped. "Maybe one day your words will sink in."

"It's not my words that will save you. Once God's Word leaves His presence, it's like a boomerang. It won't return until it accomplishes and prospers what He wills for it to do."

"You're so deep, Philip. I believe Jesus died for my sins on the cross and don't need church to remind me of that."

"I'm not trying to be too spiritual, but one day if you surrender, God will reveal the church within you." He glanced at her before entering the highway.

She glowed. It wasn't the outer beauty. It was as if God allowed him to have a peep into her soul.

Too soon for Philip, they arrived at Lambert Airport, and she pointed to the drop-off sign. He wasn't having it. "I'm parking in the garage. I want to walk you inside—you know, carry your luggage." She eyed her carry-on, and they laughed.

He parked, then gave her hand a gentle squeeze. "Jesus, give Queen traveling mercies, and guide the aircraft to its destination. We asked in Your name, Jesus. Amen."

"Amen," she whispered and stared into his eyes. "You pray for everyone, but who prays for you?" She lifted a brow and placed her soft hand on his heart. It responded with forceful beats as if it was in the process of resuscitation. "Who prays for you? Not the pastor, son, or brother, but the strong man of faith that I know you to be?"

Stunned by her touch and question, Philip couldn't move fast enough as she stepped out of his car and began her strut toward the airport entrance, leaving a trail of admirers along the way.

He scrambled out of his vehicle and hurried to catch up. Like Grandma BB had escorts, Philip was Queen's, whether she wanted him or not.

Chapter Three

Queen's heart fluttered at Philip's text, which awaited her when she touched down in Tulsa.

Next time you're in town, you, me, and dinner. Miss Jamieson, you're my inspiration.

Philip didn't need any inspiration. God gave him plenty. He was her rock and didn't know it. Whenever she was around him, she felt safe—odd because Queen didn't frighten easily.

As she sent a group text to everyone to let them know she had landed and it was great seeing them, her mind drifted to Philip, and she fumed. She never wanted to see him stressed out that way again—ever.

What are you gonna do about it?

The thought reminded her of childhood taunts over petty disputes like commandeering a bike or not paying for a five-cent cup of lemonade at a makeshift stand.

After she and Suzette had their share of fights with bullies, their father showed them how to box, saying no one would ever suspect his beautiful daughters would be capable of throwing the first jab. Samuel Jamieson was right. She smiled at the memories.

Ignoring the internal dare, Queen unpacked, showered, then prepared for bed. She whispered her customary prayers, but it didn't seem enough as the question nagged at her. What was she going to do—could she do—to help?

She padded across the floor to the guest bedroom. Kami had left a Bible in there when she visited one summer. Cracking it open, the pages parted at First Timothy.

In the commentary, Paul wrote the letter to Timothy who was an evangelist and ordained as a deacon, to provide pastoral care and guidance to a young church leader. The apostle wanted him to reside in Ephesus until his work was done.

Queen paused. Who was guiding Philip in this...this profession? She lost her place and somehow found herself reading another commentary: *Philip's name symbolizes a person who ran with swiftness, as does a horse—a fitting name for a New Testament evangelist who ran to carry the Gospel message.* Yep. That described her Philip to a T.

Philip had four daughters who prophesied.

Wait. Hold up. Four daughters? *Hmmph.* "They better know how to pray and take care of him. That's all I'm saying."

Without realizing it, she had taken the Bible back into her room and curled up with it in the bed. She read until she dozed. When she woke in the middle of the night, the Bible was still nestled in her arms as if it was a pillow.

Monday morning, Queen strutted into the office of *The Journal for Engineering & Science* where she oversaw the research and articles for publication as senior editor. Bored with her previous position as a mechanical engineer at Tisdale & Associates for ten years, Queen welcomed a change.

That evening at home, Queen spoke with her best friends, Cori and Trice. Before the night ended, she reached for the Bible to read more in Timothy. She *tsk*ed and concluded that Philip, like Timothy, may be dealing with some hardcore stubborn folks.

If they didn't want to follow their leader, stay home. Just like there were hypocrites in the workplace, those same people traveled to church.

Foolishness was the very reason she didn't join anybody's church. That was Queen's story, and she was sticking with it.

For days, Philip stayed on her mind. She was tempted to call him to give her assessment of his situation.

Why call when in-person visits were better?

She decided to fly into St. Louis on a clandestine mission. Queen would attend Philip's Sunday morning service—and leave without a trace of a footprint that she had been there. Queen wanted to observe the shenanigans for herself that had him agitated. Plus, the whole four-daughter thing she read about had her off balance.

On Sunday morning, the Transportation Security Administration screener at the airport remembered her from the previous week. "Are you a model?" the man asked.

Suzette would have been proud folks thought so about Queen. "No, I'm not." She handed him her license and ticket.

"You're too beautiful not to be."

"Nah." Queen scrunched her nose in gist. "Too short. Don't let these heels fool ya. I'm nowhere close to five-eleven."

"You're beautiful any height. I can't help myself but flirt, so come through my line anytime." His name badge read Terrence. He smiled and shouldn't have. He needed a toothpick.

On paper, Total Surrender's membership was about a thousand. Philip wouldn't profess to knowing most of them by name, but he had an idea who was missing by where they sat.

Philip was drawn to a woman on his left midway to the front. She sat regal in a wide blue hat and fitted dress with a gold-and-blue printed cape that stopped at her elbows. It was something about her body language that seemed familiar, yet the brim of her hat hid her eyes until she angled her face a certain way. *Queen?* Why was she here?

For salvation, God whispered as if he should have known. *Focus on My Word.*

With his heart pounding, he continued his sermon from Romans 13. "Verse eleven says, '*And that, knowing the time, now it is high time to awake out of sleep: for now is our salvation nearer than when we believed.*' God is flashing warning signs before our eyes.

"Playtime is over," he continued. "This message is for you today. Wake up. Listen to what God is saying to your heart. He's knocking. Open the door to your soul…"

As he pleaded with the congregation, a vision took Philip to a place where he was conducting a tent meeting. Hundreds were drawn from the streets and packed under the tent. So many of them answered the call for salvation, there weren't enough altar workers to help minister and baptize them, but he had preached, believing God would add countless souls to His church as mentioned in passages throughout the Book of Acts.

In a blink of an eye, Philip returned and stood before his congregation again as souls raced to the altar, weeping and crying out for Jesus to save them. He glanced at Queen's direction. She hadn't moved.

Awake! God's voice snapped him to attention. *I go after the lost sheep. Minister to those I send you.*

With that, he rested his microphone and walked down the steps to those who had formed a line. He listened and prayed, rebuked, and prayed, then spoke God's Word for healing. The line swelled, but God gave him supernatural strength to minister.

As the crowd thinned, he glanced up and caught sight of Queen moving his way. When she was within feet of him, instead of continuing, she took a seat on the front pew and watched him.

He swallowed the disappointment and smiled at her. *God, she's Yours*, he thought.

At the close of service, Nathan gave him the salvation report of those who wanted the baptism in Jesus' name.

"God was busy today through you." Nathan nodded. "About a dozen people are rejoicing in tongues like in the Book of Acts' upper room. It's Holy Ghost fire in there."

"Yes." With no music, Philip danced in place onto the Lord. The Spirit hit Nathan, and others joined in until Philip's spirit calmed.

He mouthed to Queen he would be right back as he left with Nathan.

"I enjoy these services where the Spirit is high, and the Holy Ghost gives us a workout." Nathan kept in step. "I was sure that woman in blue was coming to the altar for prayer or salvation."

Philip grunted out his amusement. "*That* woman is my sister's cousin-in-law. She's back in town. I don't know why, but God's going after her."

"You mean the same one you took to the airport?" Nathan looked stunned. "What family gathering did you have this weekend and left me out—again?"

Shrugging, Philip couldn't recall. "I must have missed an invitation myself." He detoured to his office, showered, and changed in no time so he wouldn't leave Queen by herself too long.

Refreshed, he returned to the sanctuary where Queen and some teenagers were having a conversation. They stopped when he approached.

"Hi, Elder Dupree," the girls sang in chorus.

"Miss Queen was telling us about the clothes her friends design. I'm going to be a model when I grow up," Tabbie said, and the other nodded.

"Don't forget beauty and brains," Queen said before they hurried off. She scooted over, and he joined her. She grinned. "You preached."

He squeezed her fingers—long and soft—when he would have exchanged hugs. Every church had prying eyes. His included. "Woman, what are you doing here? I'm speechless."

"That's because you used all your words preaching."

"There's more from the Source. Trust me, so why are you back in the Lou?" He stretched his legs, then rested an arm on the back of the pew.

"I was hungry, and you promised me dinner the next time I was in town. I had an Uber drop me off from the airport." She struck an indignant pose.

Was she serious? Philip didn't stop his lips from curling upward. "Well, who am I to let you starve when you passed up hundreds of churches and restaurants to get a free meal— spiritual and physical nourishment." Philip tugged on her hand. Forget the busybodies. "Come on, my Queen. Let me feed you."

She gave him a seductive stare with her signature one-dimple smile. "I hope your wallet is thick," she sassed, "because I worked up a serious appetite watching you preach."

"I got this." As they crossed the parking lot to his SUV, he noted her heels. Did the woman own any slippers? *Ouch.* "When are you leaving?" He opened her door.

"After dinner." She smiled as she clicked her seatbelt.

"Today?" His jaw dropped, and he blinked. "Are you serious?" Shaking his head, he closed her door and then walked around and slid into his seat. He faced her without starting the engine.

"Yep. My flight is at nine-ten. I don't mind waiting at the airport."

"Not happening." Philip wrinkled a brow and drummed a finger on the steering wheel. "What's the real story?"

Queen squirmed in her seat. "I wanted us to talk."

Something was wrong. Philip's heart stopped. He swallowed and braced for earth-shattering news that couldn't be discussed over the phone or on Zoom.

"I've been praying for you." Sincerity shone from her eyes. Conviction filled her voice.

Philip had heard folks say the same thing more times than he could count, but coming from Queen, they were more than words. "Thank you, but I sense I should ask why."

Removing her hat for the first time, Queen angled her body, restrained by the seatbelt, to look at him. One glance revealed she had stuffed her curls under that hat. "After reading First Timothy, I know you've got some real challenges, dude."

Dude? An old soul. Philip dared not belittle her statement. "Thanks for your assessment, Madam Jamieson, and for your prayers."

"I may not be a prayer warrior, or a regular in church, but I'm serious when I said I've got your back. I had to read to know what you're up against. Let me just say, Timothy had some traitor characters up in his church. Now—" she straightened her frame and looked ahead—"I'm hungry. Feed me."

Chapter Four

"The food is scrumptious." Queen closed her eyes and dabbed her lips. Stuffed, she relaxed in her chair. "This was worth the trip."

"For the food, huh?" Somehow Philip saw through her facade. His expression said he could play whatever game she wanted.

She anchored her elbow on the table so she could rest her chin on her hand. "That and to support you. Last weekend, I wanted to be there for Victoria. Today was your day." She glanced at her watch. "I can't believe we've been here this long. Drop me off at the airport. You don't have to babysit me."

"I will in two hours." He grinned that brilliant smile and moved his brows in a gesture that reminded her of bodybuilders bouncing their pec muscles. "Since I don't have to share you with the family, consider this is our 'you-and-me time.'"

"If I didn't know you were a pastor, I would call you a tease," Queen lowered her lashes. "I like the sound of that. It is hard to have a personal conversation around family."

Philip suggested a Sunday drive after he paid the bill. As they cruised through Forest Park, Queen received a text from

Ace: **Hey, sis. Your niece is coming early. I know you were just here, but you wanted to be here when the baby came, so… I'll see you whenever you can come back.**

"What's wrong?" Philip stared at her.

"Ace's baby is coming early." She'd missed the births of her other nieces, so Queen was hyped. "Yes!"

"You want me to take you to the hospital?"

Reality hit. "No. I'm not supposed to be here, remember? This was *your* surprise visit."

"And I very much enjoyed my gift. Pencil me in for a next time, but what do you want me to do about now?" Philip looked clueless.

Queen gnawed on her lips, her in-and-out scheme had backfired. Her family would get ideas if they knew she and Philip were together, but they knew better than to try matchmaking. Philip was another story. Gabrielle and the other Jamieson wives were on a mission to set him up. Fine, but Queen wanted the honor to vet her.

"Well, I could take my flight home, pack some clothes, then catch an early morning flight out."

Rubbing his forehead, Philip didn't seem to like her idea. "Or you can just stay a couple of nights with them."

And she didn't like his. "I'd rather get a hotel room and be in more comfortable clothes." That's what she got for wanting to make a fashion statement. Heels and hats had an expiration time frame.

He parked. "What is the beauty and brains hatching up?"

"Hold on. I'm booking a hotel room." She tapped on an app on her phone. In minutes, the task was done. "Okay." When she looked up, he was smiling at her. "What?"

"You're something special, Miss Jamieson."

"*Ummm-hmmm.*" If Philip were another man, and she mentioned a hotel room, Queen would guess his thoughts. Not this evangelist turned pastor. "I still need you to take me to the airport so I can get a rental, then I'm going shopping."

"It's Sunday. The malls just closed."

Queen cringed. No malls. Options? Anything online wouldn't be same-day delivery. She sighed and surrendered to the only option. "Suzette would strangle me, but I guess I'm going to Walmart."

"I'll take you."

"That's sweet, but trust me. I'm a serious shopper. Plus, I've taken up enough of your day. I'm glad I came. I feel better seeing you."

She texted Ace back: **I'll be there early in the morning.**

"Oh. I see how you do a brotha. I take you out to dinner, then you dump me for a Walmart run."

A laugh escaped, and he joined her, then she rested her hand over his on the steering wheel. "Never." They stared until a text alert broke their connection.

Thanks, sis. Love you.

Philip shifted his SUV into drive and pulled back into traffic. "Walmart, here we come. You're going to need help in those shoes."

She rummaged through her oversized bag and unfolded her dance slippers. "What ya say now?" Queen fluffed out her hair while he watched. The man acted like he hadn't seen his mother, or a woman primp.

Once they arrived at the discount store, Philip held her hand and led the way. "Where to first?"

At that moment, she spied a Ross for Less Store in the distance but decided to make the most of the shopping trip instead of changing her mind. "Clothing, then health and beauty." He didn't complain or seem impatient as she selected a couple pair of skinny jeans, sweaters, and a casual jacket. Next, flats. After grabbing sample sizes of toiletries, not trusting the hotel to have the brands she preferred.

At the register, she was aware of Philip's closeness. When it was time to pay, he gave the cashier his card. "My treat."

She grinned. "Shopping, dinner, what's next…bearing your four daughters?" Queen thought about the Bible commentary she had read.

"Huh?"

"Never mind."

Next stop was the airport for her rental. Philip was the definition of attentive because he trailed her back to the hotel instead of parting ways. He continued his chivalry as he escorted her to the counter. "I guess this is good night. You made my day."

"You made mine, too, and so is my little niece." She hugged him, then headed to the elevators. She imagined the questions her family would ask after learning she was in town to see Philip and not them.

Once she was secure in her room, she pulled out her tablet and emailed her boss to take a couple personal days. There went her perfect attendance.

Thirty minutes later, her phone rang—Philip. He needed his own ringtone. "Hey, didn't I just see you?"

"You did." He chuckled. "I wanted to make sure your room is satisfactory."

"Actually, it's not. I'm a little annoyed." She rummaged through the chest drawers. "Aren't hotels supposed to have Gideon Bibles?"

"Thank you, Lord," Philip whispered instead of answering her question. "Want me to bring you a Bible? I have plenty."

Shaking her head, Queen stifled a yawn. "No need. I'll download a version on my tablet."

"Okay. Make sure the doors are locked and have a good night."

"I will. Night." She told him she was about to read, but tiredness overpowered her. She drifted before the download finished.

The next morning, Ace's ringtone stirred her awake at five-thirty. "Hello."

"She's here. My angel… Your niece. She's so beautiful," he rambled on.

"Congratulations," she mumbled until realization hit, and she sprang up in bed. "She's here. She's here. I'm on my way."

"I thought you would be up and heading to the airport."

Clearing her throat, she got her bearings. "I got here yesterday. I'm at the hotel."

"Well check out and come to my house."

"Okay, bossy brother." She rolled her eyes and giggled. She didn't have time for makeup or to primp. Her niece had arrived. She showered, dressed, and grabbed a Starbucks coffee and muffin.

Suzette would scold her for being seen unpolished. Today was an exception. Queen wouldn't turn heads. When she arrived, Queen strutted inside the hospital and asked for directions. Once she opened the door to Talise's room, Ace stood for a hug. "Wow. You look like you just rolled out of bed."

She stuck out her tongue. "I did."

"That was quick. You beat Mom and Kidd here, Oklahoma girl."

"And you look like you need a bed. Where's Lauren?" Queen glanced around the room.

"I dropped her off at Kidd's. Here. You have to put this gown over your clothes." Ace held it up for her to slip her arms through the sleeves after she washed her hands.

Next, Queen set her eyes on the newest member of the Jamieson clan in Talise's arm. She glanced up. "Hey, sis."

Queen stepped closer with the same awe as she lifted the baby girl out of her mother's arms. Words caught in her throat. "She looks like…"

"You," Ace said with a chuckle. "She favors you."

Talise agreed.

Although she welcomed the compliment, Queen corrected them. "No. She's a carbon copy of my sister's baby pictures. Amazing." As she rocked the babe in her arms, she cooed. "What's your name, little sweetheart?"

"We had so many picked out. We narrowed them down to four, then when she got here, none of the names seemed to fit my bundle of pure joy." Talise *hmmm*ed. "But now. I see your features, Queen, all over her face."

Queen tilted her head and studied her sister-in-law. She and Talise had rich dark skin, delicate features, and a lot of hair, and could pass as sisters. Queen thought Lauren resembled her mother but possessed her brother's temperament.

This baby without a name had the Jamieson nose and one arched brow. The lips and cheeks—maybe. The child was beautiful. "What you see is a clone of my sister, Suzette."

"Maybe." Ace rubbed his chin as he stared at his second daughter in awe. "She has satiny brown sugar skin. She's my precious…" His eyes widened. "How about Diamond?"

"Diamond Queen." Talise nodded. "I like the ring of that."

"How about Diamond Suzette?" Queen countered as another memorial to her sister, but this couple was in their own world.

Talise rocked her head, giving Queen's suggestion some thought. "*Hmmm.* It doesn't have a flow to it." She gave a tentative smile as if not to hurt feelings.

"Then it's settled." Ace stood and took the gift from Queen's arms. "My wife likes Diamond Queen, and so that's our princess' name."

"Princess Diamond sounds better. Just sayin'." Queen shrugged with a snicker.

"Nah." Talise laughed, and so did Queen.

The newborn's only grandmother, Ace's mom, waltzed into the room, tying the sterile gown behind her back. Beaming with excitement, Sandra Mayfield and her husband, Raimond, were a distinguished couple—too stunning for anyone to call old.

"Where's my little princess?"

Queen eyed Talise and mouthed, "Told ya."

Sandra scooped the infant from her son's arms and kissed Ace on his cheek. "Congratulations, Daddy. Proud of you, son. What's her name?"

"Diamond," Talise said.

"Queen," Ace added.

Sandra eyed her daughter-in-law and son before glancing at Queen. She blinked as if seeing Queen for the first time. "She could be your child. Those Jamieson genes are strong." A hint of sadness touched her face before Raimond hugged his wife.

Queen suspected Sandra thought about her role in continuing an affair with Ace's father, even after learning he was married. Raimond brushed his lips against her cheek as if he were forcing the bad memories away.

"I told her, Mom." Talise winked at Queen.

"I am blessed with more grandchildren. Thank you," she said, choking, "but this little one is ten days early. Raimond and I are supposed to leave in the morning for the Black museums conference." She pouted and looked at her husband. "I can't go now. Granny duty calls, but take plenty of pictures of the exhibits, honey, especially that children's plantation and the Black dressmaker's wardrobe." She capped off her disappointing news with a smile.

Her husband of five years nodded it was okay while looking heartbroken, so Queen volunteered. "Nope. Go ahead, Sandra. That's when aunties step in. I can stay until you get back."

Raimond and Sandra widened their eyes. "Are you sure?" they said in unison as the baby stretched in her grandmother's arms.

"I appreciate it, sis, but didn't you take a new job? Do you have the time off?" Ace asked. "We could sure use the help. Although I love my daughters, I'm kinda scared of newborns. They're so tiny."

"I'm sure." Queen lifted her shoulder and waved her hand. "I should have accumulative vacation days. If not, I can work remotely. But I don't have enough clothes for a week's stay, so I'll have to go shopping."

"Of course, you do," Ace mumbled with mirth.

The ladies laughed as Philip appeared in the doorway. Where Queen wasn't quite polished, Philip was well-groomed. Well-dressed, although in casual attire. His presence commanded attention. "Good morning. I hear there's a new baby added to the family."

"You're right in time to bless Diamond Queen Jamieson." Talise couldn't stop smiling.

He lifted a brow at Queen and winked. "A befitting name."

Was it getting warm in here? Queen fanned her face with the first thing she could grab.

"It's too many of us in here anyway, Raimond and I will step out," Sandra offered.

That wasn't it. Philip's charisma had a way of triggering Queen's shortness of breath.

Chapter Five

Philip's hospital visit was to see the new baby, but he couldn't keep his eyes off Queen. Her beauty radiated without the need for makeup or designer clothes. Diamond was a beauty like her aunt.

Seeing Queen cuddle her niece stirred a yearning for a family of his own. He wasn't getting any younger. Forty was on his trail and would catch him in a few months.

He blessed the child, asking God to provide for the family and give the parents wisdom to lead her to the Lord's salvation. "And in these evil days, send angels to protect Diamond from sexual predators—"

"Before I get to them." Ace balled his fists.

"Yes, please, Lord, before the Jamiesons take matters in their own hands," he finished. "In Jesus' name."

The women sniffed. Raimond patted Ace on the shoulder. "I've got your back."

As protective as the Jamiesons were of their own, and after learning of Victoria's horrific treatment in foster care, Philip wouldn't be surprised if the godparents were undercover bodyguards.

Philip brushed a kiss on Diamond's head and inhaled the baby-fresh scent of her skin. "Well, it appears my job here is done. I need to head to church for a meeting. Congratulations again." His chest swelled as he turned to Queen. "Walk me to the elevator."

Queen agreed. He doubted she was aware of her graceful movements as she stood from her chair.

He slipped his hands into his pocket as he slowed his stride to match her struts. It seemed like forever since he had seen her. "You look cute—pretty."

"Ha," she spat out a laugh. "I would call you a liar if you weren't a pastor—"

"In training," he corrected. The board wouldn't let him forget his probation period. His friend Bishop Henderson said it was protocol.

"You'll clinch it. But as I was about to say, I feel like a rag doll. I dare not leave my house like this, so no pictures."

Philip glanced at Queen. The woman wasn't smiling, but he did. This Jamieson woman was fierce. When they reached the elevator, neither was quick to push the button. He'd much rather be in her presence than the deacon board, excluding Nathan. Before doing so, Philip drew her in with an intense stare that nothing would break their connection. "When I see you, even if my eyes were closed, I'm in awe of your beauty. A gift from God that needs no further perfection. Your niece is blessed to resemble you."

"Diamond looks like Suzette."

This stubborn woman refused to accept the compliment. He imagined she was a handful as a child—at the same time adorable. She had missed her calling as an attorney, which suited her smarts and personality. But engineering was just as challenging. The lady could do anything.

"How long are you planning to stay now?" He jingled his keys, reminding himself he had an appointment. Philip wasn't ready to leave Queen. He wouldn't mind another dinner for two.

"A week until Sandra and Raimond return."

The elevator doors opened without being summoned—or maybe it was God telling him to take care of His business. Sighing, he stepped inside. "I'll check in on you—and Talise and the baby, too."

Queen laughed. "You are so not smooth. When did the evangelist become bashful?"

"I find myself being that way lately."

"*Hmmm.*" She didn't share her thoughts on that. As the doors closed, she shouted, "Hugs. Bye."

Philip forced an opening with all his strength and hopped out, startling her. "About that… Here's your hug." Her closeness brought a sense of calm, an ability he doubted Queen knew she possessed.

Do I have to release her?

"I'll stop by later. Let me know if you need anything, Nurse Queen." He winked. Before he could push the button, the elevator doors opened. Kidd and Eva stepped out. He held his daughter's hand while his wife had a grip on their niece Lauren.

He exchanged greetings with them and stepped inside the elevator. During the short drive, Philip's thoughts were about babies, a wife, family, and his calling. Being in Queen's presence initiated those thoughts.

Once Philip parked in his spot at church, he pushed back those desires. Entering the building, he waved at the cleaning staff as he strolled to his office.

After greeting his secretary, he unlocked his door to prepare for his appointment. Counseling was one of his least favorite duties as the pastor. It was heartbreaking when he poured energy into a situation for a resolution, and they don't take heed.

A knock on his door proceeded Sister Heather Baxter and her daughter Tinah. The church member was a single hardworking mother of three daughters. He stood to greet them with "Praise the Lord."

"Thank you, Elder Dupree, for seeing us," the mother who couldn't be much older than him said. The girl appeared to be fourteen or younger and pregnant. The girl's eyes didn't meet his.

"No problem."

Taking his seat, Philip listened to the mother's complaint while gauging Tinah's expressions. When Sister Baxter exhaled, he looked at her daughter.

"Sister Tinah, what do you want for yourself and your baby? Being a mother means grown-up responsibilities."

"I want my mom to stop nagging me and let me and Mark stay together." The girl rolled her eyes.

"Are you saying you and Mark are getting married so you can live under one roof as husband and wife and put your child first?"

Tinah scrunched her nose as if she had smelled something foul. "I'm too young to get married."

"I agree," Philip said, folding his hands and leaned back in his chair, "but how do you feel about becoming a mother?"

The tedious one-hour appointment dragged into two hours. The conclusion was one meeting wasn't enough. Tinah needed intervention to navigate adulthood, and she didn't want it from her mother. Philip was able to get a commitment from Tinah to attend church whether the father came.

After they left, Philip bowed his head and prayed for them and himself. "Lord, give me wisdom to guide Your people in situations foreign to me. Speak to them through me. Thank You. In Jesus' name."

Drained, all he craved was a hot meal, which he would get if his sister cooked, then he would go home. That was the norm if Queen hadn't been in town. In a few days, she had changed everything.

Philip made a pit stop to Dierbergs, a local grocery chain, for some to-go dinner plates and desserts. At checkout, he grabbed something extra.

"Hey, Auntie. Hungry?" He called Queen.

"I'm too tired to eat. I thought babies liked to sleep—ugh. Sweet little Diamond ain't having any of that."

He chuckled at her plight, glad she had volunteered, even if she sounded exhausted. "Text me the address. I have food. We can share another meal, then I'll head home."

"Did you have a good day?"

How could he answer without coming off as complaining?

"Let me say God gets His money's worth out of me."

"Well, I'm here if you want to talk."

"Thanks. Same here, but I think you have enough on your plate." He snickered.

"What's funny?" Her weariness seemed to have left her.

"You don't know how many times I've heard those same words coming from women who had ulterior motives."

She barked out a laugh. "Trust me. I may flirt, but what you see is what you get. I don't play head games with men. Either I like you or I don't."

"I hope I'm in the first category." The woman was tugging on his heartstrings. "Yeah, I'm starting to see that. Be there soon."

He got the text, tapped his navigation, and followed the directions until he remembered his way. If Queen lived in St. Louis, would they develop at closer relationship? He pondered this on his way to his destination. He parked and grabbed the sacks, then added pep to his steps.

Queen opened the door, her shoulders slumped with tiredness, but those gorgeous eyes of hers lit up. As he entered, he towered over her. Very few times had she been without her heels. He liked her height. Philip kissed her cheek.

"Food smells good. Suddenly, I'm real hungry now." She grinned and reached for the bags.

"And flowers, one for you and Talise." He bought them from behind his back.

"*Awww*. Thank you." Queen sniffed them. "You're so sweet."

Talise appeared and smiled. "Thank you, but my husband says no man better bring his wife flowers. No offense, but Ace is serious, and I kinda like him that way." She blushed.

Maybe one day Philip would understand where the man was coming from. To keep the peace, he yanked the tag off the flowers meant for Talise and added them to Queen's.

As if cued, Ace strolled into the living room, cradling Diamond. "And if you're bringing those for my sister, I want to know why."

Queen wasn't anybody's wife, but Philip was in the man's house. "They reminded me of her. She's a breath of fresh air from any other woman I've met."

"And?" Ace lifted a brow.

Was he his sister's guardian? Amused, but Philip dared not call the man's bluff. "Because she's beautiful."

They played this back-and-forth game a couple more times until the frustration wore Philip out. "Look, Ace, I'm tired and hungry. Not a good combination for me, and God knows it. I like your sister. Is that the answer you're looking for?"

"'Bout time. I smell food." Ace handed over his daughter to Talise and retrieved the bags from his sister's hands. "Let's eat."

Chapter Six

Queen needed to rethink this motherhood thing, she realized as she tiptoed out of Diamond's nursery for the second time in an hour. *Freedom, here I come.*

Six days later, she was packed and ready to run out of the house when Sandra walked through Ace's door. Despite the honor given Queen with her namesake, she couldn't get back to Tulsa fast enough. No telling how long it would take her to catch up on sleep.

Her aspiration to be a mother one day was on hold.

Now, Queen exchanged hugs with Sandra. "Your turn." She escaped and never looked back.

She checked in on Victoria and Kami at Grandma BB's house, then made one last stop before the airport.

Gabrielle opened her door and smiled. "You better had not left without saying goodbye."

"Never." Queen walked in and was met by the birthday twins. They offered her hugs, then crowded her space on the sofa.

"So, you're heading back to Tulsa?" Gabrielle pouted. "I guess Diamond couldn't change your mind to stay."

"Ha. Diamond is the reason I'm catching a nonstop flight." Queen snapped her fingers for emphasis. "My life is there."

"But not your family," Gabrielle said in a singsong pitch.

Cameron strolled through the doorway. His children leaped from Queen's side and made a beeline to their target. In one scoop, they were in his arms as he stayed on course to his wife.

He kissed Gabrielle as if Queen weren't there. Only when Gabrielle giggled did Cameron pull back, but he didn't take his eyes off her.

"Babe, Queen is here," Gabrielle pointed.

"Is she?" After one more peck, he faced Queen. "Hey, cuz."

Although she adored her brothers, Cameron held a special place in Queen's heart. His determination was the reason she connected with her other siblings, which she learned about from her father months before he died. Loneliness was a terrible companion after her parents and Suzette were gone.

Queen stood and placed a hand on her hip. "*Ummm-hmmm.* Show me some love, minus the kiss."

He released the twins and pulled her into a tight hug, then kissed her forehead. What was it with these Jamieson men and kissing the females in the family on their foreheads? A sign of endearment?

"You make me wish I wasn't a Jamieson so I could marry one."

"My wife gave up Dupree to be a Jamieson." He reached for her hand and stared into her eyes. "Every day I pray she won't regret it."

"I haven't." She whispered, *I love you.*

"You two are dropping so many clues for me to leave, so I am." She grabbed her purse.

"No. Stay for dinner. I made my mostaccioli," Gabrielle baited, knowing Queen couldn't resist the pasta dish.

"Let her go." Cameron feigned a good riddance wave. "If our cousin doesn't stay, there's more for me." He turned toward the stairwell and loosened his tie as he went to change.

"You know he's trying to use reverse psychology for you to stay. Come on. I was about to make garlic bread."

While Queen prepared the garlic spread for the bread loaves, Gabrielle tossed the salad. "So does all this love make you want to settle down with a hubby?" she asked as her Camille zoomed passed them in the hunt for her brother.

Queen fanned her hand. "Maybe, when a man looks at me the way my cousin focuses on you."

Gabrielle stopped reaching for bowls and gave Queen the side-eye. "Ha! Honey, you can command a room of men."

"Who are sexually thirsty but emotionally empty." She finished her task and placed the loaves on a baking tray, then rested her elbows on the counter. "I'm a novelty with a name like Queen. I need one man who is the real deal—just one." She lifted a finger.

"Then I guess I'll keep praying." Gabrielle winked.

"While you're at it, please make sure he's a sweetheart."

"Done."

Minutes later when the bread was done, Gabrielle proved her sincerity after Cameron blessed the food on the table, she added a footnote. "Jesus, with You all things are possible, so please send Queen a handsome, sweet, and saved man who will love and cherish her."

Queen rolled her eyes and helped herself. "I was waiting on for better or worse, from this day forever." She shook her head, humored by her cousin's antics.

With leftovers, Gabrielle suggested Queen make a to-go container for the plane.

"I'm not about to say no." She did, then Gabrielle walked her to the door. She opened it and almost collided with Philip.

He gave her a smile that reached his eyes. As he steadied her, Gabrielle mumbled something about prayers answered.

"Leaving without telling me goodbye?" He lifted a scolding eyebrow.

"Goodbye, Philip." She offered him a brief hug then continue to her car. He was on the list of who she would miss.

"Hello, Big Brother." Gabrielle squeezed him tight. "What a pleasant surprise. You must be hungry."

Yes, but his thoughts were on Queen. He was feeling some type of way that she was about to leave without telling him goodbye. He snapped out of his musings and returned his baby sister's hug. "I was hoping you can spare leftovers—or did you give them all to Queen? I'm coming from church."

"Always, for you." Gabrielle's eyes sparkled. Cameron kept his sister happy, and that's all a big brother could hope for. "If I bless God's servant, then I'll be blessed. I'm mostly a stay-at-home mom, so I always cook three balanced meals."

"That's the answer I wanted to hear." Philip hugged the twins, washed his hands, and sat at the counter. "Where's the old man of the house?"

Gabrielle laughed. "He's only a few years younger than you." She slid a plate of pasta, bread, and salad in front of him. She claimed the stool next to him as he said grace.

"Amen."

Anchoring her elbow on the counter, she rested her chin in the cup of her palm and grinned.

Philip chewed on crisp red beans that she liked to mix in her salad and eyed his sister.

"So…" She tilted her head. "You like her, don't you?"

There was only one woman who came to mind. "Who?"

"Queen." She smirked.

"She's a beautiful woman, kind, and caring." Philip bit off a hunk of garlic bread to keep from saying more.

"*Ummm-hmm*. That's what I thought. You've got that look." Gabrielle tee-heed.

"What look?"

"Men are so clueless. Maybe you need to talk to our daddy about 'the look.'" Gabrielle nodded. "I can't wait for them to relocate to be closer to us. I'll have a babysitter, and you'll have two more church members."

Their parents' move wouldn't happen for a couple of months. Although Philip owed them a phone call, it would not be about this foolishness. "Gabbie, I'm too tired to work my brain. Just tell me what the look *supposedly* means."

"You're going down. Hail to the Queen. The pastor and the princess—sounds like a movie or a book."

"That would be interesting." Philip added nothing more. An attraction was undeniable between them, but their lives were hundreds of miles apart. Plus, a big stumbling block kept their friendship from developing into more. They weren't on the same Christian walk—and that mattered, especially for a man of God.

The next day at church, Philip led the prayer to begin the meeting. He sat before the deacons in the hot seat after several congregants complained about his methods. Nathan had given Philip the heads-up on the agenda.

Deacons Albert Johnson, Wayne Davis, James Spearman, and senior deacon Theodore Larson kept straight faces while Nathan gave him a look of sympathy.

Deacon Larson cleared his throat and read silently from a sheet of paper in front of him. "Elder Dupree, you're doing a fine job, however, I'm uncertain of your counseling skills. Brother and Sister Claxton said their sessions with you didn't lead to a reconciliation, and Brother and Sister Amos said they didn't feel the anointing when you prayed for them. As a matter of fact, the tension in their home has abounded."

Philip didn't hide his annoyance as he rubbed his head. He prayed before he answered with the wrong words and tone. "The Claxtons came to me declaring they were getting a divorce regardless of what I said. From the beginning, their minds were made up. After a lengthy conversation about a middle ground, I suggested they read a copy of *His Needs, Her Needs* by Williard F. Harley, Jr. They didn't want to read a book and wanted a summary, which I gave, then put them in the hands of God."

"They're changing memberships and taking their charitable contributions with them." Deacon Larson frowned. "Your job is to add to the membership, not drive them away."

No, my job is to add souls to God's kingdom. Philip waited for God to direct him on how to respond. "There's a preacher for every one of God's creatures. There were twelve apostles, and none of them preached the same, but they all were effective in winning souls. If another pastor can help them, I say amen."

For the next hour, the board wanted to know his plans to rid the sexual immorality hinted of in the congregation, the guns some members were bringing to church, and the single sisters' anguish to be wives.

"Some of them would be good first lady material," Deacon Larson added. "You might better counsel married folks if you were a husband yourself."

"Only Jesus bared all our infirmities." Philip repeated the words the Lord whispered into his ear. "Do I need to have cancer to give an encouraging word? Do I need to be married to talk about reconciliation? Do I need to be a single parent to discuss teenage years when I was once a teenager? The Lord told me to feed His sheep and He will guide me."

"Good answer. I motion to adjourn this meeting," Nathan said, and they did.

Nathan followed Philip to his office and apologized for the grievances. "Sorry. It's not fair that you're getting hit with all this. Stoney hearts." He looked angry and ready to fight Philip's battle.

Between Nathan and Queen, Philip had warriors. "I imagine it was worse for Moses, and God didn't abandon him. Either God will send help or be my help. Otherwise…"

"What?" Nathan pressed, but Philip kept his thoughts to himself.

"Elder Dupree, I'm more than your armor bearer and deacon. I'm your friend and brother-in-Christ. I'm praying for God's will in the matter of this church. I've got your back."

Philip couldn't help but admire Nathan. "I'm counting on it."

That evening, he went straight home and cooked a dinner of chicken breasts and a can of green beans. While he went through the motions of enjoying his meal, he called his older brother.

"Hey. What's up, Pastor Brother?"

"Judge Drexel." After they exchanged the pleasantries, Philip asked, "Do you ever think you picked the wrong profession?"

"Me? It depends on the foolishness the plaintiff brings to my courtroom, but in your case…" Drexel paused. "God picked you."

"You're right. Didn't want to hear that though." Philip read the sugar and sodium content on the can of soda. He never did that. Why? "I've had a rough day—no, make it a week."

"Whoa, bro. At least God has your back. Me—nah." Drexel's sigh matched Philip's. "I had to make a ruling today, according to Illinois law, and it wasn't popular. Whenever it involves Black defendants before a Black judge, people think it's my duty to let them off the hook. My job is to make sure their punishment fits the crime, whether it's their first offense or not. One thing I will not do is discriminate against my people and others of color by giving them a higher sentence than whites. That's what I owe my people—fair treatment. That doesn't mean everybody is going to be happy. I had protestors, and my office was flooded with phone calls…"

Philip groaned. Had he hoped for a sympathetic ear? "And I thought I lost the popularity vote." After Drexel finished his vent, he encouraged Philip to release his woes, and he obliged. Growing up, they had always been close. That's one reason the church in St. Louis was appealing to Philip. Drexel lived in Springfield, Illinois, ninety minutes away.

Almost an hour later, Philip's spirits lifted as they talked sports, their parents' pending move, and clearing their schedule for the next ballgame. "I look forward to it, Brother Judge."

"Okay, Pastor Bro. Night."

There was one more person Philip desired to talk to— Queen—but he was exhausted and might fall asleep on her. Dreaming would be the next best thing until he could hear her voice again with clarity. The sooner, the better.

Chapter Seven

Queen created snow angels under the covers of her own bed. Undisturbed sleep was priceless. The solitude made her giddy.

Diamond was precious, but Queen learned a valuable lesson—enjoy her singlehood for as long as she could.

She eased back into her social butterfly routine with Cori and Trice. Thoughts of Philip brought smiles to her face throughout the day. At night, Queen read some chapters before going to bed in case she stumbled upon a Scripture that could help Philip. She laughed at herself. A Bible student? Her girlfriends wouldn't believe it.

One Saturday evening, Queen returned home from shopping for Kami and Victoria's graduation gifts. While relaxing and sipping her drink, she checked her email. A notification from Ancestry.com.

She couldn't remember the last time she'd used or renewed her account. Queen had signed up because she became thirsty for any kind of blood connection when her immediate family passed away.

For almost eight years, Queen had known nothing but contentment since the St. Louis Jamiesons welcomed her with open arms. She was beyond blessed to have the extended family, even if some of her half-brothers in Connecticut resented her presence.

Queen verified her password and signed into her account. There was a message from FredRobnett07.

Hello beautiful,

My name is Frederic Robnett. I see we are distant cousins from Queen Pokou. I would love for a chance to chat and compare our family trees. Here is my direct email…

Cameron was the point person for genealogy questions, so Queen ignored Freddy's request. His message might be a duplicate sent to all her cousins.

The following week, she left work early to drive the ninety miles to meet with the committee at the University of Central Oklahoma. The spring semester was ending, and members were evaluating if the fashion design/marketing curriculum was worth maintaining.

Queen wanted to do more in her sister's memory than donating money to the Lupus Foundation of America. Since Suzette's passion was anything—clothes, hair, modeling, and more—Queen had approached the University of Central Oklahoma at Edmond about what they were doing to attract minorities in the fashion field.

Queen arrived, parked, and scurried across the campus to the fine arts building. She rushed through the glass double doors to join the committee of three women and two men at a sleek glass table. Although the meeting was business casual, she and the department head, Nan Yeager, demonstrated their fashion style. The woman was tall with a thin frame. Tailored clothes complemented her while the third plastic surgical procedure deprived Nan of her beauty.

Nan waved her to the table. Once Queen was settled in her chair, the woman proceeded. "Thank you, Miss Jamieson, for your eagerness for our fashion department. It started off strong three years ago with an enrollment of thirty-two students. The second year, it was twenty. This year, it was only thirteen. Not good." Nan removed her thin reading glasses and shook her head. "The steady decline indicates, it's in jeopardy of being canceled unless we double the enrollment."

"No," Queen shrieked, then regained her professional demeanor. They didn't have to include her in this meeting, but her persistence and money she had been able to secure for the program opened doors. If Queen had to drain her 401(k) to fund an endowment scholarship for talented students, she would. But even that wasn't enough funds. Queen would have to up her efforts to research grant money.

An older tanned man who liked to be addressed by his last name—Block—raked his fingers through his thick white hair, then rocked back in his chair, which had no wheels. "Students attend if they have more class choices. The instructors we have now can't handle more. If we can bring in a healthy number of new students, the university will add instructors to the payroll."

Queen tapped her nails on the executive table. "I appreciate your dedication to put Tulsa on the map as the fashion capital in the South-Central region. I'm working diligently on securing larger endowments."

An hour later, Nan concluded the meeting. "Remember, our presence is required at the upcoming the spring fashion show."

On the drive back to Tulsa, Queen called Jennifer Heath, a well-known blogger with roots in the area and a big supporter of Queen's initiatives.

"Hey, Q. What's up?"

"Jen, I'm leaving a university meeting. If we don't get a stampede for the fashion program, it will be archived."

"Yikes, girl. Not good. That means next week's silent auction must be a blowout. I'll rally supporters on my end. This program is important."

Some of Queen's stress subsided. "Thanks for your support."

"Girl, I can't wait to see the spring collection. I'm ready." Jennifer was an influencer and big spender at the event, which did more than fund scholarships but connected graduates with employment opportunities from top fashion design houses, paid internships, and study abroad programs.

"I think streaming it live will be a big plus." Queen checked her rearview mirror and changed lanes. It was a good thing she was driving on autopilot because her mind was elsewhere. "See you next week."

When they ended the call, Queen exhaled. She grunted and shook her head. "And Philip thought he has problems. Try coming up with several thousand or millions of dollars."

Pray on it, she could hear Philip say—or maybe it was God's voice.

Queen was back in St. Louis. Wiggling in her cushioned seat at the Stifel Auditorium, she held her breath. It seemed that every local Jamieson, plus Grandma BB and her escorts, Chip and Dale were there. The trio stood out as they sported the classic black-and-white Stacy Adams shoes. Philip snagged the open seat next to her—or rather her family had left it available.

"Hey, beautiful. I've missed you."

"I've missed you, too. *Shhh*." She scooted to the edge of her seat, waiting for the principal to call Kami Jamieson followed by Victoria Jamieson to receive their diplomas. Queen leaped to her feet and screamed the loudest. Her family provided the backup chorus with whistles and one family member shouted, "Yes! The Jamiesons are in the house."

The principal paused for quiet, then moved on. Queen reclaimed her seat and composure.

"You skipped out on your calling. You're a one-woman pep rally."

"Hey," she sassed him over a shoulder. "My nieces are the next generation to carry on the Jamieson legacy."

The ceremony concluded in an hour with over three hundred graduates accepted to one hundred and eighty-something colleges, universities, and vocational institutions.

Afterward, Queen and Philip shuffled through the maze to find their graduates. Parke had so many balloons, it surprised her he cleared the doorway.

Kami and Victoria where under a decorated archway taking selfies. Queen had never seen Victoria looked so happy—at peace with herself and the world. Queen was glad Parke advocated for Victoria to walk across the stage. Through perseverance, she had earned the accolades.

"Those two sisters are superstars," Philip said aloud to no one in particular.

Queen smiled. "Yes, they are."

When Kami looked up and saw family heading her way, she waved. "Dad!"

"My favorite daughters." Parke handed them each a bouquet of balloons. "My ladies." He wrapped his arms around Kami, squeezed her tight, and placed a kiss on her cheek. Next, he eyed Victoria and opened his arms.

"He would wait all day if he had to for Victoria to respond." Queen sniffed.

It was as if the surrounding buzz froze as the family held their breath, wondering if Victoria would finally let the Jamieson men in her life. Victoria nodded, then walked into Parke's embrace and hugged him with no hesitation as if it was commonplace. The Jamiesons released celebratory cheers.

"I'll always be here to protect you," Queen heard Parke say, choking with emotion.

Touched, Queen patted her chest, then angled her phone to capture the moment.

"She's going to be all right." Philip reminded her of his presence.

"How do any of us really know?" Queen fumbled with the pearls around her neck. She listened for his answer, but none came.

"Come on, Mom," Victoria beckoned toward Cheney. It was as if the diploma opened her heart. Next, she called her brothers to join her and Kami.

"Wow. Wherever that breakthrough came from, thank you, Jesus," Ace said, handing over Diamond to Queen so that he, Talise, and their daughter, Lauren, could get photos with the superstars.

As Queen cuddled her namesake in her arms, she had no problem biding her time in the spotlight with the girls. Cologne teased her nostrils.

Philip, who hadn't left her side, cooed at the baby. She loved whatever he was wearing. "Say 'hi, Uncle Philip.'"

"She becomes prettier every time I see her. I guess when you marry and have a daughter, she'll look like you."

"If I ever marry, then I'll get a couple of these." Queen was losing hope. She tried not to think about it. Men in the workplace and at social events surrounded her. While some captured her attention, none had captured her heart. Philip had admitted his attraction. Opposites could attract all they wanted, but nothing could come of it. In truth, their worlds were different.

Soon, it was Queen's turn with the girls. They made silly poses as if they were in a photo booth at a party.

The festivities continued throughout the evening with a big family dinner party at a hotel.

When the adults retired home, Kami and Victoria announced they were going out to celebrate with classmates, a first for Victoria. Her transformation encouraged Queen and the other family members. What the girls didn't know was Grandma BB would have Chip and Dale trail them, not to spy, but to bring back up in case the girls found themselves outnumbered by characters up to foolishness—per Grandma BB's words.

Queen giggled. Something told her those girls could take care of themselves. They were smart, clever, and Jamiesons.

Philip joined her at Ace and Eva's house because that was where she was spending the night. She studied him. He seemed less stressed this time. His smiles weren't forced, and his body language relaxed. His crisis must have passed.

She and Philip were so different in personalities, but they had similar interests outside of church. Both were old souls, regarding their entertainment preferences. They found the network that aired nostalgia and old comedies that featured black actors. Both liked tennis but were horrible.

When Philip had to step into the other room to take a call from his congregants, Queen mumbled he might as well be a medical doctor. His life seemed to be a constant interruption.

They that are whole have no need of the physician, but they that are sick: I came not to call the righteous, but sinners to repentance. God's voice seemed to boom in her quiet space.

Whew. I stand corrected, Lord, she repented and grabbed her phone when alerts popped up that she was tagged in Kami and Victoria's pictures they'd posted on social media. Reading the comments, she frowned at the name, wracking her memory. Why did Frederic Robnett sound familiar?

She found her answer when she received a private message through Facebook. **Queen, you are beautiful in those pictures with your nieces. You can imagine how delighted I was to see you're here in Missouri. I and most of my—our—relatives**

live in Kansas City. I'd love to meet you in St. Louis so I can introduce myself to you, my cousin, in person.

Creepy. She scrunched up her nose at the same time Philip joined her back on the sofa. He mumbled something, then asked, "What's wrong?"

Queen showed him the message.

"Who are the Robnetts?"

Shaking her head, she shrugged. "I have no idea."

"Then they're not coming within two feet of you." Philip's expression was intense, warrior-like.

She liked warriors, but she was surrounded by them—the Jamiesons.

Resting his arms on his knees, he glanced at Ace and Kidd laughing, then her. "I think we need to give your brothers a heads-up."

"No!" She lifted her hands. "I'd rather tell your brother-in-law. Cameron's not as hotheaded. Plus, he knows the family tree better than anyone and will check out this guy."

Philip was slow to agree. "Just so you know, I can pray and fight at the same time. I competed in competitive kickboxing. I won more than I lost."

Hmmm. One more thing they had in common. They were fighters.

Chapter Eight

Philip didn't want to leave Queen behind, not when they were relaxed, watching old movies and snacks at Ace's house. Instead of asking for another dinner date, he invited her to church the next day. Without hesitation, Queen accepted.

Surprise.

The next morning, he couldn't get to church fast enough. Although God had sent His Word for Philip to preach, he prayed the message would hit Queen's heart. He wanted a knockout punch to bust the yoke that had Queen bound.

Once My Word goes forth out of My mouth, it shall not return to Me void, but shall accomplish that which I please, and it shall prosper in the thing where I sent it, God spoke, reminding him of Isaiah 55:11.

The translation was, "If it's God's appointed time to draw Queen to Him." He sighed.

At church, he couldn't focus until he sensed, and his eyes verified, Queen had entered the building. He exhaled. Nathan leaned over. "Your cousin-in-law can bring service to a halt. Wow."

Philip nodded with a slight grin. After they acknowledged the visitors and the choir sang their melodies, Philip walked to the pulpit and opened his Bible for his sermon.

"Good morning, everyone, and praise the Lord." He glanced at Queen. *Not my will, Lord, but Yours concerning her.* "In verses twenty-one and twenty-two in the first chapter of James, the Scripture says, '*Wherefore lay apart all filthiness and superfluity of naughtiness. Receive with meekness the engrafted Word, which is able to save your souls. Be ye doers of the word, and not hearers only, deceiving your own selves.*'" He paused. "Don't become complacent about church. Revelation while praying or reading your Bible should activate your faith in God to change things in your life. Come to the House of the Lord, hungry and thirsty for more. You are the church and your body the sacred temple…"

He preached until the atmosphere stilled. The true test. Would any of the sermon's morsels settle in Queen's heart when he made the altar call for sinners to repent? Would anyone accept the water baptism in Jesus' name for the remission of secret and open sins. "Receive the baptism of the fiery Holy Spirit. The evidence comes with heavenly tongues."

Philip couldn't bear to track Queen's movements. There was no need for her to know of the silent pressure he aimed at her soul. About a dozen responded to the call; all but two desired baptisms. He refused to be disappointed. It must not be Queen's time of salvation. Amen.

After Philip showered and changed, he rejoined Queen. Her smile lightened the dimmed sanctuary as she chatted with some of the teenage members.

"Ready?" He smiled back when all he wanted to ask was, why didn't you come? *God's timing,* he reminded himself.

Once they were strapped in his SUV, he drove off. "What time is your flight again?"

Queen relaxed against the headrest and closed her eyes. "Eight-thirty. I want to see whatever Cameron can track on this mysterious cousin."

The hugs, kisses, handshakes, and fuss over the twins' ritual began when they walked through Cameron's front door. Gabrielle had prepared a spread to feed an army. All this fuss because of a social media message Queen showed him. After dinner, the adults followed Cameron into his study. He tapped on the keyboards under Queen's watchful eye while Philp admired Queen.

This woman was twisting him in knots. She caught him staring twice, and neither time did he back down.

"What I can't understand is why he didn't reach out to me, Parke, or any other Jamiesons. We're the genealogy trackers." Cameron rolled his shoulders, and Gabrielle massaged his neck and shoulders.

"Honestly, I thought he had when he sent me an email earlier his month." Queen shrugged.

"What? This isn't the first time this guy has tried to get in contact with you?" Philip and Cameron whipped their necks staring at her, then Cameron reached for his phone and put it on speaker mode.

"Parke, bro, we have a situation. Queen and Philip are here—"

"A situation? Really? This was overkill," Queen said.

They were overreacting, Philip thought to himself.

"Hold on. Let's add Malcolm to this," Parke interrupted. "Sounds like we need to call an emergency family meeting."

Queen groaned out her frustration and rubbed her temples. "There is *no* emergency and no need for a family meeting."

The only girl among headstrong men, Queen was in trouble because the Jamiesons were going to have their way. "Queen—" she met Philip's eyes—"you might as well call Kidd and Ace."

Within an hour, Parke arrived first, Kidd next. Malcolm and Ace together. None of them looked happy. After their pleasantries, they grabbed some chicken and gathered in what became an impromptu war room.

"Awww nah. You've got a stalker masquerading as a cousin" was the first thing out of Kidd's mouth as he squeezed his hands into fists.

Philip wanted to tell Queen's brother to stand down. There was no threat, but he felt the same way. He might not be a Jamieson, but if it concerned Queen, he was on it, too. God help the man who married her. He would have to contend with the Jamieson men—cousins and brothers. *Nothing I can't handle.* The thought dove into his mind and swam out. Where did that that come from? Philip wouldn't deny his infatuation. It had been simmering long enough before he began his position at the church.

"Hold up. Is that what everyone called me when I was researching my family roots that lead me to you all?" Queen demanded. "I don't stalk men. They try to stalk me." She lifted her chin, not realizing she wasn't helping.

Cameron glanced at Philip. "Brother-in-law, but you might want to lead an impromptu prayer meeting because I'm going through my files and subfiles, and there's no mention of Robnetts. When I checked into my genealogy accounts, I find no messages from this Frederic Robnett."

"Awww naw." The men stood at attention. Hands balled, mouths growling, and ready to spring into action. "Nobody's talking with my sister," Kidd and Ace said almost at the same time as if they had memorized their line.

Queen folded her arms. "Excuse me. I'm still waiting for an answer. You thought I was a stalker when I reached out to you?"

"Nope. We already knew of you from Samuel's obituary that we read online," Cameron said without taking his attention off his screen.

Queen relaxed, and Philip squeezed her hand. He didn't have any sisters, but would he act this dramatic over a woman? But Queen could be fierce too. He had seen her possessiveness when it came to Kami and Victoria.

"He's not a Jamieson, so how can he be a distant cousin?" Kidd paced the room. His steps were heavy. "Nobody's going to mess over my sister." He flexed his muscles and punched his fist into the palm of this hand.

Kidd had become a new person in Christ's redemption, but his no-nonsense attitude was still in full force. The only person who could tame him was his wife, Eva.

Praise God for wives. If—a big if—things would develop between him and Queen, Philip knew she had the ability to settle his mood. Oh, how much he wanted to claim a life as a husband with the right person.

"Calm down. No one is going to hurt our Queen," Parke said, holding Kidd's shoulder. "Let's get Dad's take on it. There are predators out there, so I'm feelin' his concern." He called their father, Parke V, known as Papa P, and gave him a recap.

"You all could be overreacting," Papa P said through the speakerphone. "Tell Cam to reach out to this young man and invite him to family game night in a few weeks, then we all can vet him." He didn't seem ruffled by the news.

The Jamiesons' game night was known as a family-friendly gathering, but this upcoming one had the makings of an action-packed adventure with all hands on deck. No matter what was going on at the church on that evening, Philip planned to be in that hotel banquet room. He might not carry Jamieson blood, but his twin niece and nephew did.

He tapped the reminder on his phone calendar. It was a done deal. The Jamiesons would show this Frederic and those in cahoots with him that the Jamiesons—and this Dupree—would protect Queen at all costs.

Chapter Nine

On Memorial weekend, Queen sensed a surge of energy in the ballroom of the Embassy Suites hotel. Maybe it was the male Jamiesons' testosterones instead. She flew in for this quarterly family game night for the relaxed atmosphere of fun, games, and plenty of food. Why did it feel like a sting operation, and she was the bait?

Queen knew how to attract a man, so she dressed the part in her stilettos, skinny jeans, and a long train from her top. Her natural hair was freshly washed and rodded. She rocked. Bring on this so-called distant relative. Where was her jeweled crown, a gift from her best friends on her thirtieth birthday? She snapped her fingers.

At seven in the evening, her brothers and cousins walked around wearing dark shades. She hoped they could see. This was a game night, not a street fight.

True, Frederic's tag on social media freaked her out at first, but she knew how to defend herself. She walked up to Ace and tapped his shoulder. "Is all this really necessary? Ever heard of subtle?"

"Not this time, little sis." He kissed her cheek. "I don't like the way he went about it. They didn't call me and Kidd the bad boys from Boston for nothing. We got this." Ace straightened his body.

Shaking her head, Queen rolled her eyes. "Thought you two were practicing Christians?"

He gave her that killer smile that had won his wife over. "We practice it 24/7. Don't you know the weapons of our warfare aren't always carnal? We can take this to the street or to the Word, Frederic's choice. Either way, we got this." He pounded his chest, wearing his family's #TeamAce T-shirt.

Ace flexed his biceps. "I've studied 2 Corinthians 10:4–5: *For the weapons of our warfare are not carnal, but mighty through God to the pulling down of strong holds. Casting down imaginations, and every high thing that exalts itself against the knowledge of God and bringing into captivity every thought to the obedience of Christ.* Demons tremble at the name of Jesus, so if this guy walks up in here with any foolishness, it's going to turn into a prayer party—for his sake." He lowered his sunglasses and winked.

"Right…" She gritted her teeth and felt sorry for Frederic. He didn't know he was walking into a lion's den where God might not even rescue him from hostile Jamiesons. Queen continued to work the room, speaking with family members and their friends.

Eying Kami supervising her small cousins as they played, Queen wondered about Victoria. Queen had almost persuaded the recent graduate to attend the family function. The teenager was warming up to her male cousins and uncles, but she wasn't quite trusting yet. Then this thing with Frederic surfaced.

Parke didn't know what would go down and didn't want to further traumatize her, so Victoria was okay binge-watching some chess series on Netflix.

"One day," Queen whispered. Victoria would recover, even Queen was praying for that. She made her way to the main table with Papa P and his wife, Charlotte, three other elderly cousins they met at a reunion, and of course, Grandma BB.

Where were her escorts? Queen looked around. Chip was posted at an exit, and Dale wasn't far away in the shadows in a stiff military stance. All they needed were earpieces to set off the look of secret service. She squinted. Wait a minute. Was that a miniature phone cord behind his ear?

Good grief. Queen walked away with an extra sway in her hips. Not that she liked either escort beyond acquaintances. It was simply a distraction tactic to see if they would look.

She glanced over her shoulder. Chip did. Queen chuckled and continued her rounds, doting on the children. Eva was sitting at the #TeamKidd table, rubbing her belly.

"Sis, you want anything from the buffet?" The food staff announced it was ready.

"Yes. More fruit." Her sister-in-law grinned with delight.

There were almost eighty Jamiesons and friends in attendance, and the food line was long. Papa P had issued a new decree years before Queen met her extended family. All Jamiesons—adults and teenagers—should fast and pray the day of game night, a gathering that began as a childhood tradition when his boys were small.

Parke VI, Malcolm, and Cameron had yielded to God's call for salvation, so Papa P felt the family night should incorporate a spiritual element, so in his words, "We have to pray for the next generations of Jamiesons so they will be blameless and not guilty of sin."

Since Queen wasn't a churchgoer, she didn't think that applied to her. Papa P said otherwise.

It had been a struggle at first, but Queen learned how to push her breakfast and lunch plates aside and distract herself from salivating at food commercials or billboards. Even packaged airport snacks seemed to have a sweet aroma.

When she was within reach of a serving tong, Queen didn't waste time. She piled her plate with hors d'oeuvres, then grabbed another plate for her cousin.

Queen dropped off the fruit at #TeamKidd's table for Eva, then slid into a chair at #TeamCameron's where Gabrielle was holding Diamond so Talise could eat. Queen had team T-shirts for all the tables, depending on where she wanted to play on any given game night. It didn't appear Gabrielle and Cameron noticed her because he was stealing kisses—no delivering them to his wife.

"*Whew*. It's chilly in this room, but hot at this table." Queen fanned face. "If you two didn't have twins, I'd say get a room here."

"We did. Would tell you our suite number, but it's a secret." Gabrielle giggled. "The twins are going home with Cam's parents."

"I'll take Diamond if you want to get up and mingle," Queen offered. The finger food wouldn't keep her from eating and holding the baby.

Gabrielle jumped to her feet. "Bye, girl." She glided away with her husband.

Queen munched as she cuddled her niece. It was almost time to start. Her brothers and cousins left an empty seat in hopes of grabbing Frederic first. Maybe the man wasn't coming.

Papa P stood and tapped the microphone. "Attention, family. It's near time to get started, so please grab your food and take your seats." He squinted. "Is Elder Dupree here to lead us in prayer?"

"Here." Philip raised his hand as he rushed in the room, clearing the entrance.

Queen's heart fluttered. She loved a man in a suit, and Philip's was tailor-made. He must have come from some meeting or other business.

After exchanging a handshake with Papa P, Philip took the microphone and instructed everyone to stand where they were and bow their heads. "Father, in the mighty name of Jesus, we love You for Your blood You shed on calvary for our sins. We thank You for family, and I ask that you bless the gathering from the oldest to the youngest to the generations that are afar off. We thank You for this food for our nourishment. Please bless it and let our gathering be in peace. In Jesus' name. Amen."

"Amen," Queen repeated along with others. She loved to hear him pray, even preach. Okay, she loved to hear him talk. His baritone was deep and sexy. She admired Philip's swagger as he headed to #TeamCameron's table. He shook hands with Cameron, kissed the twins, then his sister before he brushed his lips on Queen's cheek and whispered, "My Queen."

It was the way he said her name that caused Queen to suck in her breath. They had exchanged hello and goodbye kisses before, but this time, her cheek tingled, and she shivered until the sensitivity faded. "Since when?"

"Every man has a queen." He winked.

"That's usually when the husband is the king of the castle."

He left her hanging as he hurried to grab a plate before the program started.

When he returned, he scooted his chair closer to her. His cologne was distinct and crisp. Queen refused to swoon, but his charisma was playing with her head about the attraction between them after witnessing Cameron's affection to his wife. "You're late" was the first thing she could think to say.

"Sorry. Counseling session at church ran over, which made me late for a business meeting." He gulped down most of his glass of lemonade, then attacked the meatballs. The man was serious about his food.

Rubbing Diamond's back as the baby rested over her shoulder, Queen watched in amazement. "When you come up for air, tell me about your workload as a pastor. You preach once a week and do a bible study."

He didn't say a word as he continue to feed his stomach. Finally, Philip dabbed a napkin on his mouth. "Woman, you have so much to learn. Sin, salvation, and redemption don't happen between nine a.m. to five p.m." He stood. "I need seconds. You haven't seen this Ricco guy, have you?"

A nickname? Queen got to her feet, almost meeting his eyes in her heels. "It's Frederic, and no, but I'll be happy to get more for you since you've had a long day." She handed over Diamond, then strolled to the buffet table so her emotions could recalibrate. She had dated men from different ethnic groups, professions, and ages. None had been a preacher. She needed a playbill of sorts.

Read your Bible, it was a whisper but loud enough for her to hear without a doubt.

"That's wife material." Gabrielle leaned over and nodded in Queen's direction.

"Is that so?" Philip relaxed in his chair after Ace came for his baby, watching Queen's every move. Not because he felt she was in harm's way. Her attractiveness beckoned him. Tilting his head, he didn't take his eyes off the view. "How do you know that?"

"Number one, she's doting on you by offering to fix your plate. I bet she'll cook for you if you ask, and number two, three, and four… my big brother hasn't stopped ogling her. That is the first time I've seen you do that."

"I don't ogle women," he defended and sat straighter. He fumbled with his napkin. "I'm appreciating God's handiwork. She's beautiful—inside and out."

"Yeah, that, too, but you've got that look. Don't deny it because you're wearing that look like you're wearing that suit. It's nice, by the way."

Queen returned with a little of this and that on his plate and another glass of lemonade. She slid it in front of him, then took her seat and shrugged. "This may sound strange, but I've never fixed a man's plate besides my daddy, so I didn't know what to get you."

"I don't take that honor lightly. Thank you." Philip stared into her eyes. What was he going to do with Queen Jamieson? Sweet. Kind. Fireball and off limits. He sighed.

"First on the program," Papa P said, motioning his grandson Malcolm Jr. to the front, "is MJ reciting the Jamieson Legacy."

The double doors to the banquet room opened. A good-looking imposing man entered, glancing around. An entourage followed their leader inside.

"This is a private function. Are you lost?" Papa P asked as all eyes were on the group.

"If this is the Jamieson game night, we are not. I'm Frederic Robnett and these are some of my family members." They had to be a dozen of them.

"Wow," Queen whispered. "I love his entrance."

Glancing at the others, Philip sensed the men in her family didn't share her sentiments, judging from the frowns across their faces. Kidd and the head of the households stood.

"You're in the right place. Welcome." Papa P was cordial at the same time he motioned for his sons to take their seats. He asked a staff to drape another table and add chairs for their guests.

Papa P continued. "We're about to begin our program. Afterward, you're welcome to tell us about your family tree. Now, go ahead, grandson."

"I'm Malcolm Jamieson Jr., or MJ. My parents are Malcolm Sr., and Hallison. I'm eleven years old. I'm the eleventh generation of Paki Kokumuo Jaja, the firstborn son of King Seif and Princess Adaeze." He faced his grandfather who grinned at him.

MJ puffed out his chest. "Paki was twenty years old when he and his entourage were ambushed and attacked. Paki was sold at the highest bid of $275 to Jethro Turner in front of Sinner's Hotel in Maryland. The slaveholder's only daughter, Elaine, became his common-law wife as they escaped, becoming fugitives."

He fumbled with his fingers. "They had five sons who lived. My eleventh great-grandfather, Parker, was the oldest. Descendants in each generation named a son Parker until after slavery when the 'r' was removed to symbolize they were removed from enslavement.

"Paki's brothers were Aasim, Fabunni, Sarda and Orma. My cousins Kidd, Ace, and Queen are descendants of the youngest brother, Orma, who was sold into slavery for the woman he loved." MJ frowned and scrunched his nose, then bowed.

The whistles started at Malcolm's table as others followed with a hearty applause. Even their guests seemed impressed.

Papa P beamed. "Well done, grandson. Who will be the next one to recite our heritage at our winter family game night? No child is too young, so think about it. Now, teams, are you ready?"

Everyone shouted, "Yeah."

"Impressive. Those names rolled off his tongue with little effort." The comment came from their guests' table. Loud enough for Philip and others to hear.

Except maybe for Queen who seemed posed to ring the bell as she waited for the question.

After reaching inside a box, the patriarch pulled out an index card. For the benefit of their guests, Papa P explained the rules of the game. "Now, this question comes from #TeamKidd. What are virtual free slaves?"

#TeamAce's bell rang seconds before #TeamParke. Papa P acknowledged Ace as he stood. "Slaves who openly live as if they were free. They managed a household away from the owner's residence and negotiated business affairs for their owners. Surprisingly, neighbors treated them as quasi free," Ace taunted his older brother.

"Correct! Your table is on the board."

There was no physical board today, so Grandma BB acted as the scorekeeper.

Papa P pulled another card and smiled. "This is for one of our small ones. Quote your favorite Scripture from the New Testament."

Kidd's daughter, Kennedy, raised her hand and jumped up. "Pick me, Papa. Pick me."

The elder chuckled at the child's enthusiasm. "You have to ring the bell, Little Bit."

Kidd lifted Kennedy so she could tap the ringer. She continued until her father planted her feet on the floor again. "The Lord himself shall descend from heaven with a shout. The voice of the archangel, and the trumpet of God…" She looked backed at her father for help.

"Come on, baby. You know it," Kidd encouraged his daughter.

Kennedy took a deep breath, rocked on the heels of her shoes, then became excited. "Oh: the dead in Christ shall rise first." Her eyes widened. "I hope we're still alive, so we can be caught up with them in the clouds to meet the Lord in the air, and we'll be with the Lord forever and ever and ever. Amen!"

A thunderous applause, even from the guests' table made the girl bashful. She ran into her daddy's arms, then her mother's where she talked to the baby in her mother's belly.

"Well done, Kennedy." Papa P winked at her. "Do you know where that Scripture is in the Bible?" She nodded. "You have to tell us, sweetie."

Kennedy twisted a finger in her mouth until Eva reached over and pulled it out. "Tell us."

"First Thessylone 4:16 and 17," the child shouted.

"First Thessalonians," her father corrected.

After another round of applause, Lauren jumped up. Ace and Talise's daughter, who was the same age as her first cousin, wanted a turn. Papa P granted her the floor, and she quoted Psalm 23. All six verses.

Philip was in awe of the Jamiesons commitment to the Lord and their family tree. *Train up a child in the way he should go, and when he is old, he will not depart from it.* He quoted Proverbs 22:6 to himself. Who knew what the Lord had in store for her? Maybe she would become an evangelist one day.

"The next question comes from us," Papa P said of the elders at the head table. "Name at least two infamous slave traders."

Frederic stood as Queen's fingers tapped the bell. She frowned.

"May I answer?" the leader of the group asked. "Sorry my table doesn't have a bell, but I am enjoying your game night."

Papa P faced Queen. "Queen?"

Lifting her chin, she squinted at the stranger. "I concede." Then she mumbled, "but I don't like it. I knew that answer."

"That's a first—you letting someone take your turn," Cameron mumbled, and she slapped his shoulder.

"Ouch." Cameron feigned injury.

Philip leaned over. "I believe in you." Would she recognize her own words to him? "What's the answer?"

"There were hundreds. William H. Williams was well known. Let's see if he can impress me." She leaned back in her seat and folded her arms.

Their guest stepped away from his table. "Thank you, sir. Again, my name is Frederic Robnett. Before I answer, I would like to extend our thanks for the invitation."

Cameron grunted. "It was more like a summons."

"*Shhh*," Queen warned him.

Philip sized the man up. He guessed they were both in their late thirties. Philip was taller and had more bulk. Frederic slipped one hand in his pocket as he paced a few steps, then faced everyone. "Well, let's see. There was William H. Williams who operated a slave pen in D.C."

Queen gave Philip a "told you so" look. Lord, she was beautiful. He winked, and she blushed.

"It was called Yellow House, and he trafficked enslaved men, women, and children for over twenty years." He was articulate and sounded convincing.

"Then there were Isaac Franklin and John Armfield," their guest continued, "with slaveholding pens in Alexandria, Virginia. They were considered two of the most ruthless domestic slave traders in America. It was their business and their pleasure. It was a game to them where they took pleasure in atrocities against women." He bowed his head. Was it for a moment of reflection?

Philip felt sick in the pit of his stomach. Whether they were slaveholders in the past or monsters in the present, God had reserved the Lake of Fire and brimstone for such sins. Only true repentance was their get-out-of-jail-free card.

"Besides other politicians like the mayor of Philly, Isaac Norris, or John Brown, who with his three brothers founded Brown University in Rhode Island, there was Robert Lumpkin." He glanced back at the elders' table. "He was a notorious and prominent slave trader who ironically married a light-skinned slave named Mary whom he purchased."

The room had a chilly quiet. Either the small ones were asleep or listening.

"Lumpkin's Richmond, Virginia's jail was called the Devil's Half-Acre, which was one of the largest slave-holding facilities in the city." Frederic rubbed the back of his neck. "It was just three blocks from where the capitol building sits today. It was the devil's playground for more than thirty years through the Civil War. Even St. Louis had a holding pen near where Busch Stadium is located. I'll end there."

"Thank you," Queen mumbled in a sarcastic tone.

The Jamiesons, including Philip, gave him a standing applause. "Wow."

Grandma BB stood, and her bodyguards motioned toward her, but she waved them off as she made her way to their table aided with her jewel-encrusted cane. "Here's a bell. Now we have a competition. You're on the board, but I'm watching you." She pointed two fingers from her eyes to his.

Did Philip see a smirk on Frederic's face? Grandma BB must have noticed, too, because she lifted her cane and twirled as if it were a baton.

Queen covered her face with her hands and uttered, "Please don't get her started."

"Yes, ma'am." Frederic had averted a beatdown from Grandma BB.

Philip wondered if the woman's bodyguards would have intervened.

"Well done, young man," Papa P said as Frederic returned to his table, then pulled another question. "This comes from #TeamCameron. What is the 1619 Project?"

Ace tapped the bell. His wife stood. "The 1619 Project is named for the date of the first arrival of Africans on American soil. Nikole Hannah-Jones's introductory essay. Her research shows a dark past and cloudy present, citing Americans have made less progress than they think. Blacks continue to struggle indefinitely for rights they may never obtain because of insincerity of the populous and the weak voice of white anti-racism." Talise didn't hide her disgust.

"You nailed it, babe." Ace stood and kissed her as family applauded and Papa P certified her answer was correct.

"Here's an easy one," Papa P said. "What is a freedom suit?"

Pace, Parke's oldest son, stood. Despite briefly being in the foster care system, the handsome, confident young man had just finished his freshman year in college.

From what Philip had learned in Parke's defense, he hadn't known the boy existed. Pace had been abandoned by his mother's white family after her death, and he was briefly adopted by another white family until Parke got wind of that. The young man was the oldest of all the Jamieson children, and the small ones looked up to him.

"It's the process in which a slave was brave enough to petition for his or her freedom. Contradictory to falsehoods, many were awarded their liberty. Those court cases are the reason I'm going to law school—to free the innocent and convict the guilty."

"And we're proud of you, son." Parke clapped and others joined in.

Rubbing his chin, Philip wondered if his brother could mentor Pace since he was a federal judge. Philip would mention it to Drexel, he decided as he rested his arm on the back of Queen's chair. She looked at him, and they both smiled.

For the next hour, tables vied for the winning answers until #TeamCameron was tied with #TeamKidd who was known for his family's prep to win.

Papa P seemed please as he continued, "What did Annie Parram, Anna Angales, Elizabeth Berkeley, and Sadie Thompson have in common, and why did they go to D.C. in 1916?"

Queen tapped the bell and stood with grace, beating Frederic Robnett as he got to his feet too. This time, he conceded.

"It was the fifty-fourth annual convention of ex-slaves held at the Cosmopolitan Baptist Church where one speaker was Robert E. Lee, a preacher and former slave of the Confederate general. Annie was 104 years old. Anna was 105 years old. Elizabeth was noted as 125 years old, and Sadie was 110 years old."

Papa P announced their table the winner. Philip exchanged high fives with his family while Kidd joked—or maybe he wasn't—demanding a rematch since Queen was technically his sister and should have sat at his table.

Queen laughed and stuck out her tongue before she rushed to Kidd's table and hugged her brother. When she returned to Philip's side, she grinned. "And the best hug for last."

The embrace was worth the wait. It was soothing and made everything all right in his world until Papa P gave Frederic the floor.

Chapter Ten

*S*howtime, Queen thought as a hush fell over the room as Papa P yield the floor to their guest. Frederic's stride was confident as he made his way to the front.

"Good evening again, family." He gave a curt nod and a suspicious smile as far as Queen was concerned. Their response was cordial, except Grandma BB who seemed to have "hero worship" plastered on her face.

"We are descendants of Queen Pokou, born around 1767. She was the sister of your Princess Adaeze who married King Seif—ancestors you have tracked on your father's side from Paki Kokumuo Jaja We are connected maternally from the two sisters. And we track the ladies. We cherish our queens."

Queen sat straighter in her chair. "Now that's what I'm talking about." She exchanged high fives with Gabrielle.

"Before you get swept away with the illusion that you're not cherished, think again," Philip said it in a tone that he dared her to challenge him.

"I know I am loved and cherished," she said for his ears, staring into those drugging brown eyes. *Wow*.

Frederic tugged her concentration away from Philip. "My eleventh great-grandmother Pokuo married King Kofi. In 1786, they had Bolanie, Paki's first cousin, who married Prince Ekow. They had Princess Kadida who is the mother of Queen, born in 1823. That is when our African ties were severed.

Queen felt Philip's hand's brush her shoulder. His touch gave her a sense of contentment.

"You see, on a fretful day in 1841, Queen was given to wed Issa Dembele, but their ceremony turned out to be an ambush. Both my eighth great-grandfather and eighth great-grandmother were captured and separated, never to lay eyes on each other again."

"I hate unhappy endings," she murmured as Philip patted her hand.

"Skip to the end of the Bible—and we win. That's the best happy ending," Philip said close to her ear.

Queen looked at him. Why did he have to be so spiritually minded? She was carnal in her thoughts, dress, and lifestyle, yet her heart was good, and she never mistreated anyone. She loved her life.

"If in this life, only you have hope in Me, you are of all men most miserable. But if you believe I rose from the dead. I am the first fruits of them that slept. The first resurrection is your happy ending," God whispered, *Read 1 Corinthians 15:19–26.*

She swallowed in fear. Did she hear Jesus? What about Philip? Queen reached for her purse and fumbled tapping in the Scripture God referenced, a task she would do before closing her eyes that night.

Philip glanced at the note and tilted his head. He opened his mouth, then closed it when Parke's booming voice reclaimed her attention.

"Hold up." Parke raised his hand and stood. "If they didn't marry, then they both can't be your distant grandparents."

"That's the beauty of what is meant to be—destiny," a woman from the Robnett table responded and with a catwalk stride stood next to him. "Hello, family." Her voice was sultry, and her features exotic. "My name is Queen Robnett."

There was an instant connection with Queen Jamieson. She had only met a handful of women named Queen, and they were much older.

"What my cousin should have said was although Queen and Issa never married that day, their offspring found their way to each other while in American bondage and consummated their marriage in spirit."

"Huh?" Queen mumbled with others. Even Cameron looked dumbfounded.

"We've been able to pick up the trail in the Land of the Free," Frederic said with sarcasm. "When we were able to trace our lineage from Queen's daughter, Viney, a mulatto enslaved since birth in 1842. Her enslaver and father, Duncan G. Campbell, died when she was three and promised her emancipation at sixteen years old with an inheritance of five thousand dollars."

"Right." Cameron smirked with a headshake. "Funny how those promises aren't always kept."

Queen Robnett continued, "A slave trader had other ideas and sold her in Missouri when she was six years old. They locked her up in a slave pen before Dr. John Sappington here in St. Louis purchased her like a puppy." Her voice faded, and Queen Jamieson's heart ached.

Frederic played tag team. "Viney was sixteen when he died, and she found herself on the auction block again. Our slaveholder, William Robnett, traveled from Columbia, Missouri, to make purchases on the south entrance to the Old Courthouse. He had already changed dirty hands with slave trader Isaac Franklin."

Another woman stood from the table and joined the pair. It was as if their movements were choreographed. "My name is Rejoice, and I'm Queen's younger sister. Unknowingly, William Robnett joined the descendants of the African groom and the bride. Issa Dembele was purchased blindly before he departed the ship."

Silence filled the room. The story was too incredible to believe. Queen was in awe of these women, strong fierce and one bearing the same name as her. She liked her already.

When the Robnetts finished their presentation, Papa P called for the end of this family game night and the closing prayer."

He left her side for the front. "Father, in the name of Jesus, we thank You for Your blood on calvary that erases the blemish of sins of men if we repent. Thank you for this family fellowship and bless the Robnetts and Jamiesons from this day forward. In the mighty name of Jesus. Amen."

Queen mumbled her amen and made a beeline to meet her newfound cousins. Nothing else took precedence other than embracing another namesake.

Philip blinked. If there were dust on the carpet, Queen would have kicked up a storm getting to the Robnett women. Their height didn't come in heels as high as Queen—his queen. Where his Queen had dark satiny skin, the Robnett women were fairer, a golden brown.

He returned to the #TeamCameron table. Philip wasn't family, only an observer.

"Wait until I tell Gigi she's got more cousins to love." Gabrielle's eyes were bright with excitement.

"I'm not buying that." Cameron drummed his fingers on the table.

"Definitely don't trust them." Ace stood at the table with Kidd beside him.

Parke walked up and patted Kidd on the shoulder. "That was a well-crafted story."

Cameron agreed. "Now, to double check their paper trail. I think Queen needs to proceed with caution before throwing out a welcome mat into our lives."

"You want to tell our sister that?" Ace tilted his head to the Robnett entourage chatting with those at the head table. "I believe they're exchanging phone numbers."

Instead of stewing like the other men, Philip said his good nights, kissed his sister, then he headed toward the Robnett guests.

"Queen," Philip said, approaching the group. Two heads turned and faced him. Amused, he reached for the hand of the Jamieson Queen and rubbed her fingers. "This one." He kissed her cheek. "I'm about to head out. Call me later if you want."

"Oh, the minister who gave the closing prayer—nice touch—" Queen Robnett pointed, "and definitely not family." Her eyes sparkled.

"We're in-laws," his Queen spoke up.

So that's your story, and you're sticking with it, huh? Philip wanted to question her.

"You know there's been kissing cousins, so I didn't know," Queen Robnett teased—or at least Philip thought she was joking.

"Let me introduce you to everybody. Besides Queen Robnett and her sister Rejoice, this is their cousin Sapphire." All of them smiled, then the men stepped forward to shake hands. Frederic, Dillard, Major, Sterling, and Prince. "I love their names and told them Malcolm's youngest son is Major. Two Queens and two Majors in the family line."

"Actually, there are more than two generations of Queens," Rejoice said.

Philip didn't know if he should say welcome to the family or look out for this family. He gave the safest reply. "Nice to meet you all."

When Philip turned around to make his exit, Kidd, Ace, and Cameron were glaring at him as if he had crossed enemy territory.

Lord, please keep the peace, in Jesus' name, because I'm out of here.

Chapter Eleven

The crowds. The music. The food. The taste and sound of Freedom. St. Louis' Juneteenth celebration was underway.

Vendors dotted on the sidewalks. Folks sampled dishes while others watched re-enactments of Blacks sold as chattel on the steps of the Old Courthouse.

Philip's parents had relocated here a few weeks earlier. They, along with his brothers, and sister's family were taking in the sights. He even recognized familiar faces from his congregation among the crowd. Some were downtown for the ballgame while others planned to ride the tram to the top of the Gateway Arch.

Couples. Families. Men looking and women hoping to be seen. One person missing in the mix was Queen. He smiled thinking about her. How could two walk unless they agree on the Christian walk? It was a Biblical principle that had one answer— they can't. The other thing standing between them was the distance.

"It's fascinating how different cities commemorate the freedom of enslaved African Americans in Galveston, Texas." His mother interrupted his musing while they stayed close, so not to be separated. "Imagine the U-S Colored Troops releasing two hundred and fifty slaves—definitely a Moses moment. I never thought I would see the day where this country would recognize its dark past."

Veronica held her granddaughter's hand while his father pushed the stroller where her twin Gabriel was strapped in and knocked out. Cameron and Gabrielle strolled beside them, holding hands.

Philip nodded. "I didn't realize St. Louis had such a dark history in connection to slavery. I learned an interesting tidbit about slave pens and infamous slave traders at Jamieson's game night last month."

"I admire their research," his mother said, "although America's history with Black folks is horrendous."

"Israelite slaves were also subject to cruelty, death, and harsh labor, yet God rescued them out of Egypt," Philip said. "The Lord did the same for African Americans enslaved in this country. We have to remember—especially me—anyone can repent of their past. God has no respect of persons, and His blessings are universal.

His mother stopped in her tracks and looked at Philip. Her sudden movement almost caused a collision with a couple of teenagers. "Wait a minute. I just realized you said slave pens. Here?"

The disbelief on her face matched his when Queen's cousin first mentioned them in St. Louis. "Yep. Lynch's Slave Market was located not far from here at 104 Locust between Fourth and Fifth Street."

Cameron further explained, "Missouri became a slave state after the Louisiana Purchase—the Missouri Compromise. Bernard Lynch's Slave Pens were cages for enslaved men, women, and children before they were sold at slave markets throughout downtown, not just on the steps of the Old Courthouse. Whites set up a slave stand anywhere to make a sale. Can you imagine walking to work or to some entertainment venue and hearing cries from the pens or seeing mothers wailing as their families are sold away?"

Coveting their thoughts, Philip and his family continued their stroll when they passed a table stacked with pamphlets and flyers about other local activities.   Cameron spied a vendor selling fruit cups next to it, so he bought one for everybody.

"You know, thinking about those slave pens, documents have been uncovered that describe how cramped the prison cells were." Cameron paused to give thanks, then sampled the cantaloupe. "Each victim was shackled in rooms bolted with bars on the windows. The irony of it all is these places were once private homes." "This," he said, pointing to Busch Stadium, home of the St. Louis Baseball Cardinals, "is a source of local pride, but nearby, the memory of slavery lingers just as Lynch and his slave auctions."

"Remember, history can't be changed," Philip imparted, encouraging words of hope, "but Jesus can change people's hearts, if they want Him. The Holy Ghost is available to help us love not hate others."

A woman shaped like Queen with wild hair grabbed Philip's attention. "Excuse me. I need to make a call." He stepped aside and FaceTimed Queen.

She answered with a smile that graced his phone. "Philip! Happy Juneteenth. Are you out enjoying the festivities?" She waved at someone near her before focusing on him again.

"Happy Juneteenth to you. Yes, I'm with my parents, brothers, sister, and her clan."

As if on cue, his family vied for screen time. Queen giggled.

"We miss you, Queen. I haven't seen you since my grandbabies' birthday party. I don't know if Philip told you, but we live here now, so the next time you come into town, please visit," his mother said.

"I will, Mrs. Dupree."

Philip admired her expressions. Her smile was genuine. "Speaking of next time, when are you planning to come back? There are street vendors selling all sorts of stuff, including, get this, cotton candy—blue—and we could share. I remember you mentioned it one time that you enjoyed it as a child." He wiggled his eyebrows.

"Ooh. I love it when you talk sugar." Queen showed him her cotton candy stick. "But I don't know. Maybe around Christmas. I've got a lot of things going on here."

Five whole months. Philip shook his head. Not the answer he wanted to hear. "Maybe I'll come to you."

"If you do, I'll clear my calendar," Queen taunted him.

"You just said you had a lot going on." Like Philip didn't have responsibilities there. "But I want to see you."

"I'll bump you up to priority. I'm with some girlfriends, so I've got to go. Talk to you later. Give everyone my love. Bye." Then she was gone.

Sliding his phone back in his case, Philip ignored his family's curious expressions until Drexel elbowed him.

"Really? You and Queen are an item? And here I thought my younger preaching brother was immune to seductive women." The disbelief on Drexel's face was comical.

"I want to think I am."

"Philip Dupree, you aren't ready for Queen Jamieson," his mother said.

"I might surprise you and myself." Philip snickered.

Queen joined her best friends at a merchandise booth. Tulsa's Juneteenth celebration empowered her. She hadn't missed one as long as she could remember. The Tulsa Massacre was proof evil existed in the world. Humans could be more savage than wild beasts. Now, it's a federal holiday, so no one could forget.

Cori and Trice wore silly grins with looks of expectancy for information, but Queen wasn't going to take the bait and have them in her business. The three were inseparable when it came to attending local events together.

"No wonder you're racking up frequent flyer points." Cori twisted her lips.

Trice folded her arms. "Visiting family in St. Louis, huh? From the glimpse I could see of that strong black man and his voice…" She danced from side to side. "*Ooowee.* If you're going to pass, gurl, I'll take him. When's our next trip?"

Queen laughed at the pair. They had met at a STEM symposium five years ago and had been friends ever since, traveling, shopping, and supporting each other. However, they never double or triple dated. Some dates weren't worth the long-term investment.

"Philip and I are in-laws. He's sweet, kind, and training to be a pastor." She strolled ahead of them on North Greenwood Avenue for the car and motorcycle takeover block party.

Cori's bark of laughter competed with the live music that mingled with the screams of delight from the kid zone. "You with a minister? What do you two have in common?"

"Surprisingly, more than I thought besides our love for family." Queen shrugged. "There's this vibe between us. Either I'm flirting with him and he's giving it back, or Philip's doing the flirting and I'm caught in his trap. We'll never happen. He's into church, I'm not. He lives six hours away…"

"Girl, that man called you, grinning. Fake church until you feel it," Trice advised. "Aren't you flying back to St. Louis in a couple of weeks?"

"I don't do counterfeit. Philip knows what he sees here—" Queen pointed from head to toe— "is what he gets." She shrugged. "Anyway, I think he's okay with me flirting with him."

"Something tells me the pastor is more than okay." Trice paused when a guy who looked gym certified for weightlifting made eye contact with her.

Queen smacked her friend's arm. "I thought you're on a thirty-day sabbatical from men, remember?"

Trice struck a pose meant to garner attention. It worked. "With a buffed guy like that, my memory is fading."

"What's this about your next trip?" Cori asked, pitching her trash in a nearby waste bin. "All I've got to say is I'm going to crash one of those Jamieson nights."

Trice waved her hand in the air. "Don't forget me. I'm soooo jealous. Our family gatherings—aka family feuds—are to be avoided at all costs."

Pinching more cotton candy, Queen melted some in her mouth. "Family means everything to me, and we get along— well sort of." Queen gave them a recap of the drama at the last game night.

"I'm flying into Kansas City for Royalty weekend with the ladies in the family. Philip doesn't know anything about it. Plus, I think it's only a three-hour drive from St. Louis."

"Secrets already," Trice teased.

"You know me, I'm all about family, and I met some classy cousins, including Queen."

"Get out of here. Seriously? Two Queen Jamiesons in one family?" Cori stepped back and eyed her.

Queen laughed. "Two Queens, different surnames. We clicked, so we decided to do a ladies Royalty weekend for the women in the family."

When the live band played a tune, Queen started to shake her hips and snap her fingers. "That's my song."

"You're scandalous, Queen, in that dress and heels," Trice said as her friends joined her on the sidewalk, and they danced the night away with no cares.

Chapter Twelve

A royalty weekend fit for a Queen. The girls' night out mantra with an upgrade. Queen was giddy with excitement as her plane touched down in Kansas City, Missouri.

The Jamieson and the Robnett women renamed the outing in honor of the four generations of Queens on the Robnett's side.

She decided not to mention the trip to her brothers or Gabrielle, since the men didn't trust the Robnetts. Cameron wanted Queen to hold off all contact until he finished their background checks. That wasn't happening.

Her cousin said Frederic didn't have a criminal past when she asked how he was coming along in verifying their heritage. Queen had enough love for the Jamiesons and Robnetts. She was an independent thinker. Her daddy was deceased, therefore no man ruled over her decisions, concerning family or friends.

As planned, Gigi and her two sisters coordinated their flights to arrive in the city around the same time as Queen. Within hugging distance, they screamed their delight. Next came the kisses while complimenting the other's attire in various shades of coral. It was Queen's favorite color against her dark skin.

"It's been too long since we've been together," Queen said to Lacey and Candy.

"Which is why this weekend getaway is perfect." Gigi wore her excitement in her smile. "You've straightened your hair again, and it's even longer." She ran her fingers through Queen's mane.

"Our cousin said it was royalty weekend, so I wanted to rock my crown. I thought about wearing it on the plane, but that would have drawn too much attention."

Lacey laughed. "Since when didn't you, sis?"

Samuel's first set of Jamieson daughters all looked alike. They favored their mother. Still, Queen felt the kinship.

"You mean you three. I'm the only one wearing a rock," Gigi corrected.

Rolling their carry-ons, the trio made their way to the exit and couldn't miss the *Queen's Day Out* sign that greeted them.

Queen recognized Queen "Bee" as she had begun to refer to her older cousin. Rejoice and Sapphire were there too. Three other women were fashion divas in Queen's book because their attire seemed to match their personalities.

Queen Bee opened her arms and stepped forward and gave Queen a hearty hug. "You look gorgeous, cousin."

"Thanks. These are my three sisters I told you about, Giselle, but we call her Gigi, Candy, and Lacey, the oldest."

The introductions continued. Queen Bee's youngest sister, Princess, had the longest lashes. "Sapphire, they have to be your sisters. They have the most beautiful eye color," Queen said.

"Yes, this is Jewel and Duchess. Duchess is our high school graduate," Sapphire said.

"Really?" Queen patted her chest. "My two nieces in St. Louis just graduated from high school."

For the get-together, all the women had their hair straightened with soft curls and boasted pearls for royalty day. It was a cousin convention. Queen loved it.

"Come on, family. Let's get our party started." Queen Bee led them out of the airport to a limousine.

Their driver stood straighter, then opened their door. White-beaded crowns awaited them on the seats.

"Wow. I feel special already." Gigi giggled as she slid in first, then Queen beside her until all the ladies were inside.

Nothing compared to this moment of pampering. An indescribable feeling of contentment filled Queen. She pushed back happy tears. Once the driver pulled from the curb, Queen Bee popped the cork to a bottle of champagne, and one by one filled their glasses.

Gigi declined. Queen had never seen her sister drink and suspected it had something to do with her Christian lifestyle, but she never judged Queen as she indulged.

Queen relaxed and enjoyed the view while their cousin-turned-tour-guide pointed out local attractions until the limo parked in front of 21c Museum Hotel. The entrance was elegant while simple.

One by one, they stepped out and waited for the driver to retrieve their carry-on luggage. As they were about to go inside, another limo pulled up, honked, and two men stepped out in sync.

"*Humph.* Why couldn't they have been our driver? Am I drooling?" Sapphire asked with a panicked expression as Queen recognized Chip and Dale.

What are they doing here? she wondered as Dale nodded at her before opening the door. A pearl-encrusted cane tapped the street, then one Stacy Adams shoe crushed the ground followed by the other.

Grandma BB. Amusement played on the faces of the cousins who weren't at the family game night.

Rejoice and Queen Bee chuckled. "It's Grandmother B."

Queen nudged them and whispered, "You'd better get her name right. It's Grandma BB."

Steadying herself, Grandma BB squinted. "I'm the real queen of this party. Nobody has a girls' night out without inviting me." She moved aside, and Gabrielle stepped out, followed by Talise, Hallison, and Cheney. Kami and Victoria had also come. Those two would bond with Princess and Duchess Robnett. Eva was missing, maybe because she was nearing her delivery date.

"Ah, how did you know?" Queen lifted an eyebrow.

If these Jamieson women were here, that meant Queen's brothers knew about it. Oh well. She would deal with the fallout later. Right now, it was their day she decided as she hugged each one of them.

Gabrielle raised her hand. "Me."

"Who told you?" Queen turned and eyed her sister, the likely suspect.

"Me." Gigi grinned and slipped her arm through Gabrielle's. "I couldn't come this close to my best friend and not let her know."

"What did my cousin have to say about that?" Queen didn't want the Robnetts to know they were under investigation.

Gabrielle seemed to read Queen's mind. "Nothing I can remember. Come on, who's ready for some of us time?"

"Hold up," Grandma BB said. "Where is my crown?"

"Here." Queen removed the one from her head and placed it on Grandma BB's long, gray and white hair. "From one Queen to Your Majesty." She bowed her head in gest.

Even Grandma BB seemed to choke out a whisper. "Thank you, my daughter."

Stepping back, Queen rummaged through her travel bag and pulled out hers, which she had packed for the fun of it. She didn't realize it would be a must accessory.

"We'll get crowns for you ladies, too, when we go shopping at the Village of Briarcliff after our spa appointment." Queen

Bee nudged Queen aside. "What's with Grandmother—I mean Grandma BB's bodyguards? I had to remember to breathe."

Queen snickered. "They are hot, but I've never asked anything about their personal lives. I don't know what dirt Grandma BB has on them or how much she's paying them for their 24/7 services, but they're at her beck and call. But if you want to flirt, they know how to give it back."

"Thanks for the warning." Queen Bee made a phone call, nodded, then ended the call. "After we check into our rooms, we'll eat at Piropos in the Village. You'll love it. And the spa has more than enough room for us."

As expected, Chip and Dale refused to allow Grandma BB out of their sight. They trailed the ladies' limo in theirs.

Piropos had the perfect ambience with a stunning view overlooking downtown Kansas City. The ladies enjoyed Argentina dishes while getting to know one another better.

In her peripheral vision, Queen noticed Chip and Dale outside the restaurant door. More than once, she saw them either text or talk on the phone. Kidd, Ace, Parke, Malcolm, and Cameron came to mind. Were they not only bodyguards but snitches?

As they ordered dessert, a handsome man strolled into the place. Queen Bee waved him over. He was tall and slender with dark skin and a shaved head. He kissed her cheeks then handed gift bags to the newcomers with their crowns inside.

The ladies grinned and placed them on their heads with the grace of royalty.

"Thanks, Todd." Queen Bee dismissed him.

"My sister tried to explain it to me," Gigi said, glancing at Queen, "but I couldn't follow, so how are you connected to us?"

"As far as we could find, Viney Campbell was the sole offspring of Queen Akwesi. Unfortunately, William Robnett didn't have a plantation but a cash crop farm not far from here in

Columbia. He purchased our fourth great-grandmother at sixteen for breeding…" Queen Bee paused to observe a moment of silence.

Victoria gasped and mumbled. "I hate men."

Queen heard her as the women grabbed each other's hands and squeezed. If only their ancestors could see them today—free of shackles, thriving, and reconnecting.

"She had twelve children. Ten survived, and six of those were sold to pay off his debts when he died. But the man who fathered eight of those children was Issa's descendent, Queen Akwesi's intended groom."

Queen shivered in disbelief. "Thousands of miles away and separated by time. Yet, what were the odds of them ever beginning their lineage? It's creepy."

"It was fate," Queen Bee said. "When we traced our roots, we were blown away. Viney named her first and last daughter Queen. Two Queens in the same family. My cousins—our cousins—Sapphire, Jewel, and Duchess are descendants of the Baby Queen, and she was sold on the Oregon Trail, which ended in Utah. Some descendants didn't know they were mulattos and later Black."

"Wow. I always hear about southern states' slavery, but very little about points West," Talise admitted.

"The Oregon Trail started in Independence, Missouri, not far from William Robnett's farm. If you wanted to sell human cargo, the Oregon Trail was the way to go, and it was a two-thousand-mile journey," Queen Bee explained.

"Enough talk about the past, tell me something about our newfound cousins and Grandma BB." Rejoice rested her folded arms on the table as the server collected their empty plates.

Grandma BB waved her hand to go first. Bling dotted every finger as if they were brass knuckles strapped for a punching fest. Chip and Dale appeared from nowhere as she had summoned them. "Gentleman, you're off duty."

"Whoa. I wish I could hire them," Rejoice said and exchanged a high-five with her sister.

"Not for sale. You've got to go to Vegas and get your own." Grandma BB didn't smile, then told her life story as a young woman and blushing bride and described an idyllic life with her soul mate. "Young divas know nothing about romance these days. You get it twisted with sex."

There were a few blushes on faces, but no one confirmed their guilt.

"Real love—pure love—stays with you. It never dies, even when Henry did. I became a widow, alone without children until the Jamiesons adopted me."

Grandma BB was captivating. Even Cheney, her longtime goddaughter, acted as if she had never heard the stories before. She was the oldest of all the Jamieson women, and now the Robnetts, and had been married the longest.

Each woman shared a bit of themselves, families, and careers, except Gabrielle and Talise who seemed reserved. Queen suspected their husbands' unfounded suspicions made them hesitant. Queen wasn't as she talked about the love of her big sister, Suzette. Lacey and Gigi squeezed her hands for strength. "In her honor, I'm working on an endowment scholarship for the University of Central Oklahoma at Edmund's fashion merchandise and design program. I've never written so many proposals for funding and endowments in my life. Since attendance is dwindling, I'm actively recruiting ladies interested in a fashion career, and I help host fundraisers to support scholarships. But an endowment is my goal."

"We'll help," Queen Bee said. Rejoice raised her hand.

Everyone reached across the table to place a hand on hers as close as possible. Queen didn't care what her brothers or cousins thought of the Robnetts. These ladies formed her sisterhood.

Chapter Thirteen

Philip needed a distraction as he prepared for his Sunday sermon. He missed Queen, and whenever they spoke, neither wanted to be the first to say goodbye.

If he wanted a quick break, his sister was the choice, then his mother. Gabrielle's call went to voicemail. Odd. He didn't leave a message. She was always home with the children. Minutes later, she texted back.

In K.C. enjoying a weekend with the ladies. Call Cameron. He might need help babysitting the twins.

"What?"

When did his sister go out of town? Why was his brother-in-law "babysitting" his own children instead of his parents? Things didn't add up. He called Cameron for answers.

"Hey, it's a long story. If you want to stop by, I'll fill you in." Cameron's tone didn't sound good.

Philip had one foot in the door when he arrived, and Cameron began his rant.

"I told Gabrielle not to go, and what does my beautiful, sweet wife—your rebellious sister—" Cameron pointed an accusatory finger at him— "do? She goes to Kansas City anyway."

"O-okay. I hope not by herself."

Cameron stood and started pacing the carpet. "And there lies the problem. She and all the Jamieson wives went to meet up with Queen, her sisters, and the Robnett girls. I don't like it…"

Queen was in Kansas City, too? His Queen. Why hadn't she told him? As Philip's mind drifted, Cameron's venting yanked him back.

"I am seriously hot. We had a big argument, which made her more stubborn. I thought wives are supposed to obey their husbands." He didn't hold back his frustration.

Philip dropped his face into his hands and shook his head, then eyed his brother-in-law. "No, you didn't. Please tell me you didn't bait my sister with that Scripture."

Cameron had a calm demeanor until pushed. He gritted his teeth. "Yeah, I did. The Bible does say that, you know."

"No, no, no." He was not about to let Cameron get away with bits and pieces of a Scripture. "'*For the husband is the head of the wife, even as Christ is the head of the church: and he is the savior of the body. Therefore, as the church is subject unto Christ, so let the wives be to their own husbands in everything. Husbands, love your wives, even as Christ also loved the church, and gave himself for it.* It's all in Ephesians 5:23–25: Love is patient—"

A piercing scream came from upstairs, and Cameron took off for the steps. Philip was on his heels.

Gabriel had pushed his twin sister, Camille, down over a toy. While Cameron disciplined his son, Philip scooped up Camille to comfort her. He rubbed her back. "It's okay." He was rewarded with her little arms squeezing his neck tight.

Cameron looked worried and paced the floor, shoving toys aside in his path. "Your sister might kick me out of the bedroom over this stunt. No telling when we'll kiss and make up."

Rocking chair in the twins' bedroom, Philip patted his niece. "You have to apologize."

"Me. Why?" Cameron stopped in his tracks and became indignant. "I'm the head."

"To cover your wife. But Christ is the Head of you. Lead by example. Be the bigger person. The Bible says, *Husbands, dwell with your wives according to knowledge, giving honor unto them, as unto the weaker vessel, and as being heirs together of the grace of life; that your prayers be not hindered.*"

Cameron huffed. "I guess that Scripture is there since you're a pastor. Not fair."

His brother-in-law didn't know Philip had some Scriptures loaded and ready to discharge at will. Same scenarios, different couples. "Read First Peter 3:7. You two need to fix what's broken so God can answer your prayers. You never know what you'll need from God." Stepping out of his preacher hat, Philip slipped into his role as big brother. "Plus, bro, you should have learned by now that ultimatums don't work with my sister."

Cameron said nothing as he sat in the window seat, sulking like his son instead of digesting the wisdom of the Scriptures.

"Listen, my sister loves you, or she would have never given you the time of day."

"Trust me, she didn't for a long time."

"Prayer should always solve disputes. Now, why didn't you want her to go?" Philip shifted Camille in his arms, ready to get to the bottom of this.

Twisting his mouth, Cameron stalled. "Isn't it obvious? I don't trust the Robnetts. None of us do."

The jury was still out for Philip. "Do you think my sister is in danger?"

"Well, no, because if I did..."

Lord, can You step in and soften his heart please, so I can minister to him? "Listen, I'm not married—"

"Which is your fault, man." Cameron gave him a stupefied expression. "I heard Queen say preachers are sexy. I assumed she was talking about you, so if you want a wife, she's available."

Philip didn't care if Cameron ribbed him about his grin. He earned it listening to his ranting. "So for clarification purposes, Queen said I'm sexy or preachers are sexy in general?" *How many preachers does she know?*

Cameron dropped his head back and groaned. "Man, I guess she was talking about you," he said, eyeing Philip, "or it could be one of mega preachers."

His brother-in-law was no help. Philip refocused. How many times had he counseled his members over this very same Scripture? "Life is too short for misunderstandings and hurt feelings. If the other Jamieson wives were going, I could see her feeling left out. Please tell me you two prayed before she left."

"*Awww*...Nope, too mad."

Philip slapped his forehead. "I'm sure my sister would have enjoyed her trip better if she knew her husband loved her and was the first to apologize."

If torture had a look, Cameron was wearing it. Clearly, he wasn't feeling his advice.

"I'm not a chump, man. She is not the boss of me."

"Cam, text your wife with kind words. God forbid if something were to happen to either of you and the last thing said were angry words."

That seemed to hit home. "You're right." He pulled out his phone. "Only because you're a man of God, I'm taking your advice."

"Right." Philip stood and laid his sleeping niece in her bed. Next, he took Gabriel out of his father's arms and did the same while Cameron walked away, tapping on his phone.

Alone in the children's room, his thoughts drifted to Queen. Yes, Philip wanted to be married when the time was right. At this stage in his life, he felt uncertain about his calling to pastor.

Minutes later, Cameron returned with a smug expression.

"I take it, you and your wife patched things up?"

"Yeah, we did. She even sent me a picture of them enjoying lunch. Chip took this one. Dale snapped a couple of photos too." He shared them with Philip.

He stared at the ladies wearing crowns but zoomed in on his Queen. It had been a long time since he had seen her hair straight—lovely. If he were in Cameron's shoes, would he forbid and deny his wife the pleasure of having a good time with other ladies? He hoped he wouldn't be that type of husband.

"I'm glad you two kissed and made up virtually."

"Oh, we will. Count on it." He winked. "Come on, I'll walk you to the door."

"Wait a minute. You're kicking me out now without a sandwich to go?" Philip couldn't believe the man.

"Okay." Cameron snickered. "I'm sure there's leftovers."

Back at his house before Philip crawled in the bed, he texted Queen. **I saw the picture of you in K.C. You're breathtaking. You seem so far away.**

It was a while before Queen texted him back. **I'm only 3 hours away. Heading home in the a.m. I'll see you when I come back to St. Louis. Promise.**

What if I don't wait to wait that long? He rolled over, closed his eyes, and mumbled, "I'm not talking about physical distance. I need a spiritual connection."

Chapter Fourteen

T it for tat. Not a good quality for a pastor candidate. Was Philip being petty boarding the plane for Tulsa and not telling Queen? They weren't in a relationship yet, but he planned to change that during this visit.

The invitation from Resurrection Temple couldn't have had better timing. Evangelism was in his blood, and in two months, he was would officially retire when he became pastor. Nathan and the board approved his speaking engagement if it didn't interfere with his Sunday services.

Deacons Townsend and Alford from the church greeted him at the airport. As soon as he walked outside, the humidity slapped him.

"Whew. It's just as hot here as it was in St. Louis." Philip fanned his chest with his polo shirt.

"It's going to be a hot one, Evangelist—I mean interim pastor," Deacon Alford corrected, wiping beads of sweat from his forehead, "even under the tent. But we'll have the overhead fans and bottled water to hand out. Pastor Franklin will meet you there."

Not that Total Surrender Church mistreated him, but this Tulsa church showered him with brotherly love. They made Philip feel at home.

"It's so good to have you back. Many of the souls who were delivered from one of your meetings a few years back still walk with God, and the word is out the Evangelist Philip Dupree is in town." Deacon Townsend, an older gentleman, had a slow, low laugh as he patted Philip on the back before he climbed in the vehicle where the cold air blasted without mercy.

He guessed that to them, Philip would always be an evangelist whether he was a pastor or not. Sounded good to his ears, so Philip didn't correct them.

"Amen." The praise hyped and humbled Philip. This was his calling. His comfort zone.

The conversation en route to the hotel was refreshing. He didn't have to worry about church budgets. Counseling sessions. Complaints.

For the next two days, he had one mission. Philip would labor in the harvest on the streets of Tulsa.

Once he settled in his hotel suite, he called Queen to surprise her.

"Philip," her sultry voice greeted him. "I can't wait to see you."

He grinned. "Yeah. I was hoping you'd say that." He rubbed his face, smooth from his morning shave. Philip had to look his best when Queen saw him.

"Guess what I'm doing." She didn't give him a chance to answer. "I'm packing to fly out tomorrow to St. Louis. Surprise. Will you pick me up from the airport?"

His heart and jaw dropped. Was this a joke?

"Philip? Philip?"

He sucked the air back into his lungs. "I'm in Tulsa."

"You're where?" The disbelief in her voice was the same in his heart.

Now who was surprising whom? "I'm here today and tomorrow for a tent meeting. Remember those?"

Kami had repented of her rebellious streak at one of Philip's tent meetings while she stayed with Queen last summer.

"Oh, yes. How could I forget that heat? Whew. I don't see how you can preach and pray without collapsing." Queen sighed.

"God gives me strength. I've missed you and hoped to see you. I have to fly out early Sunday morning in time to preach at my church." Philip couldn't gage from her responses what she was thinking. "Dinner is our favorite meal, so I hope you will let me take you out. There's something I would like us to discuss." His feelings were deepening. Queen needed to bring her feelings to the table, too.

"Is everything okay?" She didn't mask the concern in her voice.

"It depends."

"On what?"

"You... Since you're flying out tomorrow, it looks like tonight is all we have. I'm conducting the tent meeting at the same location as before when you brought Kami. It may be late, but we can eat and talk."

"Philip, I love you, but I'm not coming to a tent meeting." Her defiance was in full force.

He wasn't looking for platonic love from Queen Jamieson. "Saturday's tent meeting is at one. What time is your flight?"

She was quiet. "I'm going to change it and fly back with you. Pick me up for dinner tomorrow at six P.M."

Relief flowed through Philip's veins. He would see her after all. "Did you have a good time with the other queens in Kansas City?"

"Yes."

Philip could hear the "wow" in her voice. "It had been a while since I saw you with your hair straight."

"I wanted to feel like a princess for a change. I can't be a queen all the time."

"But you are." He imagined her perfect smile. "Any way you look at it, Queen Jamieson, you're royalty." He reflected on 1 Peter 2:9: *But ye are a chosen generation, a royal priesthood, a holy nation, a peculiar people; that ye should shew forth the praises of him who hath called you out of darkness into his marvelous light.* Lord, please choose Queen.

Have you not read in Matthew 22;14 that many are call, but few are worthy to be chosen? God asked him.

God wouldn't force His salvation on anyone. Queen had to choose.

"Are you flirting with me?" Queen interrupted his thoughts.

"And if I am?"

"I'll flirt back," Queen sassed. "It's been a while."

"Hold that promise until tomorrow." They ended the call.

Philip's personal life needed prayer. Right now, he prayed for God's will to be done tonight during the tent meeting.

At six-thirty, the deacons arrived at the hotel to drive him to the location. By then, God had given him the message for His people: *I Came to Save the Sick.*

Onlookers gathered around the tent as the musicians tested their sound equipment. When Philip stepped out of the car, he shook hands with those he remembered.

A crowd packed under the white top tent that stretched a block. The heat swelled despite the oversized fans. He wiped his forehead as the singers lifted their voices in praise.

Once Philip was introduced, he bowed his head to lead the crowd in prayer. "Lord, bless Your people who are here and those who want to be and aren't able. Feed their souls and bellies. Show up tonight, Lord, and show out. In Jesus' name. Amen."

Every folded chair was taken. Others stood in the back as ushers walked the makeshift aisles to pass out bottled water.

"Jesus had one purpose on this earth," Philip began, "to save the sick. Some don't need a doctor to tell you when something isn't right in your body. You just have a feelin', but you might want the doctor to confirm it. Or, are you one of those who don't want to know and would rather stay in the dark, which seems like a better choice. Since when is living in the dark a good idea? Sickness can be medical, mental, or spiritual."

Philip bobbed his head. "Jesus is the Master Physician who has diagnosed your condition before you were aware of your symptoms. Don't you want to know what's wrong with you? You don't need an appointment or transportation to visit Him. All you need is to cry out JESUS," he screamed and held the note. He repeated Jesus, and others called out His name too.

"Don't stay in the dark about your condition. Jesus is our Light, and His healing is instant…" He preached hard for about forty-five minutes to an audience that grew thicker despite the summer heat. "The prescription to receive complete healing is repentance, accepting Jesus is Lord, then the baptism of water and spirit in Jesus' name. Come on while the offer stands because there is an expiration date—the rapture."

Folding his arms, Philip stopped and watched the Spirit beckon people to the altar for healing. Wouldn't it be something if Queen was among them?

Chapter Fifteen

The heat wasn't the main reason Queen stayed away from yesterday's tent meeting. Pool parties were the solution for the summer's heat and humidity. But an outside church service? She was scared, not of Philip, but the authority behind the words he preached.

Queen didn't think she was terrible enough to warrant a change. But knowing Philip was in town, a battle brewed within her. Go.

Today, against her better judgment, Queen donned a long flowing sundress and slid her freshly pedicured toes into heeled sandals. She tied up her hair to brave the condition inside the tent. She would need another shower before dinner for sure.

Once downtown, Queen couldn't believe her eyes as she drove closer to the location. Was a philanthropist handing out money? No, it appeared Philip was the attraction. While he greeted folks at the front entrance, Queen squeezed through an opening in the back. The heat embraced her. She accepted a bottled water and took her seat. Closing her eyes, she fanned herself as the music played.

"My Queen." Philip's voice was a soft as a light breeze. She blinked, and their eyes met. "Were you hiding from me? I saw you come in."

How? Philip seemed distracted with folks. The buzz of activity seemed to freeze as they smiled at each other. Missing him, Queen was tempted to leap into his arms for a hug. She was in awe of his handsomeness, confidence, and gentleness. He was larger than life.

This was his element.

He was cool and relaxed. Queen was hot and uncomfortable. She dabbed at the beads of sweat worming their way from her forehead. "Why do you enjoy a tent when you could be back in church with a/c?"

"Because God's harvest isn't inside a building. My job is to go out into the field—the community, the cities—and invite people to God's feast. Some won't leave their homes to attend church but will listen from their porch or stop on their way to the store or running an errand." He scanned the crowd, then focused on her again. Goosebumps began to cool her skin.

"I'm glad you're here." He squeezed her hands.

"Me, too." Fear hadn't kept her away.

"We're still on for dinner, right?"

"Of course. I love it when a man treats me."

"This man. Woman, you're such a flirt. Text me your address. I'm having a rental car dropped off at the hotel."

Shaking her head, Queen objected. "I can pick you up. That's too much."

"You're not too much trouble, Queen. I'm driving." With a hurried stride, he headed to the makeshift stage in the front, greeting people along the way.

After the music selections, he stepped to the mic and prayed. "I have a simple question for you today? What is it going to take for you to come to Jesus?" He folded his arms and extended his ear to listen for responses. "God wants to know what's your hold out. When Jesus died on a splintered cross, He gave His all for us. If you knew what Jesus has in store for you, trust me, you'd take off running toward the treasure…"

Queen pondered Philip's questions. She feared God would ask too much of her. Plus, what could Queen give God.

"God is longsuffering with our foolishness, but the Lord Jesus' grace has an expiration date. Folks say drugs will kill you—true. Alcohol will kill, guns, knives…so can lightning, but one sure way to die and go to hell is not repenting of your sins. Will you repent today and let God wash away your sins in the mighty name of Jesus? Come…" He raised his arm, beckoning them. Women, teenagers, and small children formed a line. A few men with bowed heads brought up the rear.

Queen stood, debated, then veered in the direction of her car. She had to get ready for her dinner date, but thoughts of expiration dates—not on food but on her life—stayed with her.

When Philip arrived on time, he didn't resemble the same man who wore himself out preaching. He was refreshed, dressed in his collared mint-green shirt and black slacks. Queen had showered, washed her hair to air dry, and donned a simple yellow dress with the highest heels she owned.

He whistled as he stepped into her house, and she fell into his arms. Peace engulfed her, and she didn't want to leave his embrace. He chuckled. "Ready?"

"*Ummm-hmmm.*" Opening her eyes, Queen smiled at him but didn't move. Was she waiting for a kiss? She blinked at the thought as he tapped her nose instead.

"I'm hungry, woman. You comin'?"

"Oh, yeah." She blushed, embarrassed he had left her hanging. With her hand secured in his, they walked to the rental car. In between Philip following the navigation's directions, they chatted about everything from family to the heat.

Philip parked in front of Caz's Chowhouse, not far from the location of the tent meeting. "Remember this place?"

"As a matter of fact, I do." Queen smirked, recalling their tug-of-war over whether Kami should have adult privileges like calling her Queen instead of Auntie or Aunt Queen.

"Good." He unsnapped his seatbelt and stepped out, taking the scent of his cologne with him.

This wasn't a random place for dinner. A sentimental man was endearing. Philip opened the door and took her hand. "This is feeling so much like a real date." She grinned.

"Because it is." He bit his bottom lip.

Tilting her head, Queen studied him as they flirted. The two had family in common and they cared about each other. But what more could there be between them?

Inside the place, he requested booth seating. "I think it was over there." He pointed.

Queen's interest was piqued as they slid into their benches, facing each other. Their server introduced himself, gave them menus, and gave them space to place their orders.

Philip leaned back and gave her an intense scrutiny. Any other man, Queen would have guessed what was on his mind. With Philip, she was clueless.

Leaning forward, he anchored his chin on his linked hands. "Can we finish a conversation we started last summer?"

"Huh? Last summer?" Queen blinked. "Sometimes I can't remember what I did a few weeks ago."

"Let me refresh your memory. On the subject of relationships…"

"Did I miss some part of a conversation because we've never talked about relationships?" Queen squirmed in her seat, then mimicked him with her chin resting on her hands.

Philip massaged his mustache with one finger. "We started by discussing Kami not falling in love with the wrong person. I recall asking you if that assessment was from experience. You never answered."

"You remember that?"

"There isn't anything to forget about you." His eyes seemed to dance as he awaited her reaction.

His words were soft as a caress to Queen's cheek. She closed her eyes to imagine it.

That night had been idle conversation, yet he had repeated it to her verbatim. An unknown emotion washed over her. "I haven't had an emotional connection with a man in years."

"Not true. I've felt you in here." He patted his chest. "You may construct a mental fortress against mere men. I'm not one of them. You're God's work of art to be appreciated—gorgeous brown eyes, satiny skin, and toned figure scream for attention that you're available."

Queen blushed and lifted her brow in a seductive manner. "So the Pastor's been checking me out. That seems like a no-no." She waved her finger. He captured her wrist with a gentle hold.

"If I lust—yes. You're more than what eyes behold, Queen. I see your kindness, compassion, and love for others."

He gave her seduction, a cool down. She was humbled. This was one man not to play with.

"This evening isn't about a Bible study, Queen. I want an honest discussion about our relationship. We've been flirting towards one for months."

His honesty sucked the air from her lungs. She'd never heard him talk this deep about his attraction for her. "I thought you've been immune to me because you always mention this or that Scripture."

"Woman, you don't know how wrong you are. You've got me." The tables turned on him. He shook his head and looked away. "Lord, help me. We can have Bible class, if that's what you want, but I believe God is giving me grace for this conversation. Can we talk about us?"

"Okay." She swallowed as the waiter appeared with their meals.

Philip tamed his frustration for the interruption. She dared not mock his vulnerability.

"Thank you," they said in unison. She placed her hand in his for the blessing. "I have all night to listen to you, okay? I told you I would clear my calendar for you, so please give thanks because I'm hungry."

His killer smile made her cheeks ache from another blush as she bowed her head.

"Father, in the name of Jesus, thank You for this fellowship with Queen, and please reveal our purpose to each other. I give thanks for this meal, ask that You bless the hands of those who prepared it, sanctify it for the nourishment of our bodies, and remind us to bless those who are hungry. In Jesus' mighty name, we pray. Amen."

Queen eyed her shrimp and salmon, then his chicken and steak. "Yours looks yummy."

"Here." He carved off a section and blew on it as if he was sealing it with a kiss, then coaxed her to sample it.

"Tasty." It had the Philip touch. There was no sex between them, but his gesture sparked tension. God, forgive her thoughts as she sat in front of a man of God. *Get a grip, girl.*

Philip forked a shrimp from her plate.

"Thief." She chuckled, then sobered. "Why haven't you married? You're around women all the time."

"Not more than the men in your workplace and other admirers." Philip watched her as he sipped water from his glass. "When I take off my preaching robe per se and go home to an empty house—after I detour to my sister's for leftovers, of course—I want to experience what every Jamieson man has, a wife. I'm ready to be a husband, not a pastor husband. Just a man with a wife to love."

His sincerity made her feel all sorts of ways. His words drugged her. She wanted to raise her hand and volunteer.

"Queen Jamieson, I'm asking for the opportunity for us to explore a relationship—we're beyond the flirting—beginning now, with no expiration date until your heart tells you that I'm the one you want."

She swallowed and tried to regulate her breathing. "Philip, are you saying I'm the one you're choosing?"

"Yes." He nodded. "My heart is feeling that, so now it's got to make sense in my head."

"Wow." Queen's thoughts were twisted tight. *Pastor Philip wants me?* She rested her fork and reached for his hand for strength.

"My heart is recalibrating. I'm the sinner and you're the saint. We're incompatible," she argued, but secretly she wanted him to fight for it.

Philip smirked. "Not so. Queen, I think you thought we were on different sides, but God is allowing me to see you on my team. You were ready to fight for my honor. That's the lady I want in my life. We all were born with a sin gene. When God calls you to clean yourself up for His return, you've got to be ready to answer. When you're ready to make that step, I'll be there. Do you, Queen Jamieson, want to be my lady?" He toyed with his napkin. Staring at her, waiting. Was he holding his breath?

Queen exhaled for both of them, then shook her head. "I'm scared for so many reasons—distance is one of them—but I want to try." She said it. Queen was yielding to temptation.

With a slight nod, Philip leaned across the table. His eyes dared her to blink as he inched closer, then she felt something. The spark. The softness of his lips. Their emotional connection.

Queen scratched dessert off their order. The sweetness of Philip Dupree's words and his first kiss left her content.

Chapter Sixteen

Queen had said yes. It was official. Philip and Queen were a couple. That was his first thought when he woke early Sunday morning.

He slid out of bed in his hotel room and prayed, thanking the Lord for new mercies and…Queen.

One desire of his heart down. One more to go. Queen had surrendered to a relationship with Philip. Would she do the same with God? Not his problem, or was it?

Not if you give Me your burden, God whispered.

Several passages raced through his mind: Psalm 55; 1 Peter 5… The message was the same. Give her salvation over to God and trust Him to handle it.

As he checked out of his room, the same two deacons from Resurrection Temple walked into the lobby. They were dressed for church, although their services didn't start for a few hours.

"We know you don't need a ride since you're returning the rental, but we're grateful for the souls God added to the church through you." Deacon Townsend pumped his hand with an envelope containing a love offering from the tent meeting. "God bless. You'll always have an open invitation anytime you visit Tulsa."

Philip thanked him and said his goodbyes to Deacon Alford, and the men walked out together and parted ways. He got into his rental and drove to Queen's house to get her for their flight.

Queen opened her door, and her face glowed. Good. She didn't regret her decision from last night. In her black and white ensemble. Philip's greeting was a kiss on her lips, then he reached for her carry-on. On the drive to the Tulsa airport, their hands were linked, not as friends or in-laws, but a couple.

"I haven't been in a relationship in so long." Philip squeezed her hand. "This feels like home."

Queen brushed hair from her eyes and glanced at him. "I've been in relationships, and this feels different. I can honestly say that everything is alright in my world."

"You look beautiful. I've never seen a bad color on you. Everything looks good on you, including those stripes. You sure you don't want to come to church with me this morning?"

"Not this time." She smiled, and he let it rest.

"Then I'll be waiting for your 'next time.'"

"Thank you," she said, lowering her lashes before looking at him again, "for not pressuring me."

"I'm not your judge. Do me a favor: Don't keep God waiting too long."

"Gotcha," she said as they arrived at the airport and followed the signs to return the rental.

With linked hands, they headed to the main terminal. Throughout all his world travels for the ministry, Philip never had a woman accompanied him on a trip. He couldn't describe his feeling of contentment with Queen.

They were next in line when a TSA screener waved her ahead. "Good morning, Queen," he greeted without checking her license. "You brightened up my day. Have a safe flight."

"Thank you." She smiled and proceeded to the conveyor belt where she slipped off her shoes and placed them in a crate with her handbag.

Philip was directed to a shorter line and passed through security without an issue, then waited for her on the other side. He didn't blame the sly glances a TSA worker was casting at Queen, appreciating God's beauty, but as of last evening, Queen was his, and he was a confident man to know it.

Once she was cleared, Queen sat to slip her feet into her shoes. After putting her cell phone, keys, and other items back in her purse, she stood. Their hands reconnected and didn't miss a beat in their stroll to their gate.

Once they found seats together, Queen looped her arm through his. "Did you always know you wanted to preach?"

Philip forced out a grunt and shook his head. "Nope. It was the farthest thing from my mind. I was a business major in college and needed some electives." He paused to watch her as she listened to him. "I took religion and philosophy courses because I heard the instructor was good. How to Study the Bible was a spiritual awakening. The next semester, I took Bible Interpretation or Hermeneutics, which gets to the root meaning and message of the Scriptures."

Queen chuckled. "Not once did I consider using my electives on religion courses."

"Neither did I." Philip glanced at their intertwined hands. "By the time I graduated, I had enough credits to minor in Christian discipleship."

"End of story, and here we are today." She smiled.

Memories flooded him that made him grit his teeth. "Not quite. When I worked in corporate America, I became very sick. I developed a high temperature and suffered a seizure."

"Oh no." Both of Queen's hands slapped her cheeks in shock.

She did it again. Her deep-rooted concern endeared her to him more and more. "Doctors ran tests, but couldn't trace the root of the condition. Laying in the hospital, God spoke to me. 'Testify of My goodness.' The college courses came to mind. I didn't know what He meant by testify until my parents said I took a turn for the worse and was in a coma for three days. I was a healthy twenty-five-year-old man who had suffered a stroke."

Queen's mouth dropped. Shock was written all over her face. Her eyes filled with moisture.

"It's okay. The Lord gave me a testimony. I endured physical therapy, and miraculously, I recovered—completely restored. At the time, my old pastor asked me to say a few things because the church had been praying for me." Philip exhaled. He remembered the moment and the faces. "When he handed me the microphone, more than my testimony came out. I felt the power of God all around me, and my testimony took on a life of its own in the form of preaching. Soon, I was in demand to 'testify' about God's salvation, and the rest is history."

"Philip," Queen said, sniffing, "I'm so sorry you had to go through that."

"I'm all right, baby." He rubbed her hand. "Without that test, my life would have been different—or not at all."

His endearment made her smile. "The most devastating thing I've ever gone through was the death of my dad. Years later, my mother, then Suzette." Queen choked and glanced toward an incoming plane. "I felt so alone. I'd have given anything for Jesus to talk to me."

Hearing her say that encouraged him. "I've learned God speaks when He has a mission for us. For years, I preached inside church walls and held revivals under tents. I've traveled the world spreading the news of deliverance, but last year, God told me to settle in one spot and feed His sheep."

"And you surrendered to His will at Total Surrender Church. Pun intended." She grinned. "So why were you questioning what God told you?" She paused when boarding was announced for their flight.

Philip stood and stretched, then helped Queen to her feet. "I wasn't expecting so much discord among its members. Despite the hiccups in learning pastorship, the name seemed like a beacon for every soul who walks through that door, reminding them they have to submit to God to receive salvation."

Queen was quiet throughout the boarding, and Philip didn't interrupt her thoughts.

Once they were strapped into their seatbelts and Queen was snuggled next to him within their restraints, she asked, "Should we tell our families we're dating?"

"I think they knew before us." He grinned, admiring her full lips as their flight took off for the skies.

Chapter Seventeen

The big day. Philip Dupree would be voted as pastor after so many years in the evangelism field. During his trial period, he had learned a lot about people, himself, and Queen.

He strolled into the boardroom and greeted the deacons with a hearty, "Praise the Lord."

Nathan was the first to stand and shake hands. The remaining followed.

"Have a seat, Elder Dupree." Deacon Larson, the senior deacon, gestured.

Philip complied. Nathan offered a prayer, then Deacon Larson opened a brown folder. "It's been a challenging year for all of us as you settled into leadership."

Growing pains. "Yes, but God has helped us make it to this point." Philip tapped his shoes beneath the table, ready to get the vote over with.

"Amen. We had concerns about your counseling skills, but you have guided some of the most vulnerable saints—our young people—through their crises. However, you seem to struggle with marriage counseling." He frowned.

The deacon should have sat in on some of those sessions, and he would have seen the struggle was intense. Philip exhaled and rubbed the fine hairs his razor had missed.

Deacon Larson patted his hands on the table. "Again, I suggest the benefit of a married pastor to our congregation. Your marital counseling success rate concerns me, but we know it will take time, so the board has decided to extend your trial period six months until February to court one of our sisters and announce your engagement. We feel that is reasonable."

What was reasonable about a forced marriage? He did his best to keep a blank expression. Deacon Larson had to be joking. He chanced a glance at Nathan who offered an apologetic shrug. Oh boy, the board was serious. Philip had nothing against marriage. The idea was close to his heart with Queen, but he would not agree to a time frame. *God, please give me the words to say.*

Straightening himself in the chair, Philip attempted to meet absurdity with diplomacy. "With all due respect, Deacon Larson, based on our verbal agreement, nothing was mentioned about my marital status as a prerequisite for the position."

He made eye contact with each deacon. "Do I have to have cancer to minister to a cancer victim, experiment with sexual impurity to minister to confused souls, have a history of drug addiction or incarceration to minister to God's people? Solomon was the wisest man in the Old Testament, then there was Deborah as a judge. Only God has been touched by all these infirmities, and I listen for His instructions to counsel others." He refused to succumb to a headache.

Deacon Spearman cleared his throat. "Elder Dupree, we in no way meant to question the authority God has bestowed on you, but after the shameful behavior of fornication from our last single pastor, we feel it's best to address it. If you're willing to give some thought to our conversation and pray, I'm sure God will open your eyes to see a helpmate."

Shameful behavior? This was the first time Philip had ever heard this. Even Nathan said nothing. He prayed for God to calm his spirit. Between the arranged marriage and church's dark past, Philip was irked. He opened his mouth and measured his words.

"I was led to believe the vacancy was created because Elder Wynn's behavior was financial misconduct." That had not caused Philip concern. He knew how to balance books, with or without the deacons' assistance.

"Yeah, that, too," Deacon Larson admitted. "We've prayed for a leader of your caliber, wisdom, and with a good rapport. The board's vote has to be unanimous, I'm the only holdout, so please don't judge them harshly. After your appointment, the board will step back and work under your direction."

The meeting adjourned, and the room emptied before Philip could gather his thoughts. He walked into his office, closed the door, and prayed. "Lord, I have defrauded no one like Jacob, yet I feel like I'm in his shoes to earn a position that seemed promised to me."

Philip ignored the knock at his door so he could wallow in his injury before he called his good friend Bishop Henderson and got his take. A second knock prevented that. He was a big boy and had to roll with the punches.

"Come in."

Nathan popped his head inside. "You okay, brother?"

"I don't know how to answer that." Philip offered him a seat. "Why do I feel I was deceived?"

"Because you had no idea of all of Elder Wynn's shenanigans. Would you have still come if you knew?" Nathan pressed.

"With marriage as a requirement, no, but Elder Wynn's history in the church would not have turned me away." Philip swirled in his chair and rubbed his head. "In Biblical times, there were evil rulers and good ones. In these times, there are false leaders and true men of God. I am to lead this congregation with a good example. I'm surprised Deacon Larson didn't hand me an Excel spreadsheet with a list of every single sister's name, address, and phone number with the link to their health records. This proposition is ridiculous."

Nathan looked as tortured as Philip felt. "I'm not here to defend Deacon Larson because I see his point, but my vote is for you." He scooted to the edge of the chair. "Hear me out: I know you've been busy since you arrived, but we have some sweet-spirited, beautiful single sisters who attend this church. None have captured your attention?"

Philip's eyes crossed looking at his friend. "Not you, too. I've noticed them, but not for the purpose of marriage, and if this crop is so plentiful, why haven't you picked a flower from the field?"

Nathan sat back and crossed an ankle over his knee. "It's not my appointed time. Deacon Larson tried to use that same tactic on me, too. I didn't take the bait. He knew in his spirit God put me in this position, so he had no choice but to appoint me. The same will happen to you."

"I'm already in a relationship." Philip had never seen Nathan grin so broadly. Yep, Philip thought it was a big deal too.

"Why didn't you just say that? Deacon Larson would have appointed you on the spot and done away with the extension. Is it one of the sisters who get in your prayer line every Sunday, or the one of the choir directors, or—"

"It's complicated." Philip toyed with his mustache.

Nathan stood. "Aren't all relationships?"

"I guess so." Philip got to his feet and shook his friend's hand. "Thanks."

"No problem. Everything will work out the way it's supposed to. Whenever you want to share details about the who, I'm all ears." Then Nathan left, leaving Philip to his own thoughts. He would not involve Queen in this foolishness.

It was the worse week ever. Did people not know the definition of deadline? Queen's staff writers had weak excuses for not doing their research for their articles. Why did she leave her role as a senior mechanical engineer to become an editor of an engineering journal? Why when her writers tried to take shortcuts, Engineering was all about details.

Sometimes Queen wished she wasn't the boss. She found herself praying to say the right thing before she fired somebody. Eight pairs of eyes waited for her edict. "The ball was dropped. We all must put in extra time to play catch-up. I would advise you to cancel any plans and stock up on espresso so we can go to publication." She held up three fingers. "Three days. Work like you only have two."

Queen dismissed the meeting and returned to her desk where a vase of flowers made her smile. Philip. She sniffed, then read the note, *Because you're mine.* The tension in her body drained immediately.

Glad to be home hours later, an email alerted her that the fashion merchandise program was doomed. The fall enrollment numbers hadn't budged.

Queen had worked too hard to go down in defeat. She gnawed on her lips and called Gigi and explained her dilemma. "I don't know what else to do."

"Let's jump on a video call with the royal ladies. I like saying that." And Queen liked hearing it, too. "Give me a sec. I'll email everyone a link to meet within an hour."

"Okay," she whispered. What else could she do?

Pray to Me, God whispered.

She almost knew how this was going to turn out. Her prayers weren't being answered. Queen had prayed when her father was dying. He still died. She pleaded with God not to take her mother. The last straw was watching Suzette take her last breath.

The committee had made it clear that unless there was a late stampede, the program would be phased out. No.

She needed to clear her head to think, and her spacious three-bedroom ranch home seemed claustrophobic. While she waited on Gigi to send a conference link, Queen took a short stroll through the village as homeowners who lived in Gilcease Hills referred to their neighborhood.

The fog of confusion cleared as thoughts of Philip surfaced. It was Wednesday, the day Philip taught Bible class, so they wouldn't talk until later that night. Queen exhaled.

"God, why don't You listen to me? I need a miracle." Her phone alerted her of a text. "Meeting in ten minutes." Making a U-turn, she power-walked back, waving at an elderly woman working in her flower beds.

Queen was out of breath when she made a beeline to her tablet on the kitchen counter. She tapped in the code and soon, faces of the beautiful black women in the Jamieson and Robnett families filled her screen: sisters Lacey, Candy, Gigi; sisters-in-law Eva and Talise; then the cousins: Gabrielle, Cheney, Hallison, Queen Bee, Rejoice, Sapphire, and Princess. Their smiles warmed her heart, making everything alright in her world.

She grinned. "Hi, sisters and cousins."

They greeted her in a chorus of hi's and heys, then Queen Bee took the lead. "Gigi told us you need help before you signed on. What can we do?"

"Do you need us to send money?" Eva asked as she rocked her two-month-old son, Malik, in her arms.

"Whatever you need, we've got you, sis," Kidd yelled from the background. Only his folded arms were visible.

A tear dripped as Queen blinked. She choked at their love. Maybe God had answered her prayers after all through family.

"This isn't about the money. The program needs bodies for the endowed scholarships. Who isn't interested in fashion?"

"It's always about money," Gigi stated.

"How many scholarships can you provide at the moment?" Queen Bee asked.

Queen did a quick mental calculation. "About ten—max—until we have our winter fundraiser to replenish the pot."

"We need to get the word out about the program, and that's where I come in… advertising," Rejoice chimed in. "How about we pool our money and flood social media, including YouTube, with images and ads in the surrounding states. What's the deadline for late registration?"

Maybe there was hope after Queen told them the date.

Rejoice was hyped. "Let's get this out in three days tops. I'll call in favors from the graphic department. We want everyone to take notice about the program—everybody!"

"It's all about spreading the word. Count me in with three hundred dollars to add to the budget," Gabrielle said. Queen Bee matched it. Others followed with their commitments.

"Thank you all. Love you, ladies." Queen didn't check the tears flowing down her cheeks.

"Hey, we're sisters and cousins. This is what we do, sis." Gigi winked. "Well, I guess this meeting is adjourned and you'd better get busy and send Rejoice the info."

When Queen ended the call, she boo-hooed until Philip's ringtone caused her to sniff and pat her cheeks before accepting the FaceTime call. "Hi."

"What's wrong?" His budding smile collapsed. "Are you okay? Gabrielle said you're upset. What's going on, baby? Do I need to take the next flight out?"

His words were like a kiss to make things better. "I'm alright now. I had a crisis, and the ladies of royalty came to my rescue." She explained what was going on.

"Do you need more money?"

"I don't but thank you." Hearing his voice and seeing his concern relaxed Queen. She kicked off her tennis shoes and stretched out on her chaise. "I miss you."

"That's all you had to say. I'll see you on Friday. I'm booking my flight now."

He ended the call before she could protest. There was no way Queen would anyway.

Chapter Eighteen

Friday. Queen's good mood and extra attention to her attire and makeup didn't go unappreciated at the office. The few women in her department said she glowed. Accepting their compliments with thanks, it did nothing for her impatience as the workday crawled until she had to get Philip from the airport.

Some employees who greeted her at Tulsa International Airport were surprised she wasn't clearing the gates to take off for St. Louis or the East Coast.

"Not this time," she told a young ticket agent who was about to take her break.

Queen fingered the petals of a single red rose. Patience was overrated. Craning her neck, she saw him. Philip's confident swagger stood out among the rush of the travelers. She smirked at the hero worship from some women near him. Of all the men she had dated, none brought excitement and calm at the same time the way Philip's presence did.

Rooted in her spot, Queen could barely contain her excitement as Philip neared the exit.

When their eyes connected, his slow smile coaxed her to walk. She ran. Queen wrapped her arms around his waist and closed her eyes to find his heartbeat. It was strong like hers.

"My Queen." He kissed her forehead when she looked up.

Queen was back to her natural wild curls, and she didn't want the reward of his kiss to be lost in her hair. Stepping back, she handed him the flower. "I don't know if this is just a girlie thing, but…"

"I like it." He accepted, then fumbled for her hand until their fingers locked.

"I'm so glad you came." She couldn't help but smile.

"You needed me, so here I am."

Like the National Guard, he was there in the state of her emotional emergency.

As customary for her out-of-town guests, she offered him her spare room. Philip declined. "We aren't married, and there won't be any buffers to tame our temptations." He must have noticed her disappointment. "Innocent intentions could be tainted with rumors. I don't want that for either of us."

Okay. She leaned into his hug,

"I also called my deacon friends to let them know I would be in town."

"What? I have to share?" Queen pouted. "Philip, I thought you were coming to see me. Sounds childish, but I'm being transparent."

He grinned. "And it's attractive. I told them my lady lives here and I'm visiting her. My call was for my transparency and accountability."

Once they made it to her car, she grinned. Why did she feel like a hormone-raging teenager who wanted to kiss him until they fogged up the windows?

"I'm serious about not disrespecting your body or soul," Philip said as if he had read her thoughts.

How did he keep his hormones in check after their absence? She needed that control if they were to continue this long-distance relationship until… Until when? Their feelings frizzled? Queen hoped not.

"Hungry?" She started her car.

"A man is always hungry, babe." He patted his firm stomach. "Do you mind if I check into my hotel first, and then we get dinner?"

Leaving the airport, she headed toward the same hotel the local church had booked him in that summer.

He angled his body and watched her. "Feeling better about the enrollment situation at the university?"

Queen gritted her teeth and glanced at him. "Rejoice will start running ads on Monday, and we'll see if anyone will bite. Even if the school gets the applicants, it still might not be enough to save the program."

He rubbed her back when she stopped at a light. "I don't mind adding to the donation."

"*Awww*. That's sweet. A man who supports his woman. I need you to pray that God will send the students, and I'm holding you to that."

He nodded. "I can do that, all in God's will."

"Why do you end prayer requests like that?" She had meant to ask him that before.

"Because we can pray and believe all we want, but if it's not God's will, fasting and praying won't change God's decision. David in the Bible had sinned with Bathsheba, and she bore a baby. David knew what to do to get God's attention—fast and pray. Once the child died, he accepted that was God's will and he moved forward."

"You are so deep, my evangelist."

"I hope not so complicated where a person can't follow me."

"I happen to like your complicated." She blew him a kiss.

The Fairfield Inn & Suites was on North Main in the Tulsa Arts District. Queen made herself comfortable in the lobby while Philip checked in, then took his things to his room. He didn't keep her waiting long.

"Since you're a hearty eater, I thought you might like a good steak, and we could walk there."

Philip glanced down at Queen's feet and admired her polished toenails, then lifted a brow and chuckled. "In those heels. I recall a similar conversation last year, and you said you had been wearing heels since riding a tricycle or something like that."

Queen laughed and tugged him toward the entrance. "Something like that. The steakhouse is a block away." She stuck out her tongue.

"Okay. I'll walk slow."

"No need." She disengaged her hand and took long exaggerated strides to walk in front of him, then pointed. "I can race you to the door."

"Whether you run, walk, or skip, you move with the grace of a dancer, but if you think I'm going to let you outrun me, think again. Track man here."

Before Queen could blink, Philip moved quickly toward her, scooped her up into his arms and ran the rest of the way to restaurant entrance. She screamed her delight. It was going to be a great weekend.

As Philip feasted on his steak, he admired Queen's outer beauty, but it was her inner beauty that gave him peace. He wanted to be her peace, which was why he came to ease her stress.

"So, how is everything at your church?" She pushed away her plate. "Are you the official pastor yet?"

Maybe never.

Complaining church folks.

Arranged marriage—sort of.

Deadlines.

How embarrassing to tell her he had six months to get married or he wouldn't be voted pastor. He couldn't repeat such nonsense. "Not quite. There's been a six-month extension…"

Queen reached across the table and covered his hand with hers. "I'm here if you want to talk anything out, but I'm sure everything will work out." She tilted her head. "God's will, right?" She was so innocent with her concern and clueless at his plight.

"Yes, God's will." He stretched and stifled a yawn. It had been a long day, but Nathan hadn't left his side as they did repairs in some of the rooms at the church for the children. It was a one-day project that had stretched into two days. "So, what do you have planned for us tomorrow?"

"Well," she said, her eyes danced with mischief and her lips teased him, "if you're up for a road trip, I thought about a two-hour drive to the annual Poteau hot-air balloon festival. It's usually held in October, but it's this weekend. All you have to do is sit back and ride."

"No, I'll drive. I came to take care of you. Since my parents moved to St. Louis, we've taken weekend rides to Springfield. Two hours is nothing. The GPS will get us there."

"A man who knows how to take charge. I love it." She placed her hands on the sides of his face and guided his lips toward hers. His reward was the sweetest kiss that made him want to beg for more.

It took all of Philip's willpower to pull away, then he exhaled. "This is the reason we can't be alone. With our strong attraction, the devil will play us for a fool."

Queen frowned. "I guess I'm going to have to trust you on that." She changed the subject to the newest photos of Diamond that her sister-in-law had sent. "She looks like a baby doll—the lashes and eye color."

"As beautiful as her aunt."

"Thank you. I think the Robnetts are a good-looking clan, too. The women are gorgeous, and the men are beyond handsome."

"They alright." Philip couldn't get enough of gazing at Queen. "I happen to think the lady across from me is the most beautiful woman in the Jamieson clan. My sister doesn't count. She has Dupree blood in her veins." He grinned. "As far as the Robnett men, I'm with your brothers and cousins on them: watch and pray."

Queen shook her head. "My family needs to stop hatin'."

He didn't want to debate. What she called hatin' was caution. At least the Jamiesons were committed Christians who practiced biblical principles.

Once he paid their bill, they strolled back to the hotel. He brushed his lips against her soft ones, then opened her car door. "Call me when you get home."

As Queen turned the ignition, she stared into his eyes. "Thanks for coming. Being here is huge to me." She puckered her lips, and he delivered again.

Stepping back, Philip watched her drive away. In no time, she called. "Made it. We better get some rest. The festival is packed with lots of activities, including hot-air balloon rides. I hope you're not scared of heights, preacher."

"I look forward to it. Night." Philip slid to the floor for his nightly prayers, then added, "Lord, my confidence is in You— not that balloon. Please guide the wind and let us land safely. In Jesus' name. Amen."

He was ready the next morning when Queen arrived. That woman gave the best good-morning hugs. When she rested her head on his chest, it was as if she had found a safe place.

The drive on I-40 was smooth to their destination. Philip found a parking space, then they joined the crowd to check out the sights.

The monster truck rides caught his eye while Queen tugged him toward the balloon rides. Before they climbed in with a handful of other joy-seekers, Philip whispered a prayer and was glad the balloon was tethered to the ground and not given free rein.

Lift-off was up to seventy feet in the air. Queen snuggled closer, and he rubbed the soft skin of her arm.

"Is everything alright in your world?" he whispered close to her ear.

"Yes." Her tone was peaceful. "I wish you didn't have to leave in the morning."

"I wish you weren't so far away, here all by yourself." Philip wanted to suggest she move to be closer to family and him in St. Louis. One thing he knew about Queen: She did things by her own dance beat. If her two brothers hadn't persuaded her to relocate, then Philip wouldn't voice his opinion either.

"My life is here. My family is buried here, friends… Kami spent last summer with me, remember? And with my newfound Robnett cousins, I have more family to visit."

"Don't get me wrong. I'm glad you have more family, but you are here alone, so be careful who you invite into your house, okay?"

She looked up. Her expression hinted something was brewing in her brain. Was she about to be the sassy Queen he knew her to be? He waited.

"I will. If I feel a hint of hesitation, then I'll put them up in a hotel. Happy?"

In any relationship, there would be give-and-takes. With Queen, Philip would have to choose which battles he thought he could win. "Almost." He dropped the subject to enjoy the subtle sway of the hot-air balloon and Queen's perfume.

Chapter Nineteen

"Congratulations. We did it," Gigi screamed for sixty seconds when Queen had called to give her the tally. Twenty-seven students signed up during late enrollment; three were young men.

Her source in the registrar's office was confident this could be a game changer. "Yes! #TeamJamieson and #TeamRobnett. We need to throw a party to celebrate." Queen did a happy dance.

"You are the party queen, so who's on the guest list?" Gigi giggled.

"Family, of course." Queen grinned to herself. "Our Kansas City cousins have always wanted to visit, so now they'll have a reason. I doubt if any of our Jamieson families in the Lou will be able to come, especially with their small children and babies. Queen got a firsthand experience as Diamond's nanny for a week. Any last minute or short-term events were impossible with children without planning.

"But they'll be here in spirit." Tears of happiness filled her eyes.

She phoned Philip next. Queen was touched that he stepped out of a meeting to take her call. A while back, he had said her heart would let Queen know if he was the one. Her heart screamed yes.

"God heard your prayers. Thank you, Philip." She was on the verge of crying again. Joy filled her.

"Hey, I was only part of the big picture, baby." His deep voice wrapped her in a comforting cocoon. "Your family's support made it happen as well. Congratulations. We should celebrate."

"I plan to. Family, friends, and you." She put the brakes on her excitement. "How would that work? You probably won't go clubbing with us, but that's usually how I celebrate."

He chuckled. "We'll celebrate in a different way. Check your calendar, and we'll do something special. Hey, congratulations again. I need to get back."

"Okay." She threw him a kiss.

"Caught it." Philip ended the call.

In this moment of celebration, Queen wished Philip was within hugs' reach, not miles apart.

Years ago, she'd dated a pilot. Their long-distance relationship lasted nine months. Queen wasn't that into him, so they agreed to remove themselves from each other's speed dial and life. Queen had never looked back. She didn't want to fathom that same scenario with Philip.

The royal ladies from Kansas City couldn't wait. Queen connected with their free-spirited personalities.

Their bonds tightened after the weekend with Queen Bee, Rejoice, Sapphire, Princess, Jewel, and Duchess. Besides Frederic and those who attended the game night, Queen had met more male cousins: Issac and Esquire Robnett. Both were attorneys by profession.

Queen chose the date and booked the place for the festivity. Then one by one, those cousins backed out for legitimate reasons until Queen Bee, Sapphire, Esquire and Frederic remained coming. Plus, Cori and Trice who like Queen herself wouldn't dare miss a party.

Dressed for a night on the town, the plan was to drink and dance the night away before her and her cousins crashed at her home, then on Saturday, Cori and Trice would join them for brunch.

The day had come. Cori had to take a last-minute business trip, and Trice contracted a stomach virus. She was ticked she would miss meeting the handsome cousins. Queen felt bad for her friend.

But she still had family. With a ready smile and her poster, *Robnetts Rock*, Queen counted down the seconds as bunches of travelers passed by her. She wanted them to see why she called Tulsa home. Her heart raced with excitement.

She spotted Frederic, but not Queen Bee and Sapphire. Queen Bee had texted her a few days ago with the bad news that others had cancelled, and she was mad at them about backing out.

He cleared the terminal and pumped his fist when he read her sign. "Hey, cousin." Towering over her, he kissed her cheek and hugged her.

"Hey to you. You're alone?" Queen was happy to see him but disappointed her party guests were dwindling.

"Emergency." Frederic bobbed his head. "My aunt, Sapphire's mom, was rushed to the hospital with chest pains, and Queen Bee went with her."

Queen gasped and patted her chest. "Oh no."

"Yeah. They were on their way to the airport when Sapphire got the call. Hopefully, everything will check out with Aunt Ruby and those two will fly out in the morning. Tonight, you're stuck with me."

"I'll say a prayer for her." Queen blinked. She said that? Philip was rubbing off on her. Now, the party must go on. She sighed and looped her arm through Frederic's, then headed for the exit, laughing. "I guess you'll do."

"We can still have a good time." She could feel him flex his biceps. "Queen Bee and Sapphire said you cooked up a storm. I hope your place is our first stop because biscuits disguised as cookies and pretzels on the plane weren't enough for an appetizer."

Yes, she cooked, but if the others didn't show up, she would freeze some, and her neighbors would get leftovers.

Don't entertain men alone, she could hear Philip's whisper and her brothers' yells drowning out her common sense. Queen almost stumbled, but Frederic caught her.

"Steady, my Queen. You haven't started drinking without me."

My Queen sounded odd coming from his mouth. Philip had a way of saying her name as if he never had heard it before.

"I never have a one-woman party." Leaving the airport, she took the opposite direction of her house on I-44 to the Glo Best Western Tulsa-Catoosa East Route 66.

Queen parked and unstrapped her seatbelt. "Come on, cuz." The bewildered look on Frederic was amusing.

"What are we doing here? I thought we were staying at your house." He grabbed his garment bag, and they strolled in together.

"That's when it was three Robnetts staying with me. Since it's only you for the night, I think this three-star hotel will be most comfortable—until Sapphire and Queen Bee arrive in the a.m."

"Oh."

She could tell he was processing the change of plans. At the counter, Queen inquired about a vacancy and was about to pay.

Frederic wouldn't hear of it and handed over his credit card. With his room key in hand, he faced her. "Not only are we cousins, but you have the grace of royalty. Our ancestors would expect nothing less." He smiled. "I'll hurry because I'm ravished."

"Thanks for understanding. I'll wait for you down here, then we can walk next door to the restaurant. I've eaten there with my girlfriends. They have some scrumptious food."

"Sounds good. Be right back." Frederic walked to the elevator.

Not that Queen didn't think Frederic wasn't trustworthy, but she decided to double check his story. She sent Queen Bee and Sapphire a text.

Cousins, Frederic arrived without you. Is everything okay? Sapphire, how's your mom?

This is Queen Bee. I have Sapphire's phone. She's in there with my aunt. Doctor said she had a mild heart attack, and they're keeping her overnight. Sapphire is spending the night at the hospital, and I decided I'd better stay with her. My apologies, Queen. Hope you understand.

Understand? Of course. We only have one mom. Queen's heart sank. **I'll pray for her speedy recovering.**

You and Frederic have a good time celebrating. Talk to you soon.

Queen stood and walked to the counter. "Please add a second night for Mr. Robnett. Thanks." This had nothing to do with Philip's request. Rather, Queen's good common sense.

Frederic reappeared with a smile meant to be charming. Her cousin was strikingly handsome. His eyes were his best asset. While Sapphire's were a greenish-gray and Queen Bee's were a special blend of browns, Frederic was gifted with an unusual shade. There was no color to describe it. "Ready?"

They crossed the parking lot to the adjacent restaurant, Smoke Woodfire Grill. Queen was thrilled for the second location besides downtown.

"I love their menu," she said as Frederic held the door open for her.

A hostess greeted and sat them in a booth. Frederic scanned the menu, then glanced at her. "What do you recommend?"

Queen laughed. "Everything. The shrimp and grits are good. So is the smoked chicken pasta, or you might enjoy the bone-in pork chop."

"You're no help, woman." He tugged on his mustache before choosing the smoked chicken pasta with servings for two.

"After this, we'll go dancing." Queen snapped her fingers.

"I've got skills." Frederic winked and ordered red wine.

Sprite was Queen's choice. Although she was a social drinker, she never drank anything stronger than a soda when out alone with a man—friend, foe, and now cousin. She needed to stay alert for his safety because she would leave bruises.

As they waited, Frederic leaned back and studied her. "You're so beautiful. I can see why your names fits you."

She thanked him but would rather talk about something else. "How long have you been researching your family?"

She watched him sink into his element—the same one he presented at the game night. "It's been passed down from generation to generation. My grandmother's name is Queen, as you know. Queen Bee is the fourth generation Queen in the family. We're serious about bestowing majestic names on our children as descendants of royalty."

"But how did you find out that Queen Akwesi and Issa were captured during their wedding ceremony?"

"It's Issa Dembele. My brother's named Issac—not Isaac— in his memory. It had been a rumor. Viney had the name Queen tattooed under her arm. William Robnett purchased Viney for breeding." He twisted his mouth.

Yeah, she heard the story. Queen wanted to vomit too. It was an ugly history, but it was American history. "That's so horrific what human beings can do to each other." How inhumane. Queen shivered at the thought of being a baby factory for profit.

Frederic covered her hand with his. His touch was anything but comforting. She slid her hand free and reached for her Sprite when she wanted a sanitizer wipe.

"Despite the obstacles, our ancestors endured and lived unlike the Igbo West African captives. They committed mass suicide to die free rather than live enslaved."

Queen had learned about the Igbo Landing on the St. Simons Island during a family game night. Her mind drifted until the server brought their meals. Queen caught herself from taking Frederic's hands to pray. She'd rather keep her touches for Philip.

She bowed her head, waiting for Frederic to give thanks for their food as she had grown accustomed with the Jamieson men and Philip. Instead, there was silence. When she spied Frederic, to her surprise, he had started eating without her. *Okay*. Queen whispered her own blessing. She missed Philip.

"Anyway, when Viney had daughters, she did the same thing, whether or not, the slaveholder permitted such a prestigious name for a slave. The owner didn't know another captive, Jebu, was a descendent of Issa and had King tattooed under his arm."

Queen sipped on her soda. "Wow, how fascinating. I know so much about the Jamiesons. My cousin, Cameron, is helping me with my maternal side, which is a small family."

Frederic squinted. "I sensed that he isn't too friendly, but hey…" He shrugged and twisted his lips. "I'm a certified genealogist. I'm available to help, too, if you need me. We do share half of the same history."

As if knowing she was thinking about him, Philip's ringtone lit up her phone. Giddy, she mouthed to Frederic, "hold on" and answered. "Hey, you."

His deep voice mesmerized her. "Hi, baby. Did your cousins arrive safely? I hope you're having a good time."

"Only Frederic came—it's a long story—and we're out enjoying dinner."

Philip was quiet for a moment. "I hope we're not on speaker."

"We're not now."

"Queen, please tell me he's not staying at your house."

"No."

His sigh of relief was deafening. "Thank you, Jesus. Baby, be careful. You're alone with this guy who is so far up or down your tree to be a blood relative… My sweet woman is too naïve and trusting. Now, I'm going to be praying until you're at home safe and sound."

"Philip, pray for Aunt Ruby, Sapphire's mom. She had a mild heart attack. I'll call you later. Bye." She ended the call, happy to hear from him, but annoyed he misjudged her intelligence. *Men.* She rolled her eyes. "Sorry."

Frederic snickered. "Philip? Is that your man friend?"

Queen couldn't stop her lips from curling into a smile and the warm feeling settling in her heart. "He's a special man in my life."

"*Hmmm.* How special?" He sipped from his stemware.

"We're dating. He's a pastor in St. Louis," Queen explained and sang Philip's praises.

"Oh, I didn't realize you were into God and church." Frederic eyed her.

"I know who God is. His name is Jesus, as for church, I attend when the mood hits me." Queen realized it had been a while.

"I was hoping we could get to know each other better this weekend," Frederic hinted in a tone that sounded scandalous.

"We are. You know I'm glad I've met my Robnett cousins, I'm passionate about upholding my sister's memory in fashion, I'm dating a soon-to-be pastor, and I checked out your story with Queen Bee. There." Queen slapped her hands together. "You know all I want you to know."

He tapped his finger on the table. His eyes sparkled. "There's so much more to a fascinating woman like you. Your name on Ancestry attracted my attention. Since I saw you at the family game night, my heart hasn't been in rhythm since."

Queen lowered her lashes, then unleashed her sass. "You flatter me. It's best that your heart skips a beat than stop breathing due to sudden unconsciousness from assault. So, let's be clear: What are you saying, cousin?" She made sure her movements were delicate so he wouldn't suspect a punch to the jaw.

"We do share DNA, but not enough to keep us from exploring a closer relationship. There are kissing cousins in families. All I'm asking for is a chance. You see, I came to celebrate your accomplishment, and Philip's not here."

Hold up. Stand down, back up because I'm going for the mace with that line.

"From the moment I learned we're cousins, there was never a chance, and if that is your sole intention…you don't want to cross that line with me. I'll cut you. Understand?" Queen stood and reached inside her purse, pulling out a fifty-dollar bill. "Sleep on that—alone." She strolled out the restaurant to her car. Party over.

Chapter Twenty

"Lord, dispatch Your angels to protect my woman because I am not okay." Philip stopped watching TV after Queen's call. The actors from the movie seemed to stare at him. He rubbed his forehead. A plane ride couldn't get him to Tulsa fast enough.

A confident Black man, Philip knew his strength was in God, but their long-distance relationship tested him tonight. "Queen is too smart to be naïve." He eyed his phone, debating whether he should call her again.

Date rape is real. He had prayed for enough victims to know. Philip saw the way Frederic assessed Queen at the family game night. If that man touched her in any way, God help both of them because there would be some major repenting required on Philip's part and reconstructive surgery for Frederic.

Philip shut his eyes. "Jesus, You know all things. I can't outdo Your protection. Protect and save Queen for Your glory." He opened them and spied his remote to click off the program.

He looked up, wanting to see through the ceiling into heaven. "Lord, Hebrews four and sixteen says we can come boldly to Your throne of grace where we can obtain Your mercy. Jesus," Philip roared like a lion, so the powerful name would travel in the spiritual realm to make the demons tremble, "send help."

His anxiety lessened as peace descended upon him that made Philip too weak to stand.

When Queen called hours later, he didn't realize he had dozed off. "Are you okay?" was the first thing out of his mouth.

"Of course. Why wouldn't I be?"

"Woman, I don't have high blood pressure. Please don't give it to me tonight. I was worried about you being alone with Frederic, so I had a talk with Jesus. I don't trust that man—relative or not."

"Get in line. Not after tonight."

"What do you mean? Did he hurt you?" Philip sat up and gritted his teeth. There would be no need to pack clothes as he grabbed his wallet and slipped his feet into his shoes. He could take care of this business in a round trip.

"No. He says that he's attracted to me. *Humph.* My own flesh and blood. Can we say creepy?" She paused. "But no worries. I told him I'd cut him—and I will."

Philip exhaled and collapsed back into his chair. *Praise God. Thank You, Jesus.* "Baby, you've got too much going for you to be a hood girl."

"I don't have to be a hood girl to defend myself. My father enrolled Suzette and me into boxing lessons. I don't need gloves to do damage. Then Kidd and Ace made sure I learned other self-defense techniques. I've been on my own long enough to take care of myself."

Despite his frazzled nerves, Philip smiled. "Will you let me take care of you?" That sounded like a marriage proposal, didn't it? What *was* he saying?

"We're more than four hundred miles apart."

"You could relocate." There he'd said it.

"So can you," Queen countered with an edge to her voice.

"And bring the entire congregation with me?" he smarted off.

"Listen, I've dealt with one man tonight. I just got home. I'm too aggravated to be nice, so I'll say good night."

"Queen—" She ended the call without a goodbye.

"What did I say?" He punched his hand in frustration.

The next morning, after a fitful night's sleep, Philip spent time in God's presence, then he texted Queen: **I'm sorry. When a man cares about a woman, he CARES about everything in her life. Including safety.**

He wanted to say more, but not through text or phone. They needed to have an in-person conversation. Video conferencing didn't count.

He checked the time. It was eight on a Saturday morning. **Call me when you get up**, he texted his sister.

Gabrielle did within minutes. "Hey, big brother. I have two little mouths to feed. Of course, I'm up. Is everything alright? What's going on?" She rambled off one question after another, not giving Philip a chance to answer until she seemed to run out of guesses.

"What happened was…" he explained and didn't leave out any details.

"Wow. That dude needs a stiletto beat down."

His lioness sister came to life. She didn't play over her shoes.

"I'm glad he didn't stay with her. The two other male cousins we met seemed nice though."

Philip had to know what he was dealing with—one bad apple or an entire family. "Do you think Queen Bee and Sapphire set her up?"

"No. The royalty ladies are the real deal. Plus, trust me, Queen can take care of herself."

He rubbed the ache in the back of his neck. Gabrielle was missing the point. "She doesn't have to. That's where I come in."

"Queen is anything but a damsel in distress, but I'll call her once I get the twins fed and I'm out of Cam's hearing. If he knew what went down, he would be on the phone with the bad boys from Boston," she said, referencing Kidd's and Ace's nicknames. "Plus, you know my husband didn't trust them from first sight, even though it looks like Frederic is on point with our shared heritage, but Cam's not ready to make that announcement, so no I won't tell him—"

"Too late, baby," Cameron's sleep-filled voice could be heard in the background. "I'll call Queen myself."

"Oops," Gabrielle mumbled.

Philip groaned and beat his forehead against an imaginary brick wall. He'd asked God to send His angels, not the Jamieson infantry. This was not the confidential brother-sister chat he'd had in mind. "Put your husband on the phone, please."

"What's up, Pastor Brother-in-law?"

"I need you to hold your peace. Let Queen and me work this out. No family interference."

"Your request is denied. The Jamieson protect their own…" he continued to rant. "But because you have spiritual backup, I'll let you handle your woman. But…you need to put a ring on her finger after she commits her life to Christ, of course." He handed the phone back to Gabrielle.

Chapter Twenty-one

Queen didn't care if Frederic was stranded in Tulsa or flew back to Kansas City to lick his wounds after that stunt he pulled Friday night. He was smart enough not to attempt to make amends.

It was Sunday, the Lord's Day, and Queen was still mad. It was not a day of rest for her at all.

Did Queen Bee or Sapphire know of Frederic's infatuation with her? With Sapphire's mother's condition, Queen didn't want to bother them with such pettiness.

That evening, Trice called and smacked her lips, wanting the scoop.

After asking how she was feeling, Queen had no qualms about spilling the details.

"*Ugh*, and I missed that. *Oooh*."

"Girl, he made me mad. I expect other men to be jerks, but relatives?" Queen rolled her eyes as she stretched out on her patio ottoman then told her about Philip's response and Cameron's phone call.

"Girl, you'd better be careful with that pastor. He'll pray on you in a hot minute."

"Yeah, don't I know it. Can't cut him," she joked, missing his voice. Two whole days without speaking to him. They both suffered. He practically called her naïve with respect to men.

"Ah, no you can't." Her friend laughed.

"Right."

Monday morning before leaving for the office, she called Philip after he texted her a morning Scripture: **Ephesians 4:26: Be ye angry, and sin not. Don't let the sun go down upon your wrath. Translation: The sun's been setting for four days. Flowers will be waiting for you at the office. My peace offering.**

"Sorry I snapped."

"You were upset." His voice was soothing. "I get that, but I didn't mean to add more stress. Let me be clear: You're my lady, so I have a right to be concerned about your body and soul." She heard the uneasiness in Philip's voice as he continued, "I had to recall every Scripture about worrying. I was so close to catching the first plane out of here."

Awww. She could imagine that scenario. Philip willing to drop whatever he was doing was one of the reasons she found him emotionally attractive.

"I'm still willing to come."

Queen closed her eyes. "And I need a hug. But even if I bump you up to priority, we won't have any the quality time. With the fundraiser ball coming up in December, I have meetings. The best I can do is a raincheck. I'll be in town before Thanksgiving. I'm all in for the kiss and make up part." She laughed.

"I hope you will spend some of your Thanksgiving with me and my family. Weeks seem like months." He didn't hide his frustration.

"What can we do about it? This is the disadvantage of our type of relationship." She gave him a fake challenge as she exited off the highway to her office building.

"I don't know, but I'm sure the Lord will help me, so get ready as I bring in the heavy armor."

"Whoa." Queen giggled. "Bring it on then. Bye."

The Sunday before Thanksgiving, Philip waited at the airport with a bouquet for Queen's plane to touch down in St. Louis.

Philip was still dressed in his suit minus the tie. Sundays drained him more so as a pastor than an evangelist conducting tent meetings: he taught Sunday school, preached at morning worship service and then afternoon saints meeting. Yet, despite his tiredness, his heart gave him newfound energy when Queen was within his view.

"My Queen." He stepped forward with his arms ready to take her hostage once she cleared the terminal.

Not only did she snuggle in his arms, but Queen also rested her head on his chest as if she were counting his heartbeat. "I love this greeting much better. Don't tell Kami and Victoria."

"Your secret is safe with me," he murmured near her ear before one more squeeze. Philip released and inspected her from head to toe. "Yep, perfection. Thank you, Jesus, for her safe travels.

Linking his fingers through hers, Philip led the way to the baggage area. "I don't like going months without seeing you. It seems like years."

"I know. I miss your hugs." She inched closer to his side as if they might get separated through the maze of travelers.

Philip faced Queen as they waited for her suitcase on the carousel. "I wanted to look you in the eyes and say don't be angry with me for caring about you. I'll protect you with all the strength God gave me, even from afar. I've got spiritual backup."

"No knife or gun, huh?"

"What?" Philip did his best to keep from crossing his eyes in disbelief. "The weapons of my warfare aren't carnal, but mighty through God. Please tell me you don't carry weapons."

Queen grinned and rubbed her nose against his. "Only a knife."

Philip looked toward heaven. "Lord, this woman You gave me is going to give me gray hair." He squinted at her. "Promise me you'll be careful not to get into situations that might cause you to use it—please," he pleaded as the buzzer alerted them to new luggage.

"I promise, but—"

"No buts," he ordered, placing a finger on her soft lips.

Queen complied by kissing his finger. "It feels so good to have you close."

"It does, doesn't it?" He grinned.

With her luggage in tow, they made their way to the parking garage to his vehicle. "My first stop, Grandma BB's house. I want to see Kami and Victoria."

He did her bidding. Twenty minutes later, Kami and Grandma BB greeted Queen then him with hearty hugs. Victoria offered him a smile and wave. Philip would take that.

Although Philip would rather have taken Queen out to dinner before he had to relinquish his time with her, he or Queen couldn't pass up Grandma BB's pasta.

As they sat around the table, Kami chatted away about the courses she was taking at Wash U where her brother was a student and Cameron was department chair and taught. "I was even in a class with Pace. Someone thought we were boyfriend and girlfriend." She gagged.

"Victoria, what about you?" Queen said in between bites. "Any plans?"

The girl shrugged, but Grandma BB answered. "She just needs some down time before going off to college—if she wants to go. Right now, she and Kami are helping me to compile a journal of my life."

Queen eyed the woman. "Are you sick? Is there something we need to know? Something Philip needs to pray for?"

"Hush, chile." Grandma BB frowned. "I ain't ready to see Jesus yet."

Literally, Philip kept to himself. And that was the problem, Ready or not, everybody will see Him. If only Grandma BB and Queen could sense the urgency in securing their eternity while there was still time.

Queen wiped her mouth and stood with her empty plate and grabbed his. Philip liked to watch the way she moved. She was graceful and confident, and that's what attracted him to her at first sight.

Soon, their visit ended when Philip helped Queen slip her arms through her coat's sleeves.

"You're rocking that coat, Auntie." Kami pointed.

"Everything a woman wears should feel uniquely hers like no one else can wear it better. This is a design from a talented woman in the fashion program at the university," Queen said in a singsong tone as she modeled the embroidered patchwork coat from side to side.

"We still on for the Black Friday or bust shopping? I'm counting down the days." Grandma BB grabbed her purse and pulled out a thick roll of cash and grinned. "If this isn't enough," she reached back in and displayed her credit cards. "One for shoes, another for clothes, this one is for gifts, and these three are for impulse shopping. Oh, and I'll save some cash for the red kettle. Say the word, and I'll be ready on Friday to slip on my Stacy Adams and meet y'all there."

Philip laughed at the older woman's antics as Queen invited him to tag along. "Can't. We have community service. Our church is passing out hot meals, warm blankets, and wool socks to the homeless."

Queen gnawed on her pouty lips and frowned. "I guess I should break the Black Friday or Bust tradition and do the volunteer stuff, huh?"

"I'm not trying to make you feel guilty." Philip sighed.

"Too late," Grandma BB interrupted. "I feel guilty, but I'll get over it." She winked as the couple, opened the door, and left.

"I can shop anytime and anywhere but spending time with you is better than being at the premium malls." Queen stared into Philip's eyes.

That's exactly what he wanted to hear. Queen choosing him. "I appreciate that." Philip tugged her closer by her collar and stole a kiss. "Thanksgiving dinner at my parents'?" He wanted confirmation that she hadn't changed her mind. "They're doing it big. This will be their first one since moving here, then I'm willing to share you with your family."

"Who said I wanted to be shared?" she sassed him, lifting her chin in a challenge.

"Tell him, Queen," Grandma BB popped her head out the door, snapped her fingers, and rolled her neck until arthritis seemed to get the best of her and she couldn't move. "That's what I told my late husband…" Either the woman had a hearing aid, or he and Queen were talking louder than he thought.

Victoria and Kami appeared on the porch.

"We've heard this story. Hurry and go," Kami warned. "She's been telling us her whole life's memories, reflections, adventures, love story… We're starting volume three."

Once he and Queen were inside his car, he linked hands. "In all honesty, I don't want to share you either. I'd rather kidnap you to make up for all the times we couldn't be together."

"*Oooh*. I like your naughty thoughts." Queen grinned and wiggled in her seat.

Philip chuckled. "Pure thoughts. I wish you lived here, so our time wouldn't be rushed. Have you kind of thought about it at all?"

Queen lifted a brow and was slow in answering. "Yep. I imagined the reverse scenario with you moving. Tulsa is my home."

And there lies the problem. Philip pulled away from the curb.

Chapter Twenty-two

Weeks later…

What man got on a plane wearing a tux and snow boots? The forecast called for one inch. Philip Dupree stomped through three inches to the airport to surprise his woman.

He had three reasons for his flight to Tulsa—to support Queen at the annual fundraiser to raise scholarship money for the fashion design program. She said the silent auction of the students' designs on display was the highlight of the evening. Philip heard her passion every time she mentioned it.

Frederic was the second reason. He had since called and texted Queen his apologies until she'd blocked his number. If the man tagged along with his cousins under the guise of apologizing in person, Philip wanted to be there. He had fasted and prayed for this moment.

The third reason would happen before the night was over. Closing his eyes as the plane took off, Philip gave into exhaustion. He had attended the Christmas play at his own church, then left after the second act to catch his flight.

God knew he labored with the people without the official title. His only beef with the board was the "add-on" stipulation that the pastor had to be married. That should have been an upfront clause. If anything, dating Queen was proving he wasn't good at multi-tasking.

He drifted off with tormented thoughts and didn't stir until the plane touched down. He stretched and waited, counting the minutes until he could retrieve his carryon and get going. The ball had started.

Philip was never in a hurry, but on this chilly Saturday night, he rushed through the Tulsa Airport to pick up his rental car, then drive to the Harwelden Mansion. Good thing it was only ten minutes from the airport.

When the winding road ended in front of a four-story palace, Philip was tongue-tied as the valet waited for him to step out.

"One moment." Philip exchanged his boots for his dress shoes before handing over his keys and a tip.

He whistled as he climbed the first of three sets of stairs. Philip straightened his tie, not breaking his stride.

The brick-and-stone estate was intimidating to commoners like himself until he recalled John 14:2–3: *In my Father's house are many mansions: if it were not so, I would have told you. I go to prepare a place for you. And if I go and prepare a place for you, I will come again, and receive you unto myself; that where I am, there ye may be also.*

God's promise stayed with Philip as he approached the grand entrance with massive carved wood double doors that seemed ten feet high or more. No wonder formal attire was required. Two young ushers—possibly students—were also decked out in tuxes.

He entered the foyer where it appeared an entire forest supplied the flooring and exquisite stairwell. Now, to find and surprise Queen.

Philip mingled through the maze of guests adorned in festive holiday colors. He snagged a couple of hors d'oeuvres during his covert mission. After scouring three ballrooms, with no sighting, he was about to call her when she appeared in a doorway chatting with a group. He recognized Queen Bee and Rejoice Robnett. Were there more? Was Frederic among them?

The answers didn't matter as Philip admired Queen from afar. She was a fashion statement with whatever she wore. Tonight, his woman was stunning with her hair swept up into a ball on top of her head. She had trimmed bangs and a pinch of long strands dangling on the sides. Her earrings sparkled from the light. The long gown that graced her figure reminded him of a ballerina as it fanned out from her waist. Gold and red were her colors.

Moving out of sight, he called her. As it rang, Philip observed her open her purse and search for her phone. When she saw his name, she smiled. He caught himself smiling, too, as she answered.

"Philip! I miss you. I wish you were here. The turnout is great." Her voice was breathless. "Where are you? out?"

"I miss you too." He walked her way. When he was within a few feet of her, he whispered, "Let me be your plus one tonight. Turn around."

She did a graceful pivot, and a scream of delight escaped her lips as guests watched. Queen hugged him with strength he didn't know she had.

"You're here." It was a tossup between whether she was going to cry or laugh.

"I am, but I'm hungry." The appetizers could only do so much for a man who had been on a spiritual fast since midnight.

"Philip!" Queen Bee reminded them of her presence. "It's good to see you again." She leaned closer and graced him with air kisses from cheek to cheek.

Rejoice hugged him after asking Queen's permission. "You just made my cousin's day. My sister and I are going to get into some good trouble." She winked, then looped arms with Queen Bee and strolled away.

"They seem nice."

"They are family. I love them." She linked her fingers—soft—through his. "Come on. I'll fix you a plate, and there's more seating in the next room."

When Philip sat, he could have melted into the cushion. The sectional engulfed his body in comfort. Queen returned with a plate piled with food and a tall glass of punch. She was attentive to his needs. She forked a meatball, sampled a bite then fed it to him. Yeah, he was enjoying the moment being the king of this castle.

Yes, Philip had made the right decision to come, even if it was for one night.

Queen didn't want to leave Philip's side. He was her highlight of the night. She squeezed his biceps to make sure this wasn't a dream.

She admired his fresh haircut, clean shave, and tux while he ate. "I thought you had a play at church tonight."

He swallowed and nodded. "I did. I made my appearance. After an hour into the program, Nathan drove me to the airport. It had started to snow again, so I prayed my flight wouldn't be cancelled." He took another bite and chewed. "I had reasons for coming. The main one is to look you in the eyes and say I love you with a love so strong that I would do everything within my power to make you happy."

"Are you sure?" Her heart was full of love for this man. She opened her mouth to speak, but the words choked in her throat. Her misty eyes blurred her vision. She sniffed to keep from bawling. "I love you, too… so much. You make me a better person."

"I've been sure for a long time."

Her mind documented the moment, place, and the time Philip professed the three words. "Thank you, Philip Dupree, for coming all this way to tell me. That means a lot to me. You look very handsome tonight."

"I was a bit overdressed at the children's Christmas program."

Queen grinned. "I'm sure you were the best dressed man there."

"My parents attended, and my mother thought so, too." He kissed her nose, and his energy seemed restored. "You sounded so disappointed when I told you our plans clashed. I had to find a way to meet my commitment to the church and support the woman I love." He glanced around the room. "I'm glad a lot of people are here to support your vision, baby, and this mansion is just…wow. When I see the riches of this world, my mind reminds me of what God has prepared for me and those who love him."

She was in awe of him. "I kinda like how you compare this world to God's, but yes, this place is fifteen thousand square feet. The Harwelden Mansion is popular for anything lavish — weddings, corporate events, plus non-profit fundraisers like tonight, which cost us nothing, and it's even open to bed-and-breakfasts."

Philip scanned the room from the ceiling to the floor. "This place is majestic. Now, I'm ready to meet your people." He stood and patted his stomach. Philip guided her to her feet, then twirled her around. "I can't help but to love you."

Queen shivered under Philip's scrutiny. It wasn't lustful, but admiration. She had no regrets letting her guard down with a man who she thought they had little in common, but they had found love.

"So old Freddie boy couldn't make it—too bad." Philip didn't crack a smile.

"I say good riddance to his foolishness. His cousins wouldn't let him on the plane. Queen Bee and Sapphire were so embarrassed and mad at him after a stunt like that. The elders were hot that he attempted to disrespect me. He may be banned from some of their future gatherings. Besides Queen Bee, Rejoice, and Sapphire, they brought Jewel, who said she might be interested in the fashion program. She's been asking a lot of questions and wants to visit the campus. I think this event has won her over."

"Congratulations. I'm sure your sister would be proud of what you're doing in her memory." He squeezed her hand.

"That's so important to me." Now, Queen took a deep breath. "Follow me."

His presence completed her. This was the first time she could introduce him to her circle of acquaintances, close friends, and board members.

Since he mentioned he was flying out early to get to church, she refused to leave his side. The only exception was when she was asked to give the guests a history of the Suzette Jamieson Scholarship Fund.

Philip helped her up on the elevated platform and stayed close.

"Tonight has been fabulous," she greeted the crowd. "Your presence and generous donation to UCO's fashion scholarship endowment will help the next graduate realize her or his dreams of their fashion making a statement on the runaway, in movies, in the stores… The possibilities are endless."

She paused at their applause. "I'm sure you've admired the fabulous creations from this year's senior class. Take a second look and place a generous bid for the silent auction. Remember, the winning bid comes with a personal designer who will design three outfits for you as part of their semester credit. Thank you." She accepted Philip's hand to step down.

Feeling like Cinderella, they only had until midnight to be together, then they would have to part ways to his hotel and her to her home. Queen planned to make the most of it because she didn't know when they would see each other again.

Chapter Twenty-three

P hilip and Queen's first Christmas was a bust. Zoom was good for business meetings and staying in touch with out-of-town family, but a terrible substitute for romantic relationships.

He did his best not to complain while Queen's eyes glowed as she opened her first gift box. "To the love of my life who has everything." Gabrielle helped him pick this one. "It's a jar of inspiration. You can put it on your desk at work or in your kitchen."

"I love it, and you. Thank you… I miss you." She fingered the clean crystal jar that was decorated with red and gold ribbons and a fake flower.

She twisted off the top and pulled out one of the miniature scrolls which contained a famous quote or a Scripture. "I have the perfect place for it, beside my bed to greet me every morning and whisper good night."

Philip's heart vibrated like a cymbal on a drum set in response to her words. He grinned. His sister had picked a winner. In addition, he bought her a single pearl necklace and a spa gift card.

"Your turn."

He tore off the wrapping and lifted the lid. "Wow." He examined the treasure before looking at Queen through his computer. This was another moment he wished there was no barrier between them so he could show her his appreciation.

Someone had captured a photo of them at the fundraiser. Queen had the image created in 3D, then encased in a crystal-clear block. The snapshot was one of many times that night he had stared into her eyes. He read the caption. "I Believe You're God's Best Man for Me—Your Queen." He recalled when she'd first said that she believed in him. "Thank you."

"I hope you like it." Her smile was uncertain. "I wasn't sure what to give a pastor."

"I'm your man first, and this touches me right here." He patted his chest, loving her more and more.

Tilting her head to the side, Queen appeared seductive. "When the event photographer showed me this, I knew it would be my keepsake. I ordered one for myself and you. That night, you made me feel like Cinderella—the black version." They chuckled together.

"The other gift was what Gabrielle told me you would always need."

Ah. Gabrielle and gift in the same sentence meant socks and ties. Sure enough, when he opened it, Philip snickered and thanked her.

"Just so you know," Queen said, lifting a shoulder as if she was posing for a photo, "I found a matching pattern in women's socks." She left her computer and returned with the socks in hand and a mischievous grin. "When I come back to the Lou, I'll wear them with my jeans."

"Woman, you are too much. I never thought I could miss someone so hard like I am now. Do you ever think about how much time we could spend together if we lived in the same city?"

"A little." She bowed her head, then looked up. "I'm comfortable hopping on a plane whenever I get lonely."

"Then come to me." Philip had spoken his thoughts. In his head, he was summoning her to St. Louis for Christmas, which was two days away. Judging from her expression, his words had shocked her as well. He didn't take them back as they stared at each other, then her tortured expression made him speak first.

"I know you're flying to Hartford to see your other siblings for Christmas, but I wish your flight had a layover in St. Louis. I would be at the airport in a flash."

A smile blossomed across her face. "And I believe the pastor. American had a layover in Charlotte or Chicago, but that would make my trip almost five hours. The timing in the St. Louis layover would put me on the East Coast too late for my sisters to pick me up."

As the solo single Jamieson and baby girl, Queen divided her holidays between the two families—Kidd and Ace in St. Louis and Gigi and her husband, Candy, and Lacey in Hartford. Sometimes the older brothers made an appearance. She learned not to expect it. While their father had abandoned them, Samuel showed unconditional love to Suzette and Queen.

"When you return from Hartford, think about 'us' time. Again, I don't regret our long-distance relationship, but it's time to make a change."

"Yes, sir." She gave him a mock salute. "I mailed my St. Louis gifts to Grandma BB's house. She likes to dress up in a red elf costume with striped stockings when they come to get them."

Philip laughed. "Please don't put that image in my head. Now I can't get it out." But his mind was already plotting. The next time they saw each other, Philip would have a ring, flowers, and a list of moving companies for her. He couldn't wait.

Queen stumbled in her tracks at the sight of her welcoming committee at the Hartford airport. In addition to sisters and Gigi's husband, her dad's first family of sons was there too. That never happened. Ever. A tear fell at the sight.

Twins Jayson and Mayson and Benjamin were cordial. The oldest, Saul, had died years before Queen had a chance to meet him.

The youngest, Zaki, was a no-show. He was bitter from their father's betrayal. Zaki tolerated Queen, but refused to acknowledge Ace and Kidd since Samuel never married their mother Sandra, even though Zaki and Ace could pass as twins.

Queen tucked away the brief family history and walked into Gigi's open arms. "Hey, baby sister." She squeezed Queen tight enough that she could feel it through her thick wool coat, then rocked her from side to side.

"You've had your thirty seconds." Lacey, the oldest sister, bumped Gigi out of the way. "My turn." She hugged Queen and whispered, "You see three of our four knucklehead brothers are here. I think they want to give an olive branch as a Christmas gift."

"I'll take it." Queen welcomed the reconciliation. She loved her siblings and cousins—full or half, even the Robnetts. They were building not only a friendship but a bond. She was willing to cut her losses with Frederic.

Candy hugged her.

Then Mayson stepped forward and offered a platonic embrace—at least it was more than a handshake. "Nice to see you again."

His eyes reminded her of Kidd—a rich dark brown. After the other twin's hug, Benjamin added his welcome. "I'll come over to Gigi's before you leave so we can catch up."

"I would like that." Queen blinked back the moisture, but she couldn't mask her surprise. Now, she wished she had brought gifts for them, too—bummer.

If you're going to celebrate Christmas, celebrate Christ and give Him your best, Philip had said when she asked him what he wanted for Christmas. She sent a donation to his church, then went shopping with Cori and Trice.

As a group, they trailed her to baggage claim where two of her three checked suitcases contained gifts. She would stack the empty one inside the bigger one for her return flight.

Once Benjamin retrieved her luggage, the group headed to the parking garage where they parted ways to their homes, except for her sisters and brother-in-law. The hugs her brothers gave her this time were heartier. The bonus was their kisses on her cheek.

When Benjamin said, "See you later, sis," Queen wrapped him in a bear hug and didn't want to let go.

Releasing him from her grip, she sniffed. "I'm glad you came."

"Me, too." He grinned at her, then walked toward his car.

"Whew. I wasn't expecting that," Queen told Gigi.

"Honestly," Lacey said, dabbing a tear in the corner of her eye, "none of us were. I guess it's the miracle of Christmas."

"Peace on earth and in our family. I'll take it." Gigi climbed in the car.

Back at her house, Gigi's husband, Jacob, showed off his culinary skills by preparing a meal for the sisters. The couple had been married for a while and suffered through two miscarriages. Queen didn't know if they would try again.

After the late light dinner, Queen passed out her gifts.

"Jacob, because you take good care of my sister..." He was a bookworm, so she tried to watch out for author events to get him signed books and gave him a copy of *Run: Book One* by John Lewis and Andrew Aydin.

He accepted with a grin. "More goodies for my collection." He opened the book and saw Andrew Aydin's signature. "Thanks, sis."

Queen reached for three identical boxes. "These are for my three favorite sisters." She grinned.

The three exchanged snickers. "We're your only sisters," they said in unison, then Gigi frowned. "Unless there are more out there."

Lacey shook her head. "I wouldn't put it past our father."

Queen shrugged. "The man your family and Kidd and Ace describe wasn't the father I knew. Daddy was the kindest man who confessed to Suzette and me before he became ill that we had siblings, and he asked for our forgiveness. Our mother knew about his other children before she married him."

"I guess what's hard, especially for Zaki, is Dad stepped out on our mother, not yours. With Kidd and Ace's mother, Sandra knew he was married when she had Ace," Gigi said. "One thing I admire about Sandra is she admitted her wrong and tried to apologize to Mama. I respect her for that. She said when she repented and was baptized in water in Jesus' name, the power of the Holy Ghost allowed her to forgive herself. Okay, I'll get off my church soapbox."

Queen waved her hand. "I hear stuff like that from time to time. You forgot I'm dating a minister—pastor."

"And so how is that going for you?" Gigi tugged her legs under her body on the sofa.

"I think that's my cue to say good night, ladies. Looks like I have a date with a book." Jacob brushed a kiss on his wife's lips then his sisters-in-law's cheeks.

"Perfect. I'm so in love with that man." Queen released a whimsical sigh.

"We are talking about Philip, right? I want to make sure since you were watching my husband." Gigi laughed.

"Philip, of course." Queen slapped her leg. "I was waiting for him to get out of the room."

"Like we didn't know that. Philip is one sexy pastor, and he has two brothers. One is too young for me." Lacey lifted a brow. "So, when are you moving?"

Queen grunted. "I'm not."

Her three sisters exchanged glances before Lacey continued. "I don't know how the hierarchy of church works. But can pastors quit if God tells them to stay like we do on a regular job?"

"I don't know, but I'm not moving. Why does the woman always have to quit her job and sacrifice her life for love? I'm not that type of woman, so I don't know how our fairytale is going to play out."

"*Ummm-hmmm.*" Gigi huffed and squinted. "Stubborn like a Jamieson."

"So are you planning to break it off with him?" Lacey gave her an unreadable expression. Queen couldn't decipher if she was serious or baiting her.

"What? We're not breaking up." She lifted a brow. "Have you two heard something I need to know?"

"No. Wondering how much longer this long-distance love will last," Lacey said.

"I believe in living life in the moment. Tomorrows aren't promised. If I have taken my time to evaluate the pros and cons about dating Philip—a pastor with a church, four hundred miles away, and more things—I never would have taken the plunge. We're moving at a slow pace, and I know he's there for me."

"You can't be my sister?" Gigi dragged out a groan. "You don't take true love for granted. It's like getting struck by lightning, and once isn't enough."

"Noted." Queen wanted to change the subject. Yes, she and Philip missed each other, but uprooting one's life was a major decision, not for a man who wasn't her husband. Then she swallowed. Queen didn't want to think there could come a day when they would have the "talk" to go their separate ways. That nagged at her for the rest of the night.

On Christmas Eve, the sisters called the Jamiesons in St. Louis to wish them a Merry Christmas and watch them open gifts on video conferencing.

Philip's ringtone woke Queen early Christmas morning. The second she answered, his melodious voice serenaded "Joy to the World" in her ears.

"And he sings, too," Gigi mouthed with a giggle. "See you downstairs for breakfast."

"Merry Christmas, Philip." She stretched her body. It was their first Christmas together as a couple, yet they were apart. How could they fix this, so it wouldn't happen again on the next holiday?

Pray on it, she heard God say.

Queen blinked. There lies the problem. She had no idea what to pray for as she got up to enjoy breakfast with her family as they ended the call.

Chapter Twenty-four

Queen's estranged brother, Zaki, showed up at Gigi's house. He was the missing piece Queen longed for. The Connecticut siblings played board games, watched movies, and talked about their lives—minus any discussion about their father. It was the best Christmas week ever.

The night before Queen was due to fly out, Gigi called for a group prayer. They formed a circle around Queen and bowed their heads.

Her sister tapped the speaker phone. To Queen's surprise, Philip was on the other end. "Lord, in the name of Jesus, bless this family. Strengthen their bonds. Let them forever remember You in their lives…." His voice was strong. His words powerful.

All the Jamiesons mumbled and whispered their amens.

Philip was her heartbeat that crescendoed, then exploded into a gentle breeze.

How could Gigi disconnect knowing Queen would want to speak with Philip? She blushed as all eyes were on her when she called him back. "Hey, babe. Thanks for praying for us."

"It's what I do." His chuckle was deep. "Call me when you get home."

"I will." She was about to end their call when Philip stopped her,

"Hey, I mean before your plane takes off…and when it lands too," he added.

Her siblings snickered. Any other man, Queen would have reminded him of his boundaries. Not with Philip. His concern was endearing. Perfect. She felt so loved.

"And you're going to let him go?" Candy laughed. "If that man asked me to move to Jamaica, I would pack nothing but swimsuits."

The next day, Queen exchanged tearful goodbyes and emotional hugs until next time. Her spirit was high when she strolled through the airport to fly home.

Queen did as Philip had requested when she landed and en route to her house. "Home at last. No more traveling for a while. I'm looking forward to bringing in the new year with my girlfriends." Her console showed they were still connected. "Philip, can you hear me?"

"Yes, babe. How about we celebrate? Our church has watch meeting on New Year's Eve. We'll be praying out the old year and praising God for the new. Join us. Then you and I can do something special on New Year's Day."

"*Ummm-hmmm*." Queen was tired of travel. "Will you say a prayer for me?"

"Always. If you don't want to come here, you can attend a watch meeting. I'm sure Resurrection Temple is having one. That's the church that sponsored the tent meetings."

Night church? "Sorry, babe. Cori, Trice, and I have plans, but I'll call you before I go out. Hey, I'm pulling into my driveway. Home."

The next night, about ten P.M., Philip called Queen before he was about to enter the sanctuary for the testimony, prayer, and praise service. "I want to pray for you before you go out."

"Yes, please do."

"Lord, in the mighty name of Jesus, we thank You for this time You've given us. We thank You for Your blessings. You've never deserted us. You're faithful, even when we aren't. I ask that You forgive us of our sins. Help us to walk right before You, to honor, to have a desire to please You. We ask for new mercies in the morning..."

Queen experienced a tug-of-war inside of her during the prayer. One part of her wanted Philip to hurry and finish while another part wanted to relish in it.

"In Jesus' name," Queen repeated with him, then glanced at the time. She couldn't recall him praying that long, then He spoke with God in heavenly tongues. It sounded beautiful. Even if she didn't understand the conversation, she felt God's presence.

"Love you, my Queen. I have to go. Be careful and call me when you get home."

"Will do. Have fun at church." After a few air kisses, Philip was gone.

An hour later, Queen was dressed and ready to bring in the new year. She would meet Cori and Trice at Miami Nights Restaurant & Lounge. Besides serving the best authentic Cuban cuisine, the owners sponsored jazz nights and Afro Caribbean Day parties, so bringing in the New Year was the place to be for the countdown and ball drop.

It was only a fifteen-minute drive from her house east on I-244 to East 21st Street. While en route, she reflected on Philip's prayer. "I do have a lot to be thankful for." Her siblings. Her expanded family—new babies and the Robnetts.

Plus, Queen hadn't felt this secure in a romantic relationship in years. "God, I might not be at church tonight, but I am grateful and thankful. In Jesus' name. Amen."

Miami Nights was buzzing when Queen stepped inside. She scanned the crammed place as Cori waved at her. Trice was chatting with a handsome gentleman.

"Now we can get this party started," Cori said with a hug and a drink in hand. The trio watched out for one another to make sure they didn't overindulge. Soon the countdown began, and the disco ball started spinning at midnight. The crowd moved outside to watch the fireworks.

The ladies called it a night at one-thirty.

"Another year." Cori grinned and lifted her hand for a high five.

"Let's do brunch soon," Trice added with her hug.

Security escorted them to their cars. Queen jumped on I-64. A new year, new possibilities, she thought, smiling to herself, cruising at a steady speed. She was eight minutes from home when she heard a pop. Glass shattered. Queen screamed and lost control of her car, slamming into something. As she dangled upside down, her airbag deployed and punched her into darkness.

Philip's own snoring woke him. As he was about to roll over, his phone rang. *Ugh.* A man of God was always on the clock to pray, give counsel, or referee a domestic dispute, but he wasn't feeling it tonight.

Wait. That was Queen's ringtone. He jolted up and grabbed it before it went to voicemail. "Queen?" He spied the time. It was after two in the morning.

"I'm at the Trauma Emergency Center—"

"What!" He roared. "I'm on the next flight out." He didn't need to hear more as he slipped out of bed and reached for the first clothes he could find. Philip didn't know the circumstances or the severity. Didn't matter. He could have lost her. But God said different.

"Please don't tell Kidd and Ace. I'm fine. My car is probably totaled, but your prayers saved me."

"I can't agree to that, babe. I'm not the only man who loves you. I have to call your brothers." Philip gave God thanks Queen was alert. As she talked, he packed.

He threw toiletries in his travel bag. Underwear, socks—including the ones she bought him—pants and sweaters were tossed in his carryon. Anything else, he would get there. "Okay, baby, rest. I'm coming straight to the hospital from the airport."

Philip took a deep breath, then made the dreaded call. Ace first.

"Hello." The sleep in his voice was thick.

"Ace, this is Philip. Queen just called. She's been in an accident—"

"What do you mean? What happened? Is she alive? I guess she is, I mean she called you…"

While he rambled, Philip added Kidd to the line.

"What?" Kidd's shriek had to wake not only his house, but the neighborhood. The sound hurt Philip's ear.

Philip repeated what he knew. "She's alive and alert. Praise God for that. I'm booking the next flight out."

"We'll meet you at the airport." Kidd disconnected.

Ace concurred and ended the call.

In the back of Philip's mind, he wondered if this would have happened if she had gone to church instead of clubbing. "Nope, I'm not going to entertain that thought." Time and chance happened to the just and unjust. He recalled Ecclesiastes 9:11.

Behind the wheel, Philip realized he hadn't brushed his teeth. He'll take care of that at the airport.

It was too early to call Nathan. He texted him instead, hoping not to wake him until he got to Tulsa and knew more.

At Lambert, he cleared the gate and headed to the designated terminal. He'd just taken his seat when he saw Ace speed-walking in his direction. Philip stood to greet him, and they exchanged a handshake, hug, and pat on the back.

"Man, you alright? How did you get here so fast?"

"You said my sister was hurt. That's all I needed to know," Ace said. "Plus, I didn't need to shave and get pretty to see my sister. She's used to my ugly face."

A face that could have used a second washing to get the tiredness out. Philip kept that to himself.

Although the terminal wasn't crowded, travelers seemed to create a path for Kidd as he marched toward them. His greeting was curt. "Now repeat what you said to me again." He folded his arms, and Philip recounted the questions he'd asked Queen and her responses.

Ace glance at the overhead. Among the first flights out this morning, theirs was on time.

"This was your job." Kidd's nostrils flared as his fists rested at his waist.

"Excuse me?" Philip frowned.

"You're supposed to be taking care of my sister. Why was she even at a lounge? Why wasn't she going to a watch meeting?" He rattled off one accusation after another.

"Listen, man," Philip said, using his calm pastoral voice to diffuse the situation, "I have no right or authority to tell Queen what to do. You and Ace have planted the seed of salvation in her heart, and I've watered it without flooding the harvest, it's up to God for the increase."

Kidd scowled. "I'm familiar with that passage somewhere in the Bible, but I'm not feeling that right now."

"It's First Corinthians 3:7," Philip said, '*So then neither is he who plants anything, neither he who waters; but God who gives the increase.*'"

"I can't comprehend that right now." Kidd held his head.

Ace sat for the first time and anchored his elbows on his knees and looked down. "What I can't understand is why you haven't married my sister and made a decent woman out of her."

"Huh?" Philip squinted. "Queen is already an honest woman, and I would marry her in a minute if she would commit to God first."

"Again, that's your job." Kidd twisted his lips.

"I don't care how you do it, but you need to get my sister to marry you and move her to St. Louis, sooner—like yesterday—rather than later."

"Glad I have your blessings. If only it was that easy," Philip whispered as the ticket agent advised passengers to line up for boarding.

Chapter Twenty-five

We're here, Philip texted Queen as their plane landed. **See you soon. Love you**.

We? I don't have to ask, Queen texted back. **They are finally discharging me. I was about to call Trice.**

Stay put. I'm about to get a rental, then I'm coming to get you. Kidd and Ace are with me.

The trio followed the signs to transportation to pick up a rental car.

"How's my sister?" Kidd rubbed the back of his neck.

"We'll find out as soon as we get to the Trauma Emergency Center." Philip exhaled without him recalling taking a deep breath.

Once they were strapped in, Philip programmed the address into the GPS, gripped the steering wheel, and took off. The ache in his heart resurfaced when he thought about what could have happened. "Jesus, Thank You for watching over her."

"I'm talking to God right now about Queen moving to the Lou." Kidd sighed from the passenger seat.

"I'm too upset to pray. I can't imagine our lives without her, and my baby girl not knowing the aunt whose name she carries," Ace mumbled from his perch in the backseat.

Philip spied Ace shaking his head from the rearview mirror. He didn't want to imagine that scenario. He had found a woman who inspired him, beautiful, kind, generous—all the qualities that attracted him. Only her salvation commitment stood between them.

The twenty-minute ride to the ER entrance seemed like an hour. Now, they were spying out a parking space. Done. They hurried out of the car at the same time. Philip glanced back to make sure the vehicle was in park.

They cleared the double doors. Philip rushed to the nurse's station. "I'm looking for—"

"We're looking for Queen Jamieson," Kidd interrupted, showing his driver's license.

Maybe Philip was talking too slow, or out of breath as a morning run wasn't part of his daily regimen.

The nurse tapped on the keyboard and tilted her head. "Thank you, Mr. Jamieson. I do show your name listed as next of kin in case of an emergency. She's in room 335—"

The trio took off for the elevator as the nurse yelled, "But it was only for observation. She's about to be discharged."

In the elevator, Philip's finger shook as he pushed the floor number. He braced himself for the unknown. It seemed like forever before the doors opened. In a hurry to get out, their buffed bodies bottlenecked the exit until Philip pushed his way through.

After scanning the signs, Philip took off to the right. Queen's brothers were on his trail.

Philip entered the room and almost stumbled at the sight of his beloved Queen. She was dressed, sitting up in bed. Her eyes closed. Face puffy. Arm in sling. Neck in a brace. What had happened?

As he stepped closer, slivers of glass glistened from her curls, evidence of the trauma she had experienced. Her lashes fluttered as she opened her eyes, and the realization that he was there brightened them.

"Philip!" Her attempt at standing was thwarted with a sharp pain, and she fell backwards.

"Hey." He snagged a chair and dragged it to her bedside. "I'm here. So are Kidd and Ace. What happened?"

She struggled to answer when the doctor strolled in with her discharge papers. He paused at her visitors. "Sorry. Are you family?"

"Yes, we're her brothers and this is Elder Dupree," Ace answered. "We just flew in from St. Louis."

"Can you tell us what happened?" Philip's patience was leaving him fast.

The physician nodded. "Miss Jamieson sustained bruised ribs, a concussion, and a sprained arm when a gunshot shattered her car window. She lost control of her car and rolled over. She's lucky to be alive."

"God kept her alive." Philip smiled.

Kidd planted his fists on his waist. "Are you telling me someone was shooting at my sister?" His nostrils flared.

"No. She and a few other unfortunate drivers happened to be in the wrong place and got in the crossfire of gunshots from a nearby celebration. She was grazed on the arm, which caused her to lose control of the wheel."

Queen moaned. Her brothers joined Philip at her side.

"I've prescribed medication for her pain and instructions on her discharge papers. If she has any hemorrhaging, intense headaches, or vomiting, she needs to return to the ER immediately. Otherwise, she should follow up with her primary care doctor in a week but limit strenuous activities for six to eight weeks."

They thanked him. As Dr. Shane exited her room, a nurse appeared with a wheelchair and retrieved her personal belongings from the closet.

Once she was secured, Philip took her hand to walk beside her wheelchair as his phone alerted him of a text. It was from Nathan. Philip would reach out to him once he got Queen settled.

"I've got to call Trice or Cori to wash the glass out of my hair," Queen mumbled.

"I'll do it," Philip volunteered, watching her brothers walk ahead to get the rental vehicle. When they pulled up and opened the back door, Philip lifted Queen in his arms and gently placed her in the backseat, then slid in next to her.

The short drive to Queen's home in Gilcrease Hills was quiet as Kidd sent and responded to texts. When they pulled into her driveway, Kidd took Queen's purse to locate her keys.

Her brothers made themselves at home, taking charge. Queen refused to lie down until she washed the glass out of her hair.

Putting on cleaning gloves, Philip worked gently, washing her hair and running a comb through it to get out the bits of glass. After the third rinse, fewer slivers fell out. He wrapped her hair in a towel as Ace and Kidd appeared in the doorway.

"Now what should I do?" Philip asked.

Kidd shrugged.

"Don't look at us," Ace shook his head. "Our wives comb our daughters' hair, but every Jamieson in the city of St. Louis wants to know how you're feelin'."

"Sore," Queen mumbled without opening her eyes.

"Babe, how do I detangle your hair?" he whispered close to her ear. "Disclosure: I've never braided hair in my life."

"Conditioner," she mumbled, still drowsy from the drugs, then fell asleep.

Kidd patted his stomach. "While you take care of that, I'll raid her fridge. I'm starved."

"Me, too." Ace followed.

Philip was conditioned to fast for days, so skipping a snack to take care of Queen took precedence. While he attempted to do what she had asked, Philip prayed blessings and restoration over her life. "God, please bring her closer to You…."

By the time he finished with the conditioner, one of her girlfriends arrived. Introducing herself as Cori, she was barely consolable.

Trice arrived minutes later, hysterical. Philip *shh*ed them and whispered, "I know she's sleep, but can one of you give her a sponge bath in case there is glass elsewhere?"

"We got this." Trice spoke up, so Philip joined the men in the kitchen.

He straddled a stool at the counter and dropped his head into his hands. Now that he was still, exhaustion gained speed on him. Kidd slid a plate of egg whites, toast, and sausage patties in front of him. He said grace and dug in.

"So, what's the plan?" Kidd asked. "Because I ain't going nowhere for a couple of days. Eva ordered me not to show up until Queen can get around on her own."

"Well, you heard what the doctor said—six to eight weeks," Ace said.

Philip chewed on his toast, thinking. "I'm staying, too, until she's up, but if you two leave, I'll get a hotel room."

"Understood." Kidd took the empty plates and piled them in the sink.

"Preacher, if you don't marry my sister and bring her back home, I'll buy a ring myself and say it's from you." Ace didn't crack a smile.

Blame it on his tiredness, but that statement rubbed Philip the wrong way. What was it with people telling him who he had to marry and when? "I can buy my own ring, thank you, and I'll ask when I'm ready. Not a day or minute before." He didn't mean to snap, but that's the way it came out, and he wouldn't apologize.

"Whoa." Ace held up his hands. "Sorry. I'll back off a bit, but not too much longer. I don't like to be away from my wife and daughters." Ace stood and stretched. "I'm going to take a nap in the guest room with the twin beds."

Kidd claimed the other bed, defaulting the other guest room to Philip.

But Philip stretched out on the sofa and closed his eyes to wait for Queen's friends to report their progress. Next thing he knew, it was late afternoon, and the house was quiet. Once he got his bearings, he went to his rental and retrieved his travel bag. That's when he noticed Queen's friends' cars were gone.

Back inside the home, he padded down the hall in search of the available guest room. Queen's door was cracked, and he peeked in to make sure she wasn't in any pain. Despite what she went through, she was still beautiful. "Thank You, Jesus, again, for Your mercy," he whispered and continued on.

He smiled, listening to her light snoring. Philip unpacked his things. The guest bedroom had its own shower, so he indulged since it was the first chance he had to freshen up. When he stepped out, Queen's brothers were making a fuss with pots and pans from the kitchen.

After getting dressed, he left his room to investigate, peeping in on Queen first. She was awake.

"Hey, beautiful." He smiled.

"You must love me." Her voice was weak. "I'm sure I look anything but beautiful."

"You're beautiful to my eyes. Hungry?"

She nodded.

"Okay. If my nose is correct, I smell grilled cheese sandwiches and maybe soup. I'll fix you a plate."

Queen stopped him. "Thanks for coming."

"Thanks for calling me." He stared into her eyes. "I'll always be here for you. The distance between us is the only delay."

A few days turned into a week's stay before Queen convinced her brothers to go home to their wives and Philip to his congregation.

Queen was surprised she got any rest at all from the St. Louis and Hartford Jamiesons, and then the Robnetts who refused to be left out of the loop.

Although she was still sore, her pain had subsided from a scale of ten to three.

"Babe, I don't want to leave you." Sorrow filled Philip's eyes as he rubbed the back of his head in frustration. "Every night I've been praying outside of your door before I turn in."

"I've heard you." Queen smiled. "I'm going to kinda miss that."

Could that have been the reason she got urges to read her Bible during odd hours of the night? Queen stood from her chair and hugged him, resting her head on his chest, and listening to his beating heart, a heart that belonged to her—in a sense.

Kidd and Ace took their turns with their goodbyes and instructed her what to do and not to do. Kidd had already spoken with the insurance company about settling the claim on her totaled vehicle. "If I can't come back when it's time for you to get a new one, FaceTime me, and I'll put the fear of Kidd Jamieson in the salesman."

"The fear of the Lord would be worse, but I got this," Philip told him. "Stand down."

Ace grunted. "'Bout time you stood up."

Their stare-down made Queen ignore their cryptic messages. She was ready to get her house to herself—finally—even if she was still sore and limited in activities.

"Oh, and one more thing," Kidd said, "Victoria and Kami are en route to stay with you for a couple more weeks to make sure you're okay."

"Are you serious? I'm fine." Queen wanted to scream. The joy of a big family was overrated. Privacy was a premium now. She paused. When Kami stayed the summer with her, it was fun. This would be Victoria's first time in Tulsa. Why not? They would be less stressful. "Sounds good."

The men didn't leave until an Uber driver pulled up and Kami and Victoria stepped out with their designer luggage. Those had been their Christmas presents a few years back.

Queen stood in the doorway and waved. The girls dropped their bags and ran at full speed toward her. She braced herself for impact, but it never happened. Philip intercepted.

"Remember, ladies, Queen is still sore, so help her out," he reminded them.

"Yes, Uncle Philip," Kami said, and Victoria repeated the affirmative.

Once the men were gone, Queen sat on the sofa. "Kami, do you mind changing the linen in your old bedroom, then ordering groceries?"

"Okay, Auntie."

Queen convalesced a few more days, then the trio left the house with Kami behind the wheel of a rental car. They gave Victoria a tour of Tulsa. The day after that was a shopping spree. Queen rested while the sisters modeled clothes they liked.

Kami turned into a mother hen and said they were staying in and watching movies. Queen was tired and didn't put up a fuss. Later that night, they enjoyed reruns of old Black movies, including *Coming to America*, and the newer version, *Coming 2 America*.

"Wow." The costumes and pageantry amazed Victoria.

Queen understood. "Ruth E. Carter has some serious designer skills. She was the first Black woman to win an Oscar for her *Black Panther* costumes, which were nominated for Academy Awards for best costume design. She received a Walk of Fame star and has more impressive accolades. Ruth definitely makes us proud."

"I want to be like her when I grow up," Victoria said more to herself than Queen and Kami as she didn't take her eyes off the television.

"Fashions are more than fashion shows." Queen stayed on top of fashion news through her blogger friends. "I won't be surprised if some graduates from the University of Central Oklahoma land positions creating impressive designs for film and television."

"Auntie," Victoria said, "I'm not ready for on-campus education yet, but I think I've found my inspiration."

"I'm glad. Queen wiped imaginary sweat from her brows. "We can't have you putting our innocent black men in jail because God gave them melanin. All men aren't like the ones from your past."

Victoria hid her smile. "Maybe I'll get my general courses out of the way online, then I'll be ready to stay on a campus."

"I'll be right here to make that happen," Queen assured her.

Finally, Queen's home was a guest-free zone—no brothers, nieces, and Robnetts. She decided to use the day spa gift card from Philip. Cori and Trice joined her. The massage felt soothing to Queen's back and shoulders.

Without warning, Queen experienced a few nightmares where she relived the accident. One night, she woke screaming and damp with a sweat.

She padded her way to the bathroom for a cold towel. Patting her face, Queen reminded herself she was safe. She didn't want to close her eyes and relive the horror.

Without thinking, Queen grabbed her Bible and sat on her storage bench at the foot of her bed. Instead of reading random passages, she started from Genesis. She envied Adam and Eve that they could talk with their Creator.

"What did that feel like?" she wondered. Queen closed her Bible, then kneeled by her bedside. Minutes later, she slid back under the covers.

I have called, some have answered, but few will be chosen. Matthew 22:14, God whispered

Queen drifted off, imagining that she was jumping in place, trying to get the teacher's attention, yelling, "Choose me, choose me."

Chapter Twenty-six

Queen's new Range Rover was parked in her garage. True to his word, Philip flew into Tulsa to accompany her to the dealership. He didn't hover or second-guess her decision. Philip asked her opinion about features, then gave his thoughts. His visit was too short because he flew back the same night to prepare for his sermons and church services.

Reading her Bible before bed again made Queen appreciate all the hard work he put into reading, studying, and listening to God for understanding and the message for His people.

And somehow, she had wormed her way into his life as a needy woman. Queen smiled. How many times had she asked him about certain passages, and he would explain them to her with patience and without judgment? She picked up her phone and texted him. **I love you.**

Philip's reply came fifteen minutes later. **I love you more.**

She smiled. Their love was the source of a friendly competition, but the more she reflected on their relationship, Philip had never let the distance keep him from her when she needed him.

With Valentine's Day coming, Philip would return so they could celebrate their first Valentine's together. She couldn't wait. Queen found nothing at her favorite boutiques, so she shopped online for the perfect red dress and gold shoes.

Then there was a change of plans. He called her right after she ended an editorial meeting. His voice eased the irritation she felt, reminding the staff that their engineering journal relied heavily on research of new prototypes, science, and designs, not seventy percent interviews. At times, she questioned her decision to leave her career as a senior mechanical engineer.

"Baby, I'm sorry. I won't be able to come. Nathan reminded me of the congregation's couples Valentine's Day banquet. I can't believe I forgot."

No! Good thing he couldn't see her disappointment and pout. *Say something.* "Ah…I understand. As the pastor, you need to be there." Queen was not returning that red dress. It highlighted her legs.

"Yes." His voice deepened. "As your man, I need you, so I'm asking you to ease my guilt. Do you feel up to traveling and celebrating Valentine's Day with me here—and my congregation? This is an annual event to nourish healthy and faithful marriages."

Queen nodded. She could do that. The gold shoes would work. She needed to buy another red dress that covered up her best assets. "You'll get no guilt from me. I'm ready to get out of this house anyway. I haven't gone anywhere in months."

"I know."

Queen arrived in St. Louis the Friday before Valentine's Day. Philip met her at the airport. To see his beard from a distance was better than on FaceTime. Instead of quickening her footsteps, she slowed so she could take in his slow appraisal of her, and she could do the same of him.

As soon as she cleared the terminal, he approached her with his signature swag. He restrained his embrace. "I'm not hurting you, am I?"

"No, I'm fine." Queen assured him with a smile. "My nephews' hugs pack more punch than that."

He grinned. "Can't let that happen." He squeezed her tighter so she could rest her head on his shoulder. "Better?"

"Much." They shared a brief kiss before he presented her with a dozen red roses. After he grabbed her luggage, they walked outside into the brisk air.

Someone had spilled their red rose petals along the crosswalk. She pouted for the recipient and pointed. "I feel for the woman who won't get her red roses."

Philip said nothing as the trail of petals continued. They ended at his SUV. She spun around. "You did this?"

"Yes, for my Queen. I don't know if anyone will consider it littering since the wind will blow them away." He winked and held open the passenger door. "You haven't been here since November, and I wanted it special since you have to share me with my congregation tomorrow."

"*Awww.* Thank you." She kissed him before he closed the door. Seconds later, he slid behind the wheel. "The first stop—"

"I know. To Grandma BB's to see Kami and Victoria. Those two won't let me forget." Philip chuckled, checked his rearview mirror, then backed out.

"No. Actually, Grandma BB's bodyguards treated the ladies to a Valentine's treat with a limo ride, so they're probably gone."

"Even Victoria went?" Philip didn't hide his surprise when Queen nodded. "Good for her. You're staying with Ace and Talise, right?"

"You know it. I have to hold my little namesake. They're taking a new family photo. Talise asked if Diamond could wear the baby dress Suzette and I wore for our one-year-old photos. I was honored." She crossed her arms over her chest. "Plus, I sent the girls their first set of pearls for Christmas, and she's dressing Lauren and Diamond in them." Queen couldn't help but grin. She loved her nieces. Eva had already purchased some for Kennedy.

"You are the best auntie." Philip glanced, and she was sure he caught her blush. "Are you up to us going out tonight just us?"

Queen faced him and couldn't help herself from touching his smooth silky beard. "Oh, I love the idea of a pre-Valentine dinner just you and me."

"I was hoping you would say yes. Do you want to wear what you have on or change?"

"I'm changing." It was the norm for her to pack extra clothes for "just in case" moments.

At Ace's home, Queen didn't keep him waiting too long as she slipped on a purple dress—she only brought one red one—and her pearls. She kissed her nieces. "Don't wait up for me. I'm going out with the pastor."

"Lord, help that man," Talise teased.

Back in his vehicle, Philip linked hands with Queen and brought them up to his lips. "Did I say you look pretty."

"Your eyes did."

The entrance of the restaurant in the Central West End was inviting with pink ball lights. Philip parked and helped her out. Looping her arm through his, their steps matched as they climbed the stairs.

The place was crowded, but the hostess who greeted them led them to a cubby hole with a window view to Lindell Boulevard. Instead of perusing the menu, Queen admired Philip's handsome features. He seemed just as mesmerized with her as he played with her fingers.

"You scared me last month with the accident."

"I was afraid, too, and not much scares me," Queen admitted.

"But God."

"Yes, but God rescued me." After seeing the damage her vehicle sustained, Queen knew her bruises could have been broken bones.

The waitress appeared to take their orders, and they weren't ready, so they scanned the selections. Philip chose ribeye steak while her mouth watered for the parmesan chicken.

"I know we haven't gotten our meal yet, but do you mind if we pray?"

She squeezed his hands and bowed her head.

"God, in the name of Jesus, we are in awe of Your goodness and mercy unto us. I can't thank You enough for sparing Queen's life so that I can have a love of my own. Thank You again and for the food we'll eat. In Jesus' name. Amen." Philip exhaled. "I had to get that out of the way."

His prayer was touching. She dabbed the corners of her eyes, careful not to smudge her eyeliner. "I love you. I wanted to get that out of the way."

"Oh, I knew way back before the ball." He winked. "But every time I say I love you or hear you tell me how much you love me, it's like my ears are hearing it for the first time."

Queen's heart fluttered. Before their food arrived, they enjoyed flirting, air kisses, and holding hands. When their plates were placed before them, they sampled a few bites. "Tell me about this Valentine's Day program at your church. What should I expect?"

"Three couples will celebrate their silver anniversaries. Mostly all coming are married—we have several engaged couples and some newlyweds. I've performed two weddings since I've been there."

"Sounds like fun. I'll be with you, so that's all that matters to me." Then for some reason, she asked him about passages she had been reading, and he opened her understanding.

Soon, they shared dessert, and Philip paid their bill. He then faced her. "It's time, Queen, for you to surrender."

"I will." Queen wasn't fully persuaded she had a lot to repent for. As she pondered that, Philip stood and knelt on one knee.

She stifled a scream, and she covered her mouth. What was he doing? The softness in his eyes wouldn't let her blink. She gasped for breath. Her heart skipped beats. Was he... Was he about to propose?

He pulled out a velvet box from his pants pocket, then Queen lost it. She swiped at her tears until Philip took her left hand. She couldn't stop shaking.

"It's alright, baby," he whispered. "Take a deep breath."

She tried to follow his directions as everything around her became surreal.

"Queen Jamieson, you are my heartbeat. This past year, you've shown me what's been missing in my life—your love. I need you to be complete. Will you take this journey with me and be my wife?"

Speechless, Queen nodded, but he coaxed her. "Breathe, baby, and find your voice. I need to hear you say yes."

Leaning toward him, she rested her forehead on his for strength, then looked into his eyes and cupped his bearded chin. "It will always be yes with you."

Philip leaped to his feet and pumped his fists in the air. "She said yes."

The room exploded in applause as he guided Queen to her feet, careful of any tenderness that lingered with her ribs. He twirled her around, then slipped the ruby-and-diamond ring on her finger.

Nothing else mattered the rest of the night. Queen Jamieson was engaged.

Chapter Twenty-seven

"**I** had a hunch that Queen was more than an in-law." Nathan shook Philip's hand and snickered. "You're engaged to a classy lady."

"Thank you." Philip grinned. "We had to start somewhere, and this is where the journey took us." He adjusted his bow tie as he and his friend waited for the Valentine Day's program at their church to begin.

"The board will definitely be pleased and vote you in as a permanent pastor." Nathan bobbed his head. "I, for one, am relieved."

Why did Nathan's words make him sound as if he were a puppet? Philip huffed but kept a smile in place for anyone who was watching him. "Marrying Queen doesn't make me more qualified as a pastor. I believe her caring spirit will make me a better man. She's so much more than picture perfect."

"Sorry if that came out the wrong way," Nathan said in a low voice as couples waved at them. "Since you've come here, I've known you as an independent thinker. Queen gets you, and if you didn't love her, you wouldn't have taken the next flight out to make sure she was okay after her accident."

"That was the worse day of my life." Philip scanned the room for his beloved.

Queen reappeared from the ladies' room, and Mother Ross snagged her attention. He didn't take his eyes off her. The red paper hearts, white roses, and pink balloons created an impromptu photo shoot to capture Queen's beauty.

Philip noticed everything about her tonight—from the ring on her finger to the way Queen wore her hair. She glowed, stunning in a long red velvet dress with a satin bow and ruffles at the front side that ran the length of her leg—classy, original, and eye-catching, but no peep show.

The best part was Queen didn't fight her love for him. He thought about giving their relationship a year, but after her accident, he was reminded that life was precious, and he wanted her sooner than later.

Excusing himself, Philip went to Queen's rescue. If not, his woman—fiancée—would miss her meal exercising politeness. "Praise the Lord, Mother." He smiled, then reached for Queen's hand—the one he had slipped the ring on. "Excuse us. I believe we should take our seats so the program can start."

"You're, right, Elder. We'll talk later, sugar." She patted Queen's other hand.

Round tables draped with red tablecloths were sprinkled throughout the hall, except for the long head table reserved for the pastor-to-be and his new fiancé and the deacons and their wives. Nathan didn't seem bothered by being the lone man out. Musicians entertained their guests with love ballads as teenagers served food. During the meal, a dozen couples shared stories about how they first met.

"Did you know I was the one when we first met?" Queen whispered close to his ear as she linked her fingers with his.

Philip stared into her eyes then admired the curve of her lips before he answered. "I didn't know what to think except you were any man's biggest temptation. God opened my eyes to see your heart."

"I was expecting you to say, 'of course,' but I like your answer better."

"Your turn," Philip said as he continued to gaze at her lips. He couldn't wait for her to be his wife.

"I never thought you would be attracted to me… I figured a church girl would snag you."

They applauded with the others as another couple shared the highlights of their marriage, then he turned back to Queen. "You are exactly who I want and what I need." He chuckled. "I thought I annoyed you when we first met."

"You did." She laughed but clamped down to listen as a newlywed spoke about how different she and her husband were.

"Marriage has made each of us better, and we've grown spiritually," Sister Reynolds said, holding her husband's hand.

Philip squeezed Queen's hand. His woman made him better mentally. He was sure others had seen Queen's diamond rock, but Nathan was the only deacon to comment on it.

Countdown to the vote. The deacons wanted their pastor to have a wife, and that was what Philip was going to give them. His choice. His timing. His love.

What about My Will? God whispered.

Philip's heart skipped a beat. Immediately, he knew what God was referencing—his proposal to a woman who had not accepted God's plan of salvation as outlined in the Bible. Philip had intended to hold out as long as it took for Queen to surrender spiritually to God. Her accident and the fear that taunted him made Philip ignore the Lord's edict not to propose yet.

If he wasn't the interim pastor, pastor-in-training, or whatever title the church wanted to give him, Philip would counsel himself.

He hadn't been engaged three days and already he had doubts.

After a restless night, Philip woke early Sunday morning and checked the time. It was seven a.m., on the East Coast. His friend and confidant, Bishop Henderson, was about to get a wakeup call.

Bishop Henderson greeted Philip with sleep in his voice.

Philip gritted his teeth and rubbed the back of his neck. *Here goes.* "I have some news."

"Good, I hope."

"Well," Philip twisted his lips, "I'm engaged."

"Congratulations, my friend!" The excitement in his voice was genuine. "I knew sooner or later, one of those sisters at Total Surrender would catch your eye."

Rubbing his face, Philip braced to give the bad news. "My fiancé isn't saved." He counted the seconds of Bishop's silence. "I made a mistake."

"Exactly, what do you mean by 'I made a mistake?' Unless you have no problem being admitted to the hospital, you can't take it back."

Philip sighed. "Yeah. Queen was in a car accident. All I could think about was I could have lost her. I proposed because I love her."

"My friend," Bishop Henderson said, "you can't unpropose. If you exchange vows, you will disappoint God. If you don't exchange vows, you will hurt her."

"I know." Philip's heart ached at his dilemma. "What would *you* do?" He stood and paced his bedroom floor, agonizing over his plight.

"The same thing you would tell anyone you're counseling— pray and trust God."

"I expected that." After taking a deep breath, Philip nodded to himself. "Thanks." He ended the call.

Hours later, Philip preached the message God gave him from the pulpit, hoping now that Queen was engaged, she would respond to God's invitation to salvation. Glancing a few times at her, Queen seemed to be swept up in the Word. Maybe today was the day for her spiritual surrender.

"The best love story ever written is God's long suffering toward us and His forgiveness. You can't buy salvation nor earn it, yet it's invaluable…."

Dozens answered the call for salvation when a soloist sung a rendition of "Falling in Love with Jesus."

After service, Philip and Queen made their rounds to their families to share the news of their engagement, only to learn Ace had leaked the scoop after his wife noticed Queen's diamond ring. However, Philip's parents were surprised and ecstatic that one of their sons would finally give them a grandchild.

Queen's brothers gave him hugs, then fist bumps.

Kidd snickered. "'Bout time."

Grandma BB was blissful. "I knew it. After she had that accident, I'm surprised you waited this long. I won the poker bet with Chip and Dale. They didn't think Queen would give you the time of day."

He and Queen shared an amused look.

The time sped by until they had a few hours before Queen's flight home. They ate dinner near the airport. Once their orders were placed, Philip lifted her hand and kissed her ring finger.

"When I look at its brilliance, I'm in awe that you picked me." Queen admired her hand. "Chip and Dale betted against you, but I'm the winner."

"No, with all your secret and bold admirers, I'm the one you chose."

Her eyes watered. "You chose me, Philip. You saw me, not the hair and clothes and everything else but the real me I've never revealed to any other man."

"Thank you."

Too soon, their dinner was over. When he parked in the airport garage and escorted her inside, a heavy sorrow filled him. "This is hard," he admitted. "I don't like us being away from each other."

"Me either." She kissed him goodbye and walked toward the security checkpoint.

That was the hardest part, watching her leave. Stuffing his hands in his pockets, Philip retraced his steps to his car.

The next morning, the board would deliver their decision—finally. Nathan assured Philip his engagement to Queen was a game changer. He grunted as he slid behind the wheel. No, his engagement was a life changer. Would Queen change her mind to relocate if he became pastor?

Monday morning, Philip was ready to get the vote over with as he led the deacon board in prayer.

"Elder Dupree," Deacon Larson began the meeting, "we were happy to see your fiancé on Saturday night. You have fulfilled our requirements to be voted in as our permanent pastor."

Finally. "Thank you, Deacon.

"However," Deacon Larson said, lifting a hand as if to say not so fast, "as pleasant as Miss Jamieson is, has she fulfilled God's plan of salvation with the water and fire baptism in Jesus' name?"

"No, sir, she hasn't."

"And you still plan to marry her?" Deacon Larson pressed.

"I have no doubt in my mind that God is working on Queen—no doubt." He shook his head. "Our engagement is as much a commitment as Joseph and Mary in the Bible. I'll remain faithful to her and God until she surrenders to the Higher Authority—Jesus."

Nathan nodded his approval.

The other three didn't seem sold on Philip's answer.

Deacon Davis cleared his throat and sighed. "Elder Dupree, although that sounds admirable, we need leadership now. We have extended your trial period by six months. Are you asking for another extension?"

"In Elder Dupree's defense," Deacon Johnson cut him off, "we are the ones to blame for this confusion. We know God is not the author of such nonsense. We should have spelled it out in a written contract or told him upfront what our ideal pastor should be."

Their mission statement was to win souls for Christ, and God had placed the anointing on Philip to draw hundreds to Jesus through his evangelism ministry.

Time's up. Vote, deacons, so we all can move on. Philip was silent as they discussed his fate as if he weren't present. *God, I didn't sign up for this. I'm ready to return to the evangelism field.*

Who can I send to feed my sheep? God whispered.

Bowing his head, he repented of his grumbling. He knew his answer had always been, "Send me, Lord."

Deacon Spearman, the quietest one, spoke up. "I think Elder Philip Dupree has done a fine job as interim. Our membership has grown, and eighty percent of the congregation has voted for him to be the permanent pastor. I vote to extend his trial period for another six months—up to two years."

Again? Philip wanted to yell out his frustration but held his peace.

Displeasure was plastered on Deacons Larson and Davis' faces, but Deacon Davis voiced his opinion. "Our church has been in limbo since Elder Jolley left abruptly."

"And God sent me."

"Yes…but we have guidelines that must be followed," Deacon Larson stated.

"Added at a whim," Philip said. "The Bible has guidelines that are written in hundreds of languages. And for the record, I asked Queen to marry me, not out of a sense to meet your requirements, but because I love her, and she has always had my back. As far as her salvation, no one is more eager for her to submit to Christ than me. Only God knows her appointed time." *And I wish the Lord would give me a heads up*

The board took another vote, three-to-two in favor of another extension.

Chapter Twenty-eight

Queen added the perfect dress to her suitcase for the family photo with Ace, Talise, and the girls. This was the first time she had ever packed her Bible as a must-have accessory. Although she tried to be consistent in reading, some days she skipped.

Sometimes stories in the Old Testament were hard to digest. While her heart ached for the Israelites when they displeased God, she questioned if she would have survived during that time with all the laws and decrees.

The Lord had little patience for their foolishness and indecisiveness. Complaining got them in trouble every time. Queen had her whining moments. Would she have been doomed?

I came wrapped in human flesh as Jesus, not to condemn the world, but to save it, God whispered John 3:17.

The fact that the Lord was aware of her thoughts gave Queen hope she didn't have to be lost.

Arrived. She texted Philip when she landed in St. Louis on Friday afternoon.

Praise God. Can't wait to see your gorgeous face in a few hours. Still in meeting. XOXO

By default, the Jamieson sisters resumed their rights as her escorts from the airport. She was overjoyed to see Kami and Victoria. They were stunning in skinny jeans topped off with denim dusters. They belonged in the world of fashion.

Kami wasn't interested in the fashion industry as a major. She had a full scholarship for a psychology/criminology degree. Victoria had enrolled at the University of Central Oklahoma's fashion design program for the upcoming fall. One of the Robnett's cousin would be her roommate until Kami transferred there. Victoria wouldn't be alone.

"I've missed you two." She hugged the sisters.

"Not as much as Uncle Philip I bet," Kami teased. "You're not even spending the night with us. Is it because you're his fiancé now?"

"Absolutely not." Queen feigned a pout for forgiveness. "Our engagement doesn't change my love for my nieces. I'm staying with Ace. Aren't you two going to the Easter concert at Philip's church tonight?"

"Nope. Victoria and I are praise dancers at our church's service tonight," Kami told her as they made their way to the baggage claim area.

"I wish you were coming with us," Victoria said.

"Philip asked first." Queen smiled.

"Good thing I love Uncle Philip." Kami *hmp*hed.

"He is kinda cute." Victoria giggled.

Queen suffered a minor whiplash as she and Kami's necks jerked to look at Victoria. That was the first time Queen had ever heard Victoria compliment any guy.

Maybe there was hope that she was healing, accepting that not all men were the enemy. Queen spotted her luggage. "I bought some cute tops for both of you."

"I can't wait to start the fall semester, so I can learn how to design my own clothes and Kami's too from scratch." Victoria had light in her eyes.

"And I can't wait for you to come. Both of you."

During the drive to Ace's house, the girls chatted about what was going on at Grandma BB's, the family babies, and their excitement about Queen's upcoming wedding whenever she set a date.

"Auntie, do you think Grandma BB is getting ready to die? She keeps talking about her husband and other folks who are dead." Kami had an unreadable expression.

Queen sucked in her breath, then swallowed a lump. She didn't recall Suzette talking to or seeing their parents when she was dying. "Has she been sick?"

Victoria shook her head. "No, but she's been showing us a lot of pictures lately. She was really pretty when she was young, and her husband was fine, too."

"Kami, have you mentioned this to your mom or dad?"

"Yeah." She shrugged. "They say she does that from time to time when she gets lonely and misses Mr. Henry—her late husband—but we're living with her, and Chip and Dale check on her, so I don't see how she can feel alone."

Anyone can be lonely, even in a crowd, Queen thought. "Too bad she didn't remarry. Fifty, sixty years is a long time to be a widow."

"Maybe we should set her up with somebody." Kami named a list of dating sites.

"I don't think any man—young or old—can handle Grandma BB." Queen chuckled then frowned. "And you two stay away from those dating sites."

They arrived at Ace and Talise's. Philip would pick her up in a few hours for his church's Good Friday concert.

During the Valentine's Day's couples banquet, Queen chatted with members of his church. It was a friendly atmosphere, so it was hard to reconcile these were the same people who gave Philip grief early on.

"Tell Grandma BB I'll stop by and see her before I head back to Tulsa." Queen gave the girls a kiss and grabbed her luggage at the same time Ace opened his front door and hurried to help her.

"Hey, sis." He kissed her cheek.

Inside the doorway, Lauren jumped on her toes, waving and grinning. The girl was a carbon copy of her mother. Queen squatted and smothered her niece with kisses before taking Diamond out of her mother's arms.

"Welcome back." Talise and Queen exchanged a hug. "I'm glad you're taking the photo with us, and I'll return the baby dress for when you and Philip have your baby girl after you're married."

"That may be awhile. Right now, we're feuding over me moving here. Maybe feuding is too strong a word"

Talise reclined in a chair near the window, and Lauren climbed up on her mother's lap. "Don't you want to live here?"

"Yes. I want to be wherever Philip is, but my history isn't here and that's hard to let go, especially now that Victoria and Kami will be attending college near Tulsa. It's not easy packing up and moving away. I know that seems silly, but my emotional attachment is real."

"I get it. The only reason I waited to marry Ace was because I was pregnant, and I refused to walk down the aisle with a big belly. Otherwise, I would have married him the day he asked. Pick a date and yourselves a deadline." She shrugged. "Anyway, that's my two cents. Come on. No telling when the concert will be over, so you should eat before you go."

Queen finished her meal, showered, and changed. At the door, Philip hugged her like they hadn't seen each other in years, and she welcomed the embrace. "Hello, my wife-to-be." The excitement of the prospect was in his voice and eyes.

He waved goodbye to her family, then ushered her to his vehicle. "When I'm with you, everything is all right in my world."

To hear Philip admit the depth of his feelings for her was humbling. "I feel the same way."

Familiar faces greeted them when they entered the church. Although Philip wasn't on the program to preach at the musical, he addressed those in attendance. "It's a bittersweet day for us to remember that Jesus was the unblemished Lamb sacrifice led to slaughter. God prepared a special body for Himself wrapped in the flesh called Jesus to take in all types of sins—and illnesses. His body was like a sponge—cancer, drugs, sexual immortality, murder, lying, and the sins are endless." Philip shook his head. "We know He died before Good Friday to be in the grave three nights and three days to rise on Sunday, but we celebrate Him tonight."

Queen thought about the detailed sin offerings she had read in Leviticus. How did people keep up with it? He had explained that law was for the Jewish people to obey—because of Jesus, we have grace.

"Can we worship Jesus for the ultimate human sacrifice for our redemption?" he asked as he pulled her thoughts back into the present. "Thank You, Jesus." He waved a finger, pointing upward, then walked down from the pulpit stairs and took his seat next to Queen.

The music was empowering. One soloist left Queen breathless with a tangible emotion. Her feet and hands stung with pain and agony as if she was dying on a wooden cross.

This was the first time she'd stood next to Philip in church. Usually, he was in the pulpit. She could feel the strength of his worship as he seemed to be in a zone between him and God. Her vision blurred as Queen lifted her hands in worship.

Was God letting her know this was where he wanted her to be?

"It's time," he whispered with a nudge as if he knew her thoughts, "for you to decide. Are you ready to surrender?"

"Yes." Before Queen left St. Louis, she would set a wedding date.

Philip was confused. Queen nodded. She was ready, but during the altar call, dozens flocked down the aisle to accept God's offer of salvation, except her.

What was the holdout? What was standing in her way to commit to Christ? The Spirit of God was so thick during Friday's concert, Philip lost count of how many visitors raced to the altar for salvation. Although Queen was emotional, she didn't take one step forward.

He had to tame his frustration as they spent Saturday together, visiting with his parents who were interested in the wedding details.

"I like fall colors, so October it is, if it's okay with Philip," she told his mother.

"Six months. We've got a lot of planning to do." Veronica had that spark in her eyes, and so did Queen.

Before he knew what was going on, his mother had called the other Jamieson wives with a date. Some would be there within the hour with ideas. Philip groaned and massaged his forehead. He wasn't looking forward to being stuck in a roomful of women, but he wasn't leaving without Queen, so the torture would continue.

How can two walk except they agreed? Be not unequally yoked... Amos 3:3 and 2 Corinthians 6:14 came to Philip's mind. One was God's anger against His chosen family and the other... well, maybe that was applicable to him.

Until Queen walked into the light, she would remain in darkness, and she had been exposed to the Light from reading her Bible, attending church and lately, the concert. This was getting out of hand.

He meant what he said to the board about not marrying without Queen's salvation commitment. Her accident had caused him not to seek God's wisdom, so here he was. How could he go into the room full of women and say, "Stop the wedding! Queen needs a prayer meeting, not a planning meeting."

He held his peace. Honestly, he was surprised the Jamiesons didn't press her to get right with God because she was marrying Philip. He could use their help.

The Lord didn't work on man's deadlines, so Philip had to accept there might be a postponement—or two. But he wasn't going to pray for one. This was the kind of situation he warned believers not to get into and here he was—in that same situation. *Oh, boy.*

Queen mistook his quietness for boredom when Philip was repenting big time without anyone knowing it.

Sunday as he dressed for morning service to celebrate Jesus' Resurrection, he prayed. *Lord, help me not to get in the way of Your will for Queen.* He loved her, and love was patient, right? Not with a deadline looming for a wedding.

"Whew. Talk about pressure on a brother," he told his reflection.

Cast all your cares upon Me for I care about you, God whispered 1 Peter 5:7 as Philip left the house. If he couldn't trust God, there was no one else to rely on.

When he picked up Queen from her brother's house, the anxiety that had built up seeped out with one look at her smile. As he listened at her excitement about the wedding preparations, his heart sank. Philip reached for her hand and intertwined his fingers through hers.

Lord, I'm casting my cares. I'm casting, he prayed until he arrived at church and slid into his parking space.

Philip looked out into the crowded congregation from the pulpit. He acknowledged the large numbers of visitors in attendance. The harvest was plentiful.

"Good morning, everyone. It's an exciting day as we celebrate Jesus' grand resurrection. Gone is the need for priests to perform ritual sacrifices of blemish-free goats, rams, and sheep to forgive the people of their sins. God put on humanly flesh and became the perfect sinless sacrifice for sin. He forgave you—us—on the cross. He set you free." Philip preached.

"If Jesus died for the undeserving, lying, selfish people we are, isn't that enough for you to say thank you? The alternative is dying without Jesus. The choice is yours to make—today, not tomorrow or next week. Today is the day of your salvation. Repent of your wrongdoing and consent to be baptized as Acts 2:38 says, and let God wash your sins away. Come on."

Philip tried to catch his breath because people came from everywhere with hands lifted and tears streaming down. He took a praise break to worship God, and the congregation followed his lead. When he opened his eyes, Queen was no longer in her seat. Neither was she in the crowd standing around the altar for prayer. Where was she?

"They're ready to be baptized," Nathan whispered, and out of respect, Philip stopped the service to witness the candidates' salvation. That's when he spied Queen among others dressed in white.

He dropped to his knees in worship as the baptisms began.

With one hand gripping the back of the white gowns and the other in the air, the minister's voice boomed. "My dear brothers and sisters, upon the confession of your faith and the hope we have in the blessed Word of God, we now indeed baptize you both in the name of our Lord and Savior Jesus Christ for the remission of your sins. The Lord promises to fill you with the Holy Ghost power. The evidence is Him speaking in heavenly tongues through you, according to Acts. Receive His forgiveness and the power of the Holy Ghost."

Two by two, converts were submerged under water until it was Queen's turn to step into the pool. Philip's heart pounded as he stood. His breathing deepened as he watched God answer his prayer—no, prayers.

Queen was submerged, then she resurfaced, rejoicing. Philip shouted the loudest praise.

When the last soul was buried in water as an old creature and raised a new person, Philip addressed the congregation. "The Bible tells us when Jesus rose from the dead in Matthew 27:52 and 53: '*The tombs broke open, and the bodies of many saints who had fallen asleep were raised. After Jesus' resurrection, when they had come out of the tombs, they entered the holy city and appeared to many people.*' Many souls were buried this morning in Jesus' name, and they will have that same quickening power on the day of the rapture. If you are out still debating if you should come, let me persuade you: yes."

Something like a mist seemed to fill the sanctuary. One man in a wheelchair stood at attention, took hesitant steps then took off running and rejoicing. The roar from the congregation was louder than in a football stadium. Others who had testified about their illnesses were healed before their eyes. In Philip's spirit, he felt prayers were answered as everyone shouted praises to God.

It was truly a day of miracles. As on the Day of Pentecost, Philip heard heavenly tongues spill from mouths all around him.

The two-hour service stretched to three as no one wanted to leave the sanctuary. Philip worshipped the Lord Jesus for His presence, His healing power, and salvation. When the Spirit calmed the congregation, he gave the benediction.

Philip paced the pulpit until Queen returned to the sanctuary from the prayer room. Her arms were lifted in surrender, and God was speaking through her in heavenly tongues.

Queen saw him and tried to speak, but the Holy Ghost reigned and moved her lips, so she couldn't speak on her own. He wrapped his arm around her waist, and together they danced before the Lord.

"It's real. The Holy Ghost is real," Queen uttered in a daze.

She praised God without care that she missed her flight home.

Queen literally wanted to tell the family about her Holy Ghost experience, so Philip obliged. Siblings and cousins rejoiced with her.

Kami, Victoria, and Grandma BB's house was their final stop.

Grandma BB eyed Queen the moment she opened the door for them. "News travels. I heard about what happened to you at church today. I thought you would be my ride-or-die girl."

"You're on your own." Queen glowed. "I was fully persuaded to prepare for eternity." And you need to make a change. You should have been there. I've never seen anything like it. It was like a fog or mist—something within the sanctuary, but there was no moisture. It was almost like when God appeared at the ark of the covenant in the Old Testament…"

"Hold up. You're reading your Bible, too?" Grandma BB squinted and *tsk*ed. "*Aw nah*. What is the world coming to? I'm losing the last holdout."

"Now, I wish I hadn't held out as long as I did."

"It's time," Philip said to Queen, then spoke to God. *Lord, I can't thank you enough for putting me out of my misery*, Philip took Queen's hand and lead her away to his vehicle to catch her rescheduled flight home.

Chapter Twenty-nine

Two things Queen couldn't live without—Jesus' salvation and Philip's love. Since receiving her new birth with Jesus, Philip recommended she visit Resurrection Temple in Tulsa.

She did. The weekly Sunday services and Bible classes strengthened her spiritually. The Lord had revealed to her the fashion program at the university would thrive. That Word had triggered tears of joy.

With that news, Queen made the decision to move to St. Louis.

During the following months, Queen's newfound happiness battled with the sadness of saying goodbye to her hometown. Cori and Trice threw her a farewell dinner/bridal shower. Her staff gave her a going away party, although her boss said she could work remotely. The university board, blogger, two of the graduates in the fashion design program gave her the best gift: They offered to design her wedding gown.

It was becoming so real. She would marry Philip, become a church's first lady, and live surrounded by family—all of them, the Jamiesons and Robnetts.

Cameron had connected the dots. Frederic had been on point. The Jamieson men accepted the truth. They extended an olive branch to the Robnetts—their distant cousins on Paki's maternal side.

Despite Queen's upcoming move from Tulsa, Parke and Cheney couldn't talk their daughters out of leaving St. Louis to attend the University of Central Oklahoma. Victoria was sold on the school's fashion program.

"Auntie can come visit us," Victoria said as if it was no big deal.

The sisters were worried about leaving Grandma BB. The family matriarch threatened them if they didn't leave to pursue their dreams, she would put them out. Grandma BB never bluffed.

Philip sent movers to pack up her things. Now, his plane should land any minute, so he would help her drive back to St. Louis. While waiting, Queen reminisced how many times she had cleared the terminal, traveling to this or that city. Would she miss that freedom?

Seeing Philip answered her question: no. He swaggered toward her with flowers and greeted her with a hug and kiss. "Ready?" He searched her eyes.

Queen choked. "I didn't think this would be so hard."

He looped in fingers through hers and brought her hand to his lips for a kiss. "It's a new beginning for both of us, but every time you want to come back to visit, I'll be right by your side."

"Okay." Her voice cracked.

They ate then met the movers who were loading furniture into the truck at her house. She offered to give away or sale her furnishings, but Philip liked her tastes and said to bring it to their new home.

"I know we're leaving early in the morning, so can we go to Memorial Park Cemetery today?"

"Sure, babe." Philip squeezed her hand.

Twenty minutes later, she drove into the cemetery and parked. She had purchased a dozen roses. They followed a trail that took Queen to her loved ones.

The first stop was Samuel Jamieson. She placed a rose on his grave. "Daddy, I'm leaving to get married. I know you weren't perfect, but you left behind siblings who love me. Thank you for my gifts, and now I'm getting married to a man who loves me, too."

"I do," Philip whispered beside her.

Next, she lay three roses on her mother's grave. "Mommy, I'm saved now, and I'm marrying a pastor. Funny, huh? We never saw that coming."

She rested roses on her maternal grandparents' graves and finally, the remaining ones were for Suzette Shay Jamieson.

Queen struggled to get words out before she broke down and sobbed. Philip wrapped his arms around her and spoke soothing words of comfort as he wiped the tears from her eyes.

Regaining her composure, she faced Suzette's tombstone. "Well, sis, I'm leaving you, too. I never thought I would say that." She sniffed and fought back more tears. "But I'm getting married. You would approve. I've worked hard on endowment scholarships for the fashion design program at the university. It's going to be okay. Our younger cousins, who I call my nieces, are enrolling there. You would be proud."

Philip remained silent as Queen spilled out everything that was on her heart. When she ran out of words, she turned to him. "I'm ready."

His eyes were watery, too, as he squeezed her hand. No words were exchanged as they returned to the car. When he got behind the wheel, Philip programmed the GPS back to her house. "Close your eyes and rest your mind. I love you, Queen, and I'll make sure you'll always know that."

The offer came unexpectedly a month before he and Queen were to wed. The same week the deacon board would vote to install Philip as the official pastor ahead of his pending nuptials.

"We're aware of the delays of your status naming you as pastor at Total Surrender Church. With that open door, we would like to offer you a written contract to become pastor of Resurrection Temple here in Tulsa—no waiting period, and you'll be in control to run the congregation as God gives you leadership. I've decided to retire if you will be my replacement. I believe in your anointing."

Pastor Franklin continued. "Evangelist Dupree, are you interested in returning to Tulsa and accepting the position?"

Philip was speechless. Was he still breathing? Did he hear right? His mind drifted back to the day at the cemetery as Queen said her final goodbyes to her family. It tore at his heart. At that moment, he promised to do whatever was in his power to make her happy and never regret saying yes to being his wife.

Lord, is this a joke? "Yes, of course I'm interested in hearing the details of the pastorate and reading the contract. I need to speak with my fiancée first. Most importantly, I need to consult with the Lord. As you can imagine, I thought the Lord Jesus had already spoken."

"Pray over your decision, son, and let us know within a week."

"Will do."

Ending the call, Philip sat in silence. "Lord? Speak to me." He closed his eyes and rested his chin on top of his folded hands. "Jesus, don't let Satan intercept Your answer," he said, referring to Daniel's twenty-one-day delay getting the Word because of the devil's tactics in Daniel 10:13. "I meet with the board in two days and marry Queen in a month. Lord, direct my path expediently."

Philip didn't know how long he stayed in his office praying, but when Queen's ringtone interrupted, he ended with an amen. "Hey, baby. How's your day going?"

Queen didn't answer right away. "You don't sound right. What's wrong?"

He rubbed his face. "I'm waiting on an answer from the Lord that concerns us."

"Now, you're scaring me, Philip. Can you break away for lunch?"

He checked the time. He had two afternoon appointments. "Yep. I'm on my way."

Within an hour, they were seated at The Abbey's for lunch, and Queen listened intently as he repeated his conversation with Pastor Franklin in Tulsa. Her face lit up, and her eyes sparkled. Her lips curled in a smile. "Wow."

"You think we should take the offer?" Philip was clueless what to do.

"Nope. I'm not saying that. I would love to go home, and I do like that church, but this is about what God wants you to do. You said God doesn't change His mind." She paused and picked at her napkin. "You've established yourself here. Your parents are members, and I think some of the other Jamiesons plan to move membership to help you. Grandma BB…"

Philip rubbed his forehead. "Yeah, she already told me she wants to be appointed to the mother's board. I told her it doesn't work like that. She needs to get her soul right with the Lord first before she can serve others."

She rested her hand on his. "I'll follow you as long as you follow Christ. Home really is where the heart is."

"You're amazing. I guess it's time to fast and pray for clarity before I meet with the board."

"We can do that."

"Woman, do you know how much I love you?" Philip took both her hands and kissed them. He thought she would jump on the chance to go back to Tulsa.

"I do."

"Come on, let's get out of here. Let the fast begin."

Queen gathered her purse and took his hand.

Epilogue

The movie *Coming to America,* or its sequel, had nothing on Queen and Philip's nuptials in Victoria's opinion. Queen wouldn't be a Jamieson if her wedding party didn't overflow with family. No one was excluded from the festivities—babies to the elders—except…

Frederic.

Because of his behavior toward Queen, the Jamiesons banned him from all family functions. The Robnetts, appalled, too, excluded him from most gatherings.

The Duprees and Jamieson joined forces to help with the wedding preparations. Philip and Parke's mothers took charge of the cake, flowers, venue, and decor.

Queen's bridesmaids were a family production: Talise, Eva, Gabrielle, Cheney, Hali, Kami, Victoria, Gigi, Lacey, and Candy, then Cori and Trice.

She wanted to include the Robnetts too. When she learned they could sing, she asked them to provide her music entertainment for the ceremony and at the reception.

Perfect. Queen Bee, Rejoice, Sapphire, and Duchess's vocals harmonized with Princess and Jewel's musical strengths on piano and violin.

Drexel and Dashan Dupree were Philip's groomsmen. His father, Dr. Dupree, choked with emotion when Philip asked him to be the best man. Nathan and the rest of the Jamiesons filled the empty slots.

Just when Queen thought she had the perfect wedding planned, her brothers clashed on a Zoom call. During the virtual meeting at Philip's, Queen laid down the assignments.

"Kidd, as my big brother, will you escort me down the aisle?"

"No problem, sis. Yep."

"Hold up." Jayson waved his hand. "Mayson and I are the oldest. Shouldn't we escort our baby sister?"

"Nah." Kidd smirked. "I got this. You just recently claimed her. I've been protecting her as my little sister since day one. I own that right."

Queen sighed as Philip whispered, "Should I start praying?"

"Probably," she mouthed.

"I got your back, bro." Ace didn't blink.

"If you need a vote," Parke paused, "you've got mine, Cameron, and Malcolm."

"Stay out of this, Parke," Jayson warned. "Your daddy wasn't Samuel. This is between me and my baby brother."

"Who are you calling a baby?" Ace spoke up.

"Oh, boy." Queen rubbed her forehead and muted them so she could speak. "I love all of you dearly. Our father, who wasn't the best husband and father to the first family, left me with gifts: brothers. I have no problem having my six brothers escort me to the altar. I am a queen, you know."

She snickered, meaning it as a joke. "Please don't mess this up for me. I want the day to be perfect and my siblings to get along. I may be the baby in the family and in the Lord, but I've learned how to pray." She linked her fingers through Philip's. "Satan's confusion is not on the guest list. The best wedding present you can give me is to love one another. Please."

Queen held her breath as each nodded their agreement before she unmuted them all. "I love you, Mayson, Jayson, Benjamin, Zaki, Kidd, and Ace." She called them off in the order of their birth.

"Okay, sis. We'll behave." Jayson grinned, and his dimple winked at her.

"Whew." Disaster averted. She thanked the Lord.

When the day arrived, Queen sat in the bridal chamber.

Blissful.

Hopeful.

Nervous.

Gigi placed a pearl-encrusted crown on top of Queen's silky mane, which had been straightened and styled with a mass of curls for the occasion. "You're stunning, little sister."

"What was I thinking when I agreed to a wedding?" Queen fanned her face. "I think Vegas isn't overrated."

"Nah. Not you—definitely not Queen Jamieson." Gabrielle patted her shoulder.

"We're celebrating your love for Philip. You've got everything going for you: a handsome husband who believes in prayers, family from far and near, and a congregation who has packed the sanctuary to witness the vows of their newly elected pastor and their soon-to-be first lady." Gabrielle smiled, and it reminded Queen of Philip.

"More reasons to hyperventilate." Queen inhaled and exhaled.

"Sounds like it's prayer time for my daughter-in-love-to-be," Veronica Dupree said as there was a knock at the door.

"I think they're coming to escort me." Grandma BB hurried to the door in her two-toned Stacy Adams shoes, which clashed with her formal gown.

Whatever. Coordination was the least of her worries at the moment.

Kami opened the door, and Gabriel raced inside with a small envelope and headed for his mother.

Gabrielle kissed her son. "What are you doing in here?"

"Uncle Philip told me to give it to Auntie." Gabrielle took the envelope and eyed it. "*Hmmm*. What is my brother up to? He'd better not be backing out."

Queen snatched it out of her hand. "You know things like that happen. Not funny." She read Philip's handwriting across the envelope. *To be opened by Mrs. Philip Dupree on our honeymoon night.*

Whoa. Queen's mind wondered.

"Judging from the goofy grin on Queen's face, there's definitely going to be a wedding." Cori laughed and high-fived Trice.

Gabrielle sent her son out as the violin struck the first chord.

"Thirty-second prayer." Veronica instructed the ladies to form a circle around the bride.

After the Amens, one by one, her family left, each touching her cheek, so as not to leave evidence of their lipstick.

Left alone, Queen closed her eyes and thanked God for her husband-to-be who was hidden in plain sight.

The traditional wedding march echoed throughout the church, then came a hard knock at the door. Queen opened it, and all her brothers were standing there. The lineup was supposed to be the oldest to the youngest, but somehow it was reversed. Ace and Kidd stood on either side of her with their elbows extended.

Jayson answered her unspoken question. "We decided that the first shall be last...and the last first." He winked, and she mouthed her thanks.

With her six brothers, Queen took her first step toward the aisle that led to the altar where Philip waited for her.

She locked eyes with him, and his strength guided her. Queen had never seen him grin so broadly as when her entourage stopped. Philip shook each of her brothers' hands and thanked them and promised to protect and love her. Her eyes watered with emotion.

"Who gives this woman away?" Bishop Henderson, who was officiating, asked.

Queen expected her brothers to stand, but her sisters and the Robnetts popped up, too. She'd never felt so loved.

After exchanging traditional vows, they were pronounced husband and wife.

"And," Bishop Henderson's voice boomed throughout the sanctuary, "let no man or woman come between you to break your union. Pastor Dupree, you may now kiss the first lady of Total Surrender Church as your wife."

Book Club Discussions

1. Queen wanted the fashion program to thrive in her sister's memory. Name something you've done in a person's honor after their death.

2. Philip confided in Queen about his woes with the congregation. Was this a good idea? Or discuss whether you think revealing discord in the church could hinder a person's spiritual growth or coming to the Lord.

3. Discuss Queen's relationship with her half-siblings in Hartford.

4. Total Surrender put stipulations on Philip after the fact. In your opinion, were those weighing on Philip when he proposed to Queen? Why or why not?

5. Discuss Queen's reasons for not relocating to St. Louis. Did they matter once she was in a relationship with Philip?

Author's note:

Guilty of Love kicked off my popular Jamieson Legacy series in the fall of 2007. Ten books later, Grandma BB's shenanigans and the Jamiesons' antics are still going strong. Many fans ask me if the Jamiesons are real—not in the beginning, but I have learned I had a history with Jamiesons.

Charlott (e) Jamison (a mulatto) was born in 1842 in South Carolina.

By 1850, she was believed to be in the household of slaveholder, Robert Jamison in Mississippi.

On the 1860 census, in Chickasaw, Mississippi, there was white man named John Wilkinson living in the household of Robert Jamison. John is listed as a "teacher in Academy."

He was 23 years-old and born in Alabama.

Most likely he is my great-great-grandfather. Charlott was 18 years old. John also married the slaveholder's only daughter—Artie. They had sons, including one who he named Sam like the one with Charlott(e).

In 1865, two years after the Emancipation Proclamation, my great-grandfather, William Wilkinson (Wilkerson) was born.

In 1867, the birth of Sam was recorded.

By 1880, Charlott Wilkinson was listed as a widow while in the same county John Wilkinson was married to Artie Jamison. She was living with another widow, Martha Leopard. No connection.

Her son, my great grandfather, William, died in the early 1900s in his 80s.

Both sons were considered "near White." Family rumor has Sam Wilkinson going up North to pass as white. To date, no one knows the whereabouts of his descendants.

The world of family genealogy is fascinating and in every Jamieson Legacy novel, I bring one of my ancestors to life.

The Robnetts, introduced as the Jamiesons' cousins, are real. The family held a special place in my heart as a teenager through adulthood. There are a couple of Robnett slaveholders in Boone County, Missouri. Whether they are related to my Robnetts are unknown.

About the Author

Pat Simmons is a multi-published Christian romance author with more than thirty-five titles. She is a self-proclaimed genealogy sleuth who is passionate about researching her ancestors, then casting them in starring roles in her novels. She is a four-time recipient of the Romance Slam Jam Emma Rodgers Award for Best Inspirational Romance: *Still Guilty*, *Crowning Glory*, *The Confession*, and *Christmas Dinner*.

Pat's first inspirational women's fiction, *Lean on Me*, with Sourcebooks, was the February/March Together We Read Digital Book Club pick for the national library system. *Here for You* and *Stand by Me* are also part of the Family is Forever series. Her holiday indie release, *Christmas Dinner won RSJ 2021 Best Book of the Year* and *Best Inspirational Romance*. *Christmas Dinner* and *Here for You* were featured in *Woman's World*, a national magazine. *Here for You* was also listed in the "7 Great Reads That Help to Keep the Faith" by Sisters From AARP. She contributed an article, "I'm Listening" in the *Chicken Soup for the Soul: I'm Speaking Now* (2021).

Pat describes the evidence of the gift of the Holy Ghost as a life-altering experience. She has been a featured speaker and workshop presenter at various venues across the country. Pat has converted her sofa-strapped sports fanatical husband into an amateur travel agent, untrained bodyguard, GPS-guided chauffeur, and administrative assistant who is constantly on probation. They have a son and a daughter. Pat holds a B.S. in mass communications from Emerson College in Boston, Massachusetts and worked in various positions in radio, television, and print media for more than twenty years. She oversaw the media publicity for the annual RT Booklovers Conventions for fourteen years. Visit her at www.patsimmons.net.

Other Christian Titles

<u>Making Love Work Anthology</u>
Book 1: *Love at Work*
Book 2: *Words of Love*
Book 3: *A Mother's Love*

<u>Restore My Soul series:</u>
Book 1: *Crowning Glory*
Book 2: *Jet: The Back Story*
Book 3: *Love Led by the Spirit*

<u>Family is Forever series:</u>
Book 1: *Lean on Me*
Book 2: *Here for You*
Book 3: *Stand by Me*

<u>God's Gifts series:</u>
Book1: *Couple by Christmas*
Book 2: *Prayers Answered by Christmas*

<u>Perfect Chance at Love series:</u>
Book 1: *Love by Delivery*
Book 2: *Late Summer Love*

<u>Single titles</u>
Talk to Me
Her Dress (novella)
Christmas Dinner
Christmas Greetings
Waiting for Christmas
Taye's Gift

<u>Anderson Brothers series:</u>

Book 1: *Love for the Holidays (Three novellas): A Christian Christmas, A Christian Easter, and A Christian Father's Day*
Book 2: *A Woman After David's Heart (Valentine's Day)*
Book 3: *A Noelle for Nathan (Book 3 of the Andersen Brothers)*

In *Love by Delivery*, Senior Accounts Manager Dominique Hayes has it all: money, a car and a condo. Well, almost. She's starting to believe love has passed her by. One thing for sure, she can't hurry God, so she continues to wait while losing hope that a special Godly man will ever make his appearance. Package Courier Ashton Taylor knows a man who finds a wife finds a good thing. The only thing standing in his way of finding the right woman is his long work hours. Or maybe not. A chance meeting changes everything. When love finally comes knocking, will Dominique open the door and accept Ashton's special delivery?

In *Late Summer Love*, it takes strategies to win a war, but prayer and spiritual intervention are needed to win a godly woman's heart. God has been calling out to Blake Cross ever since Blake was deployed in Iraq and he took his safety for granted. Now, back on American soil, Blake still won't surrender his soul--until he meets Paige Blake during a family reunion. When the Lord gives Blake an ultimatum, is Blake listening, and is he finally ready to learn what it takes to be a godly man fit for a godly woman?

In *Crowning Glory*, Cinderella had a prince; Karyn Wallace has a King. While Karyn served four years in prison for an unthinkable crime, she embraced salvation through Crowns for Christ outreach ministry. After her release, Karyn stays strong and confident, despite the stigma society places on ex-offenders. Since Christ strengthens the underdog, Karyn refuses to sway away from the scripture, "He who the Son has set free is free indeed." Levi Tolliver, for the most part, is a practicing Christian. One contradiction is he doesn't believe in turning the other cheek. He's steadfast there is a price to pay for every sin committed, especially after the untimely death of his wife during a robbery. Then Karyn enters Levi's life. He is enthralled not only with her beauty, but her sweet spirit until he learns about her incarceration. If Levi can accept that Christ paid Karyn's debt in full, then a treasure awaits him. This is a powerful tale and reminds readers of the permanency of redemption.

Jet: The Back Story to Love Led By the Spirit, to say Jesetta "Jet" Hutchens has issues is an understatement. In Crowning Glory, Book 1 of the Restoring My Soul series, she releases a firestorm of anger with an unforgiving heart. But every hurting soul has a history. In Jet: The Back Story to Love Led by the Spirit, Jet doesn't know how to cope with the loss of her younger sister, Diane. But God sets her on the road to a spiritual recovery. To make sure she doesn't get lost, Jesus sends the handsome and single Minister Rossi Tolliver to be her guide. Psalm 147:3 says Jesus can heal the brokenhearted and bind up their wounds. That sets the stage for Love Led by the Spirit.

In *Love Led By the Spirit*, Minister Rossi Tolliver is ready to settle down. Besides the outwardly attraction, he desires a woman who is sweet, humble, and loves church folks. Sounds simple enough on paper, but when he gets off his knees, praying for that special someone to come into his life, God opens his eyes to the woman who has been there all along. There is only a slight problem. Love is the farthest thing from Jesetta "Jet" Hutchens' mind. But Rossi, the man and the minister, is hard to resist. Is Jet ready to allow the Holy Spirit to lead her to love?

LOVE AT THE CROSSROADS SERIES

In *Stopping Traffic*, Book 1, Candace Clark has a phobia about crossing the street, and for good reason. As fate would have it, her daughter's principal assigns her to crossing guard duties as part of the school's Parent Participation program. With no choice in the matter, Candace begrudgingly accepts her stop sign and safety vest, then reports to her designated crosswalk. Once Candace is determined to overcome her fears, God opens the door for a blessing, and Royce Kavanaugh enters her life, a firefighter built to rescue any damsel in distress. When a spark of attraction ignites, Candace and Royce soon discover there's more than one way to stop traffic.

In *A Baby For Christmas*, Book 2, yes, diamonds are a girl's best friend, but in Solae Wyatt-Palmer's case, she desires something more valuable. Captain Hershel Kavanaugh is a divorcee and the father of two adorable little boys. Solae has never been married and longs to be a mother. Although Hershel showers her with expensive gifts, his hesitation about proposing causes Solae to walk and never look back. As the holidays approach, Hershel must convince Solae that she has everything he could ever want for Christmas.

In *The Keepsake*, Book 3, Until death us do part...or until Desiree walks away. Desiree "Desi" Bishop is devastated when she finds evidence of her husband's affair. God knew she didn't get married only to one day stand before a judge and file for a divorce. But Desi wants out no matter how much her heart says to forgive Michael. That isn't easier said than done. She sees God's one acceptable reason for a divorce as the only opt-out clause in her marriage. Michael Bishop is a repenting man who loves his wife of three years. If only…he had paid attention to the red flags God sent to keep him from falling into the devil's snares. But Michael didn't and he had fallen. Although God had forgiven him instantly when he repented, Desi's forgiveness is moving as a snail's pace. In the end, after all the tears have been shed and forgiveness granted and received, the couple learns that some marriages are worth keeping

In *What God Has For Me*, Book 4, Halcyon Holland is leaving her live-in boyfriend, taking their daughter and the baby in her belly with her. She's tired of waiting for the ring, so she buys herself one. When her ex doesn't reconcile their relationship, Halcyon begins to second-guess whether she compromised her chance for a happily ever after. After all, what man in his right mind would want to deal with the community stigma of 'baby mama drama?' But Zachary Bishop has had his eye on Halcyon since the first time he saw her. Without a ring on her finger, Zachary prays that she will come to her senses and not only leave Scott, but come back to God. What one man doesn't cherish; Zach is ready to treasure. Not deterred by Halcyon's broken spirit, Zachary is on a mission to offer her a second chance at love that she can't refuse. And as far as her adorable children are concerned, Zachary's love is unconditional for a ready-made family. Halcyon will soon learn that her past circumstances won't hinder the Lord's blessings, because what God has for her, is for her…and him…and the children.

In *Every Woman Needs a Praying Man*, Book 5, first impressions can make or break a business deal and they could be a relationship buster, but an ill-timed panic attack draws two strangers together. Unlike firefighters who run into danger, instincts tell businessman Tyson Graham to head the other way as fast as he can when he meets a certain damsel in distress. Days later, the same woman struts through his door for a job interview. Monica Wyatt might possess the outwardly beauty and the brains on paper, but Tyson doesn't trust her to work for his firm, or maybe he doesn't trust his heart around her.

In *A Christian Christmas*, Book 1, Christian's Christmas will never be the same for Joy Knight if Christian Andersen has his way. Not to be confused with a secret Santa, Christian and his family are busier than Santa's elves making sure the Lord's blessings are distributed to those less fortunate by Christmas day. Joy is playing the hand that life dealt her, rearing four children in a home that is on the brink of foreclosure. She's not looking for a handout, but when Christian rescues her in the checkout line; her niece thinks Christian is an angel. Joy thinks he's just another man who will eventually leave, disappointing her and the children. Although Christian is a servant of the Lord, he is a flesh and blood man and all he wants for Christmas is Joy Knight. Can time spent with Christian turn Joy's attention from her financial woes to the real meaning of Christmas—and true love?

In *A Christian Easter*, how to celebrate Easter becomes a balancing act for Christian and Joy Andersen and their four children. Chocolate bunnies, colorful stuffed baskets and flashy fashion shows are their competition. Despite the enticements, Christian refuses to succumb without a fight. And it becomes a tug of war when his recently adopted ten-year-old daughter, Bethani, wants to participate in her friend's Easter tradition. Christian hopes he has instilled Proverbs 22:6, into the children's heart in the short time of being their dad.

In *A Christian Father's Day*, three fathers, one Father's Day and four children. Will the real dad, please stand up. It's never too late to be a father—or is it? Christian Andersen was looking forward to spending his first Father's Day with his adopted children---all four of them. But Father's Day becomes more complicated than Christian, or Joy ever imagined. Christian finds himself faced with living up to his name when things don't go his way to enjoy an idyllic once a year celebration. But he depends on God to guide him through the journey.
(All three of Christian's individual stories are in the Love for the Holidays)

In *A Woman After David's Heart*, Book 2, David Andersen doesn't have a problem indulging in Valentine's Day, per se, but not on a first date. Considering it was the love fest of the year, he didn't want a woman to get any ideas that a wedding ring was forthcoming before he got a chance to know her. He has no choice but to wait until the whole Valentine's Day hoopla was over, then he would make his move on a sister in his church that caught his eyes. For the past two years and counting, Valerie Hart hasn't been the recipient of a romantic Valentine's Day dinner invitation. To fill the void, Valerie keeps herself busy with God's business, hoping the Lord will send her perfect mate soon. Unfortunately, with no prospects in sight, it looks like that won't happen again this year. A Woman After David's Heart is a Valentine romance novella that can be enjoyed with or without a box of chocolates.

In *A Noelle for Nathan*, Book 3, is a story of kindness, selflessness, and falling in love during the Christmas season. Andersen Investors & Consultants, LLC, CFO Nathan Andersen (A Christian Christmas) isn't looking for attention when he buys a homeless man a meal, but grade schoolteacher Noelle Foster is watching his every move with admiration. His generosity makes him a man after her own heart. While donors give more to children and families in need around the holiday season, Noelle Foster believes in giving year-round after seeing many of her students struggle with hunger and finding a warm bed at night. At a second-chance meeting, sparks fly when Noelle and Nathan share a kindred spirit with their passion to help those less fortunate. Whether they're doing charity work or attending Christmas parties, the couple becomes inseparable. Although Noelle and Nathan exchange gifts, the biggest present is the one from Christ.

MAKING LOVE WORK SERIES

This series can be read in any order.

In *A Mother's Love*, to Jillian Carter, it's bad when her own daughter beats her to the altar. She became a teenage mother when she confused love for lust one summer. Despite the sins of her past, Jesus forgave her and blessed her to be the best Christian example for Shana. Jillian is not looking forward to becoming an empty nester at thirty-nine. The adage, she's not losing a daughter, but gaining a son-in-law is not comforting as she braces for a lonely life ahead. What she doesn't expect is for two men to vie for her affections: Shana's biological father who breezes back into their lives as a redeemed man and practicing Christian. Not only is Alex still goof looking, but he's willing to right the wrong he's done in the past. Not if Dr. Dexter Harris has anything to say about it. The widower father of the groom has set his sights on Jillian and he's willing to pull out all the stops to woo her. Now the choice is hers. Who will be the next mother's love?

In *Love at Work*, how do two people go undercover to hide an office romance in a busy television newsroom? In plain sight, of course. Desiree King is an assignment editor at KDPX-TV in St. Louis, MO. She dispatches a team to wherever breaking news happens. Her focus is to stay ahead of the competition. Overall, she's easy-going, respectable, and compassionate. But when it comes to dating a fellow coworker, she refuses to cross that professional line. Award-winning investigative reporter Bryan Mitchell makes life challenging for Desiree with his thoughtful gestures, sweet notes, and support. He tries to convince Desiree that as Christians, they could show coworkers how to blend their personal and private lives without compromising their morals.

In *Words of Love*, call it old fashion, but Simone French was smitten with a love letter. Not a text, email, or Facebook post, but a love letter sent through snail mail. The prose wasn't the corny roses-are-red-and-violets-are-blue stuff. The first letter contained short accolades for a job well done. Soon after, the missives were filled with passionate words from a man who confessed the hidden secrets of his soul. He revealed his unspoken weaknesses, listed his uncompromising desires, and unapologetically noted his subtle strengths. Yes, Rice Taylor was ready to surrender to love. Whew. Closing her eyes, Simone inhaled the faint lingering smell of roses on the beige plain stationery. She had a testimony. If anyone would listen, she would proclaim that love was truly blind.

In *Talk to Me*, despite being deaf because of a fireworks explosion, CEO of a St. Louis non-profit company, Noel Richardson, expertly navigates the hearing world. What some view as a disability, Noel views as a challenge—his lack of hearing has never held him back. It also helps that he has great looks, numerous university degrees, and full bank accounts. But those assets don't define him as a man who longs for the right woman in his life. Deciding to visit a church service, Noel is blind-sided by the most beautiful and graceful Deaf interpreter he's ever seen. Mackenzie Norton challenges him on every level through words and signing, but as their love grows, their faith is tested. When their church holds a yearly revival, they witness the healing power of God in others. Mackenzie has faith to believe that Noel can also get in on the blessing. Since faith comes by hearing, whose voice does Noel hear in his heart, Mackenzie or God's?

TESTIMONY: If I Should Die Before I Wake. It is of the LORD's mercies that we are not consumed, because His compassions fail not. They are new every morning, great is Thy faithfulness. Lamentations 3:22-23, God's mercies are sure; His promises are fulfilled; but a dawn of a new morning is God' grace. If you need a testimony about God's *grace, then If I Should Die Before I Wake* will encourage your soul. Nothing happens in our lives by chance. If you need a miracle, God's got that too. Trust Him. Has it been a while since you've had a testimony? Increase your prayer life, build your faith, and walk in victory because without a test, there is no testimony. (eBook only)

In *Her Dress*, sometimes a woman just wants to splurge on something new, especially when she's about to attend an event with movers and shakers. Find out what happens when Pepper Trudeau is all dressed up and goes to the ball, but another woman is modeling the same attire. At first, Pepper is embarrassed, then the night gets interesting when she meets Drake Logan. *Her Dress* is a romantic novella about the all-too-common occurrence—two women shopping at the same place. Maybe having the same taste isn't all bad. Sometimes a good dress is all you need to meet the man of your dreams. (eBook only)

In *Christmas Greetings*, Saige Carter loves everything about Christmas: the shopping, the food, the lights, and of course, Christmas wouldn't be complete without family and friends to share in the traditions they've created together. Plus, Saige is extra excited about her line of Christmas greeting cards hitting store shelves, but when she gets devastating news around the holidays, she wonders if she'll ever look at Christmas the same again. Daniel Washington is no Scrooge, but he'd rather skip the holidays altogether than spend them with his estranged family. After one too many arguments around the dinner table one year, Daniel had enough and walked away from the drama. As one year has turned into many, no one seems willing to take the first step toward reconciliation. When Daniel reads one of Saige's greeting cards, he's unsure if the words inside are enough to erase the pain and bring about forgiveness. Once God reveals to them His purpose for their lives, they will have a reason to rejoice.

In *Guilty of Love*, when do you know the most important decision of your life is the right one? Reaping the seeds from what she's sown; Cheney Reynolds moves into a historic neighborhood in Ferguson, Missouri, and becomes a reclusive. Her first neighbor, the incomparable Mrs. Beatrice Tilley Beacon aka Grandma BB, is an opinionated childless widow. Grandma BB is a self-proclaimed expert on topics Cheney isn't seeking advice—everything from landscaping to hip-hop dancing to romance. Then there is Parke Kokumuo Jamison VI, a direct descendant of a royal African tribe. He learned his family ancestry, African history, and lineage preservation before he could count. Unwittingly, they are drawn to each other, but it takes Christ to weave their lives into a spiritual bliss while He exonerates their past indiscretions.

In *Not Guilty*, one man, one woman, one God and one big problem. Malcolm Jamieson wasn't the man who got away, but the man God instructed Hallison Dinkins to set free. Instead of their explosive love affair leading them to the wedding altar, God diverted Hallison to the prayer altar during her first visit back to church in years. Malcolm was convinced that his woman had loss her mind to break off their engagement. Didn't Hallison know that Malcolm, a tenth-generation descendant of a royal African tribe, couldn't be replaced? Once Malcolm concedes that their relationship can't be savaged, he issues Hallison his own edict, "If we're meant to be with each other, we'll find our way back. If not, that means that there's a love stronger than what we had." His words begin to haunt Hallison until she begins to regret their breakup, and that's where their story begins. Someone must retreat, and God never loses a battle.

In *Still Guilty*, Cheney Reynolds Jamieson made a choice years ago that is now shaping her future and the future of the men she loves. A botched abortion left her unable to carry a baby to term, and her husband, Parke K. Jamison VI, is expected to produce heirs. With a wife who cannot give him a child, Parke vows to find and get custody of his illegitimate son by any means necessary. Meanwhile, Cheney's twin brother, Rainey, struggles with his anger over his ex-girlfriend's actions that haunt him, and their father, Dr. Roland Reynolds, fights to keep an old secret in the past.

In *The Acquittal*, two worlds apart, but their hearts dance to the same African drum beat. On a professional level, Dr. Rainey Reynolds is a competent, highly sought-after orthodontist. Inwardly, he needs to be set free from the chaos of revelations that make him question if happiness is obtainable. To get away from the drama, Rainey is willing to leave the country under the guise of a mission trip with Dentist Without Borders. Will changing his surroundings really change him? If one woman can heal his wounds, then he will believe that there is really peace after the storm.

Ghanaian beauty Josephine Abena Yaa Amoah returns to Africa after completing her studies as an exchange student in St. Louis, Missouri. Although her heart bleeds for his peace, she knows she must step back and pray for Rainey's surrender to Christ for God to acquit him of his self-inflicted mental torture. In the Motherland of Ghana, Africa, Rainey not only visits the places of his ancestors, will he embrace the liberty that Christ's Blood really does set every man free.

In *Guilty by Association*, how important is a name? To the St. Louis Jamiesons who are tenth generation descendants of a royal African tribe—everything. To the Boston Jamiesons whose father never married their mother—there is no loyalty or legacy. Kidd Jamieson suffers from the "angry" male syndrome because his father was an absent in the home, but insisted his two sons carry his last name. It takes an old woman who mingles genealogy truths and Bible verses together for Kidd to realize his worth as a strong black man. He learns it's not his association with the name that identifies him, but the man he becomes that defines him.

In *The Guilt Trip*, Aaron "Ace" Jamieson is living a carefree life. He's good-looking, respectable when he's in the mood, but his weakness is women. If a woman tries to ambush him with a pregnancy, he takes off in the other direction. It's a lesson learned from his absentee father that responsibility is optional. Talise Rogers has a bright future ahead of her. She's pretty and has no problem catching a man's eye, which is exactly what she does with Ace. Trapping Ace Jamieson is the furthest thing from Talise's mind when she learns she pregnant and Ace rejects her. "I want nothing from you Ace, not even your name." And Talise meant it.

In *Free From Guilt*, it's salvation round-up time and Cameron Jamieson's name is on God's hit list. Although his brothers and cousins embraced God—thanks to the women in their lives—the two-degreed MIT graduate isn't going to let any woman take him down that path without a fight. He's satisfied with his career, social calendar, and good genes. But God uses a beautiful messenger, Gabrielle Dupree, to show him that he's in a spiritual deficit. Cameron learns the hard way that man's wisdom is like foolishness to God. For every philosophical argument he throws her way, Gabrielle exposes him to scriptures that makes him question his worldly knowledge.

In *The Confession*, Sandra Nicholson had made good and bad choices throughout the years, but the best one was to give her life to Christ when her sons were small and to rear them up in the best Christian way she knew how. That was thirty something years ago and Sandra has evolved from a young single mother of two rambunctious boys, Kidd and Ace Jamieson, to a godly woman seasoned with wisdom. Despite the challenges and trials of rearing two strong-willed personalities, Sandra maintained her sanity through the grace of God, which kept gray strands at bay.

Now, Sandra Nicholson is on the threshold of happiness, but Kidd believes no man is good enough for his mother, especially if her love interest could be a man just like his absentee father.

In *The Guilty Generation*, seventeen-year-old Kami Jamieson is so over being daddy's little girl. Now that she has captured the attention of Tango, the bad boy from her school, Kami's love for her family and God have taken a backseat to her teen crush. Although the Jamiesons have instilled godly principles in Kami since she was young, they will stop at nothing, including prayer and fasting, to protect her from falling prey to society's peer pressure. Can Kami survive her teen rebellion, or will she be guilty of dividing the next generation?

In *Fun and Games with the Jamieson Men*, The Jamieson Legacy series inspired this game book of fun activities: • Brain Teasers• Crossword Puzzles• Word Searches •Sudoku •Mazes •Coloring Pages. The Jamiesons are fictional characters that put emphasis on Black Heritage, which includes Black American History tidbits, African American genealogy, and strong Black families. Relax, grab a pencil, and play along.

In *Queen's Surrender (To a Higher Calling)*, Opposites attract...or clash. The Jamieson saga continues with the Queen of the family in this inspirational romance. She's the mistress of flirtation but Philip is unaffected by her charm. The two enjoy a harmless banter about God's will versus Queen's, who prefers her own free-will lifestyle. Philip doesn't judge her choices—most of the time—and Queen respects his opinions—most of the time. It's perfect harmony sometimes.

Queen, the youngest sister of the Jamieson clan, wears her name as if it's a crown. She's single, sassy, and most of the time, loving her status, but she's about to strut down an unexpected spiritual path. Love takes no prisoners. When the descendants of a royal African tribe on her father's maternal side show up and show off at a family game night, Queen's vanity is kicked up a notch. The Robnetts take royalty to a new level with their own Queen.

Evangelist Philip Dupree is on the hot seat as the trial pastor at Total Surrender Church. The deadline for the congregation to officially elect him as pastor is months away. The stalemate: They want a family man to lead their flock. The board's ultimatum is enough to make him quit the ministry. But can a man of God walk away from his calling?

Can two people with different lifestyles and priorities cross paths and continue the journey as one? Who is going to be the first to surrender?

THE CARMEN SISTERS SERIES

In *No Easy Catch*, Book 1, Shae Carmen hasn't lost her faith in God, only the men she's come across. Shae's recent heartbreak was discovering that her boyfriend was not only married, but on the verge of reconciling with his estranged wife. Humiliated, Shae begins to second guess herself as why she didn't see the signs that he was nothing more than a devil's decoy masquerading as a devout Christian man. St. Louis Outfielder Rahn Maxwell finds himself a victim of an attempted carjacking. The Lord guides him out of harms' way by opening the gunmen's eyes to Rahn's identity. The crook instead becomes infatuated fan and asks for Rahn's autograph, and as a good will gesture, directs Rahn out of the ambush! When the news media gets wind of what happened with the baseball player, Shae's television station lands an exclusive interview. Shae and Rahn's chance meeting sets in motion a relationship where Rahn not only surrenders to Christ, but pursues Shae with a purpose to prove that good men are still out there. After letting her guard down, Shae is faced with another scandal that rocks her world. This time the stakes are higher. Not only is her heart on the line, so is her professional credibility. She and Rahn are at odds as how to handle it and friction erupts between them. Will she strike out at love again? The Lord shows Rahn that nothing happens by chance, and everything is done for Him to get the glory.

In *Defense of Love*, Book 2, lately, nothing in Garrett Nash's life has made sense. When two people close to the U.S. Marshal wrong him deeply, Garrett expects God to remove them from his life. Instead, the Lord relocates Garrett to another city to start over, as if he were the offender instead of the victim. Criminal attorney Shari Carmen is comfortable in her own skin—most of the time. Being a "dark and lovely" African American sister has its challenges, especially when it comes to relationships. Although she's a fireball in the courtroom, she knows how to fade into the background and keep the proverbial spotlight off her personal life. But literal spotlights are a different matter altogether. While playing tenor saxophone at an anniversary party, she grabs the attention of Garrett Nash. And as God draws them closer together, He makes another request of Garrett, one to which it will prove far more difficult to say "Yes, Lord."

In *Redeeming Heart*, Book 3, Landon Thomas (In Defense of Love) brings a new definition to the word "prodigal," as in prodigal son, brother or anything else imaginable. It's a good thing that God's love covers a multitude of sins, but He isn't letting Landon off easy. His journey from riches to rags proves to be humbling and a lesson well learned. Real Estate Agent Octavia Winston is a woman on a mission, whether it's God's or hers professionally. One thing is for certain, she's not about to compromise when it comes to a Christian mate, so why did God send a homeless man to steal her heart? Minister Rossi Tolliver (Crowning Glory) knows how to minister to God's lost sheep and through God's redemption, the game changes for Landon and Octavia.

In *Driven to Be Loved*, Book 4, on the surface, Brecee Carmen has nothing in common with Adrian Cole. She is a pediatrician certified in trauma care; he is a transportation problem solver for a luxury car dealership (a.k.a., a car salesman). Despite their slow but steady attraction to each other, neither one of them are sure that they're compatible. To complicate matters, Brecee is the sole unattached Carmen when it seems as though everyone else around her—family and friends—are finding love, except her. Through a series of discoveries, Adrian and Brecee learn that things don't happen by coincidence. Generational forces are at work, keeping promises, protecting family members, and perhaps even drawing Adrian back to the church. For Brecee and Adrian, God has been hard at work, playing matchmaker all along the way for their paths cross at the right time and the right place.

In *Couple by Christmas*, five-year-old Tyler Washington wants his daddy to marry this mother. The problem is both his parents were once married, then divorced two years ago. But it's Christmas time and the holidays are not the same. This year, Derek has custody, and he knows the loneliness his ex-wife will face on Christmas Day without their son. He experienced it the previous year. His past regrets and Tyler's request have Derek thinking. Maybe, just maybe, Robyn would be willing to do things as a family again for Tyler's sake. At best, act as a couple for Christmas.

In *Prayers Answered by Christmas*, Christmas is coming. While other children are compiling their lists for a fictional Santa, eight-year-old Mikaela Washington is on her knees, making her requests known to the Lord: One mommy for Christmas please. Portia Hunter refuses to let her ex-husband cheat her out of the family she wants. Her prayer is for God to send the right man into her life. Marlon Washington will do anything for his two little girls, but can he find a mommy for them and a love for himself? Since Christmas is the time of year to remember the many gifts God has given men, maybe these three souls will get their heart s desire.

Lean on Me, Book 1. No one should have to go it alone... Caregivers sometimes need a little TLC too.

Tabitha Knicely believes in family before everything. She may be overwhelmed caring for her beloved great-aunt, but she would never turn her back on the woman who raised her, even if Aunt Tweet's dementia is getting worse. Tabitha is sure she can do this on her own. But when Aunt Tweet ends up on her neighbor's front porch, and the man has the audacity to accuse Tabitha of elder abuse, things go from bad to awful. Marcus Whittington feels a mountain of regret at causing problems for Tabitha and her great-aunt. How was he to know the frail older woman's niece was doing the best she could? As Marcus gets to know Aunt Tweet and sees how hard Tabitha is fighting to keep everything together, he can't walk away from the pair. Particularly when helping Tabitha care for her great-aunt leads the two of them on a spiritual journey of faith and surrender.

Here For You, Book 2. Rachel Knicely's life has been on hold for six months while she takes care of her great aunt, who has Alzheimer's. Putting her aunt first was an easy decision—accepting that Aunt Tweet is nearing the end of her battle is far more difficult. Nicholas Adams's ministry is bringing comfort to those who are sick and homebound. He responds to a request for help for an ailing woman but when he meets the Knicelys, he realizes Rachel is the one who needs support the most. Nicholas is charmed by and attracted to Rachel, but then devastating news brings both a crisis of faith and roadblocks to their budding relationship that neither could have anticipated. This beautifully emotional and clean story contains a hero and heroine who are better at taking care of other people than themselves, a dark moment that shakes their faith, and a well-earned happily ever after.

Stand by Me, Book 3. An uplifting story about embracing love and giving others—and yourself—one more chance

When it comes to being a caregiver, Kym Knicely has been there and done that. Then she meets Charles "Chaz" Banks and soon learns that every caregiving situation is different. Chaz takes care of his seven-year-old autistic granddaughter, Chauncy. Although Kym's attraction to Chaz is strong, she must decide whether a romantic relationship can survive and thrive between two people at different stages in life. It's a journey with a different set of rules that Kym must play by if she and Chaz are to have their happily ever after and the faith and family they envision.